COOPER'S CORNER CHRONICLE

A Perfect Wedding for a Perfect Pair

Twin Oaks Bed and Breakfast was the fairy-tale setting for the wedding reception of Wendy Monroe and Seth Castleman. Beneath a full moon and glittering canopy of stars, guests dined al fresco at linen-covered tables overflowing with delectable treats. Tiny white lights twinkled from tree branches and silvery bubbles floated upward from the champagne fountain, imparting a mood of romance to everyone there.

Visitors came from as far away as France, but most of the guests were Cooper's Corner locals, who have known the bride and groom for many years. Wendy looked radiantly beautiful in her wedding gown, and Seth was drop-dead gorgeous in his tux (quite a change from his usual carpenter jeans and T-shirts). And though Wendy was definitely the star of the evening, she jokingly admitted that she was in danger of being upstaged by her maid of honor.

Alison Fairchild, our local postmistress, has set the town abuzz since coming back from New York with a totally new look (and it's not just a new hairdo). We'll leave the details for *Chronicle* readers to discover on their next trip to the post office. Judging by the male attention Alison generated at the wedding, Twin Oaks may be the setting for another wedding in the near future.

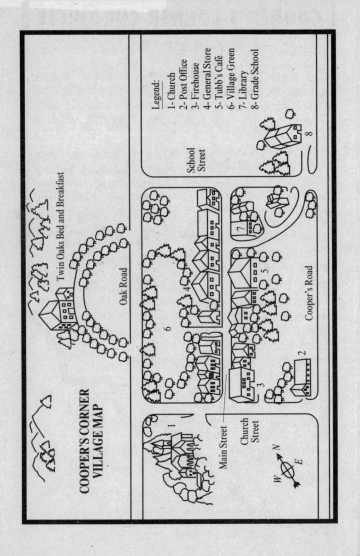

COOPER'S CORNER
VILLAGE MAP

Twin Oaks Bed and Breakfast

Oak Road

Main Street

Church Street

Cooper's Road

School Street

W N E S

Legend:
1- Church
2- Post Office
3- Firehouse
4- General Store
5- Tubb's Café
6- Village Green
7- Library
8- Grade School

COOPER'S CORNER

JOANNA WAYNE

Just One Look

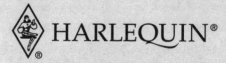

HARLEQUIN®

TORONTO • NEW YORK • LONDON
AMSTERDAM • PARIS • SYDNEY • HAMBURG
STOCKHOLM • ATHENS • TOKYO • MILAN • MADRID
PRAGUE • WARSAW • BUDAPEST • AUCKLAND

A special thanks to my good friends Pat and Steve Waters
for always being around when I have time to play a little golf or travel.
And to my husband, Wayne, for bringing
romance and happily-ever-after into my life.

HARLEQUIN BOOKS
225 Duncan Mill Road, Don Mills,
Ontario, Canada M3B 3K9

ISBN-13: 978-0-373-61260-4
ISBN-10:   0-373-61260-5

JUST ONE LOOK

Joanna Wayne is acknowledged as the author of this work.

Dear Reader,

Who wouldn't find the idea of staying in a charming bed-and-breakfast in the Berkshires inviting? Certainly not me. That's why I was intrigued with the prospect of writing one of the COOPER'S CORNER books. I was also fascinated with my characters and the chain of complex events that could be started by something as simple as a new look. The book was challenging to write, but I enjoyed the characters so much, I almost hated to see the end. Hope you enjoy your visits to Cooper's Corner, too. Bed, breakfast and happily-ever-after guaranteed.

I love to hear from readers, and you can visit me and write me a personal note by visiting my Web site at www.eclectics.com/authorsgalore/joannawayne. Or you can write me at P.O. Box 22851, Harvey, LA 70059-2851 to request a free newsletter and bookmark.

Joanna Wayne

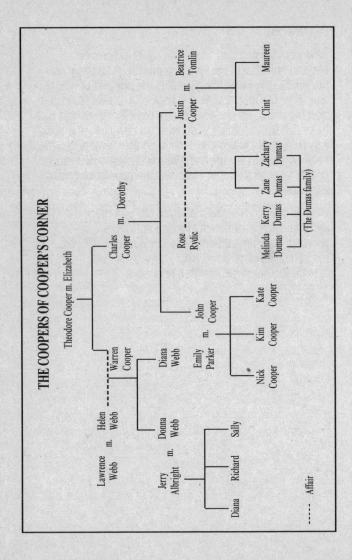

THE COOPERS OF COOPER'S CORNER

Theodore Cooper m. Elizabeth

Charles Cooper

Warren Cooper

Lawrence Webb m. Helen Webb

Diana Webb

Donna Webb

Justin Cooper m. Beatrice Tomlin

Clint   Maureen

m. Dorothy

Rose Rydic

John Cooper

Zachary Dumas

Zane Dumas

Kerry Dumas

Melinda Dumas

(The Dumas family)

Emily Parker m.

Nick Cooper

Kim Cooper

Kate Cooper

Jerry Albright m.

Diana   Richard   Sally

Affair - - - - -

CHAPTER ONE

ALISON FAIRCHILD SWERVED her light blue compact into the parking space and killed the engine. She had just under an hour before she was to be at the rehearsal for her best friend's wedding, and she was never late for anything. Then again, maybe she should be late tonight, make a grand entrance and see the look on everyone's face when they got their first glimpse of Cooper's Corner's new and vastly improved postmistress.

No, that would be too obvious. She'd just take a minute to check in with her mother and get her reaction. Then she'd be on her way. She climbed from behind the wheel and practically danced across the parking lot, her high heels clicking on the concrete, the full skirt of her silk dress swishing against her thighs.

The dress was new, a splurge from yesterday's New York shopping adventure. It was a full two inches shorter than anything else in her closet and cut low enough that a person could actually see a shadow of cleavage, if the person looked really closely. All part of her new image.

Of course, the crowning touch sat right smack in the middle of her face. The Pinocchio curse was gone, and in its place was an adorable, bobbed, upturned nose. What she hadn't been blessed with she'd just bought and paid for.

Smiling, she reached up and traced the outline of her nose for at least the thousandth time since the surgery three weeks ago. Yep. It was still there, changing her appearance so much that her own mother might not even recognize her, and making her feel—well, downright pretty. Not gorgeous. She didn't look like one of those sleek, airbrushed models in the fashion magazines or a Hollywood movie star, but for the first time in her twenty-eight years, she felt really good about her appearance.

She rang the doorbell and waited. Even after a year, it seemed strange that her mother would live in this tiny apartment while Alison knocked around all by herself in the rambling family home. But once Nora Bashelda Fairchild made up her mind she was going to do something, there was no stopping her, though Alison had tried. Her mother wanted a smaller place, a cozy spot of her own, and she'd decided that at her age she should get what she wanted.

As for Alison, she loved the family home and all its memories, especially the ones of her and her dad shooting baskets in the backyard and his reading her books like *Johnny Tremain* and *Call of the Wild* in front of the hearth on cold winter nights. They had been exceptionally close, and she still missed him. Her mother must, too. She'd never even dated another man in all the years since her husband's death. Dale Fairchild had been a man among men.

A few seconds later Nora swung open the door, glanced at Alison and then at her watch. "Alison. What a surprise! But you should have called before driving over."

"What kind of greeting is that after I've been gone for three weeks?" She hugged her mother and stepped into the room, turning so that her mom would get the full effect.

Her mother busied herself straightening the pillows on the sofa. "I'm glad to see you, of course. I just didn't know you were coming over tonight. I already have dinner plans, but I can postpone them.''

"No need. I'm on my way to the wedding rehearsal.''

"Wedding?''

"Wendy Monroe and Seth Castleman's. Don't tell me you forgot.''

"Only for a minute. I've been on the phone with your sister.''

Explanation enough. "So, what's Madge's latest catastrophe?''

"She's changing jobs. Actually, she got fired.''

"Again?''

"Yes, but don't take that tone of voice. It wasn't her fault this time. She spilled a little water on one of the customers. Can you imagine someone getting fired for something so harmless?''

No—which was why Alison figured the explanation was a gross understatement. It wasn't that she was totally unsympathetic, but Madge managed to quit or get fired from at least three jobs a year—in a slow year.

"I'm sure Madge will get another job before a week is out.'' Still no comment on her nose. Alison turned so that her mother could catch a glimpse of her profile, then walked a few steps closer and turned to face her again. Finally her mom looked right at her.

"Wendy is going to be a beautiful bride,'' Nora said. "Have you seen the wedding dress?''

"Mother, are you wearing your contact lenses?''

"I am, but I don't know what my wearing contacts has to do with Wendy's wedding dress.''

"Nothing. I've seen the dress, and it's gorgeous.''

"I do love weddings.'' Nora propped herself on the edge of the cushioned arm of the sofa, worry creases settling in around her eyes.

"I know, and you hope I'll have one someday. I still plan to, Mother, if and when I meet the right man."

"I didn't say a word." Nora stared at Alison for a minute, then stood up and walked around the sofa to straighten the pillows for the second time.

"Is something the matter?" Alison asked. "You're not sick, are you?"

"Never felt better. I was just thinking about your sister. I wish she was more like you—you know, steady and dependable. Why, you've been with the post office ever since you graduated from college."

"Steady and dependable, that's me." And mud ugly until three weeks ago. She touched the tip of her nose one more time. "Do you notice anything different about me?"

Nora tilted her head to the side and gave Alison a scrutinizing stare. "You changed your hairstyle."

"I got it trimmed and shaped at one of the hot salons in New York."

"It looks nice, but I bet you paid way too much."

"Not if it looks good." She turned again, going for the left profile. "Don't you notice anything else, something more…permanent?"

"Your dress is too short, but I hope that's not permanent. Is it new?"

"I bought it yesterday. Short is in style."

"Maybe in New York."

Hair, the length of her dress, the fact that she'd come by without calling first. The only thing her mother had missed was the one thing Alison had been certain she'd notice first. Three weeks ago, you could have hung laundry from her nose. Tonight it was cute, turned up at the end, an average size. How could anyone not notice, especially her mother?

"You seem upset, dear. Didn't your vacation with Cassandra go well?"

"The vacation went fine. I feel like a new woman."

"That's nice." She glanced at her watch again.

"It wasn't purely a vacation," Alison added. "I had rhinoplasty." There. She'd blurted it out, not at all the way she'd planned.

"You had what?"

"Rhinoplasty. A nose job."

Her mother stared at her critically for a few seconds, then slapped her palm against her cheek as if she were fighting off shock. "Oh, my word. You did. But why?"

"*Why?* The old one was hideous."

"I loved your nose. It was your dad's nose, you know."

"Dad was six foot three. I'm five-five. I wanted my own nose, one that fit my face."

Nora walked around, studying her from all angles now that she'd finally realized her youngest daughter had gotten a nose job. "I can't believe you didn't tell me you were having it done."

"I wanted it to be a surprise."

"A bouquet of flowers is a surprise. Surgery is… serious. I should have been there."

"It wasn't all that serious. The doctor did it in the morning. I was home long before dinner. Easier than dealing with Mrs. Grubecker when she comes in complaining about the price of stamps."

Nora's hand flew to her chest, as if she were holding her heart in place, a gesture she used too often for it to have an effect on either of her daughters. "What if something had gone wrong? I'd have been the last to know."

"Nothing went wrong, and you're practically the first to know."

Nora circled her, scrutinizing, as if she were checking

to see if the nose was still centered on Alison's face. "It does make you look different."

"Different as in better?"

"I'm not sure. I'll have to get used to it before I make my final judgment."

"Well, you'll have plenty of time. The other one is gone for good and this is the new me."

"I never noticed anything wrong with the old you, but if the new nose makes you happy, then I can live with it. Now, you better get going. You don't want to be late for that rehearsal."

Alison had the distinct feeling she was being rushed out of the house, but it was just as well. She did have to get to the church. "I'll pick you up for the wedding," she said, opening the front door.

"That won't be necessary. My guest will drive me."

"What guest?"

"My invitation was addressed to me and a guest. I invited someone to go with me."

"Does this guest have a name?"

"Ron Pickering."

Alison tossed the name around in her head for a moment. "I don't know any Ron Pickering."

"Then we're even. I didn't know you were getting a new nose. And call your sister tomorrow. She needs your emotional support at a time like this."

Alison would have liked to pursue the subject of Ron Pickering, find out exactly who he was and why he was going to Wendy and Seth's wedding as her mother's guest, but the maid of honor shouldn't keep the bride waiting.

She kissed her mother on the cheek and took her leave. A wolf whistle stopped her in her tracks halfway across the parking lot. Her mother's neighbor, Mr. Galloway, was standing in his driveway, a lecherous grin on his wrinkled and sagging face. The man was eighty if he was a day, but at least he'd noticed she was looking good.

She smiled and waved.

"You've got a great pair of gams, Miss Fairchild. Reminds me of Betty Grable."

"Thanks." Too bad she hadn't reminded him of someone with a great-looking nose, but she'd settle for Betty Grable, whoever that was. And Alison refused to let her mother's reaction spoil her mood. She felt great. She looked good. And she had the most incredible excitement building inside her, as if her life was about to change forever.

ALISON STOPPED at the door of the church and scanned the sanctuary. Wendy and Seth were nowhere in sight, but several of the bridesmaids and groomsmen were milling around the front. She'd known a few of them all her life. The others she'd met at the engagement party several weeks ago.

No reason for her not to join them, except now that she was here, she was experiencing a fluttering sensation in the pit of her stomach. She stared at Barry Jackson, remembered his taunts of "Allie Uglychild" and "Banana Nose" that had sent her home from school crying when she was in the third grade. The fluttering subsided.

We'll see what you have to say now, Barry Jackson.

"The women in Cooper's Corner have definitely gotten prettier."

She turned to find Kevin Bosco at her elbow. She'd had a crush on him her entire senior year, not that he'd ever noticed. Now he'd walked right up to her. Kevin, the hotshot Boston attorney. It was definitely the nose. She sucked in her breath and strove for a sexy, breathless voice. "Hello, Kevin."

"Allie Fairchild?"

"In the flesh." The look on his face left no doubt he was pleasantly surprised. "It's been a long time," she said.

"Too long. I'm living in Boston now."

"I've heard. An up-and-coming attorney with an impressive law firm, and making quite a name for yourself."

"You've been talking to my mother."

"She mentions you every now and then."

"You know moms."

Alison thought she had. After her mother failed to notice her new nose, she wasn't so sure anymore. But Kevin had noticed that she was looking good. "I didn't realize you were in the wedding party," she murmured.

"I'm not."

"Then why are you at the rehearsal?"

"I had a few days vacation and Mom talked me into coming home for the weekend. I just rode over with her tonight to help her unload and set up the brass candle-holders."

Of course. Bosco's Florist was doing the flowers for the wedding. "Will you be coming to the wedding?"

"I will now."

Heat shimmied along her nerve endings and no doubt burned in her cheeks. The blush didn't fit the image she was going for, but there wasn't a lot she could do about it. She wasn't used to this kind of attention.

"How long will you be in town?"

"I'm not sure. I have a week off, but I usually start missing the excitement of the city after a few days."

Maggie Porter, looking terrific as always, motioned for Alison to join the rest of the wedding party at the front of the church. Maggie had recently moved back to Cooper's Corner after divorcing her husband, and Wendy had asked her to be one of her bridesmaids. They'd both been competitive skiers during high school.

Alison gave her an acknowledging wave and turned back to stare into Kevin's deep brown eyes. "I guess I'll see you tomorrow night."

"Count on it." He took her left hand in his. "No diamonds. I guess that means you're fair game."

Exceedingly fair, considering she hadn't had a date in months. Kevin Bosco, back in town and looking twice as gorgeous at twenty-eight as he had at eighteen. And not only had he noticed her, he was actually coming on to her. The price of the surgery was quickly becoming the bargain of her life. "I'm still single."

"Kevin, are you going to help or not?" The no-nonsense voice of Mrs. Bosco cut into Alison's thoughts.

"Duty calls," he whispered, leaning in so close she could feel his breath on her earlobe. "Any chance we can get together later tonight?"

Yes was on her tongue, but reality checked in along with her sense of responsibility. "I'm afraid not. There's a dinner party at a restaurant in New Ashford after the rehearsal, and I'm pretty much obligated to attend."

"Then we'll hook up tomorrow," Kevin said.

"Super." She watched him walk away, not quite able to believe that she, Alison Uglychild, had just turned down a date with Kevin Bosco. Not that she'd done it by choice, but nonetheless, she'd actually said no to spending at least part of the evening with the gorgeous lawyer.

She floated down the aisle to meet with the rest of the group in front of the church. For the next ten minutes, she chatted with one friend after another, playing it cool. No one mentioned her nose job, but she knew they had noticed and were talking about it.

She spotted Father Tom Christen and was about to go over and speak to him when a cheer went up from the group. The happy couple had arrived. Wendy was radiant. Seth was beaming. Love looked great on both of them. Alison didn't recognize the man walking beside Seth, which probably meant he was Seth's best man, the one guy in the wedding party that no one had met yet. All they knew was that he was a schoolteacher from New Orleans and a confirmed bachelor.

He was no Kevin Bosco, but he was definitely not bad. Kind of hard and lean. Rugged. He'd probably look great in a pair of tight jeans. The sunglasses would have to go, though. Wearing shades inside was much too Hollywood for Cooper's Corner unless you happened to be blind. At that moment she noticed the beautiful retriever walking at his side. They didn't let dogs in…

Duh! The man *was* blind.

She'd been making fun of a blind man's sunglasses—fortunately not out loud. But you would have thought Seth would have mentioned something as important as the fact that his best man was blind. The guy was laughing at something Seth said as they walked toward her. He was paying so little attention he practically tripped over his own guide dog.

Poor guy. She'd be extra nice to him, though she hoped Seth didn't expect her to entertain him all night and at the reception tomorrow as well. Now that she'd finally worked up the courage to buy herself a new nose, she didn't want to waste it on a man who'd never notice.

ETHAN GRANGER WALKED into the Red Maple Restaurant, his pal Seth on one side, his dog, Longfellow, on the other, the damn cane getting in his way as usual. But at least this time he'd remembered to get it out of the car. They'd driven to the restaurant in Seth's truck, leaving Wendy to ride with her bridal party in a friend's van.

"How's the temperature of your feet?" he asked as Seth led the way to a private dining room in the back.

"Warm as toast. No cold feet for me. I've never been more sure of anything than I am of marrying Wendy."

"You are a far braver man than I."

"Nothing brave about it. When love is right, you know it."

"When lust is right, I know it," Ethan said. "Love is a figment of a fool's imagination."

"One of these days you're going to meet someone who knocks you right off those big feet of yours. You'll forget all about that ex-wife and beg Ms. Right to marry you. I just hope I'm around to see it."

"Then you better eat well and take your vitamins. You'll have to live a long time." Ethan kept his gaze straight ahead as he maneuvered past diners who were already seated. No need to look to the right or the left, he reminded himself. Just wait for Longfellow's lead and follow.

"So what do you think of Alison Fairchild?" Seth asked, keeping his voice low.

"She'd make my top ten list—of women to avoid."

"Why is that?"

"She's a little too sure of herself. A woman like that can do serious damage to a guy."

"Alison Fairchild? She's harmless."

"So is a rattlesnake until it bites you."

"I have to admit she's a lot more outgoing tonight than usual."

"Outgoing? She flitted around the church like a drunk

butterfly, flashing that dazzling smile at everybody and peering from under those movie star eyelashes.''

"For a blind man, you see a lot."

"It's a talent."

"One you've apparently honed quite well."

"I'm a fast learner. Which is why I'd never take a chance on marriage again.''

"Well, I've got to hand it to you. No one's even suggested you're a fake."

"And you didn't tell anyone that I'm not really blind?''

"After the way you threatened me?''

"You don't know how tough it was getting my boss to agree to this. Undercover agents do not take vacations back to their regular lives.''

"You didn't. You're still in the role—Ethan Granger, blind high school history teacher from the Big Easy. Or at least you will be as soon as you get a job. But I'm glad he agreed. A man needs his best friend at his side when he takes a wife.''

"But you did tell Wendy that I'm not blind?''

"You agreed that I could. A man can't keep secrets from his wife.''

"No, but they can sure keep them from you.''

"You weren't this big a cynic when we were teenagers.''

"I hadn't been burned to a crisp back then. So tell me about this Alison Fairchild.''

"First of all, Wendy and most of her friends call her Allie.''

Ethan gave the name some thought but rejected it. "She looks more like an Alison to me. Soft and feminine, but with man-trap eyes, great legs and a hot body.''

"I never thought of her like that.''

"Because you only have eyes for Wendy. You're as good as a dead man where other women are concerned."

"You're right, but it's not just that. Most of the time Allie just kind of fades into the background. Wendy says she's sensitive about her nose."

"She has a terrific little nose."

Seth snapped his fingers. "Son of a gun. That's it. It's the nose. She must have had it…worked on."

"Was it broken?"

"No. It was big. Really big. Now it's not. That's why she was prancing around like a kid with a new pair of shoes."

Good-looking woman flaunting a new nose. That had promise. "How about making sure I sit by her at dinner?"

"Why? You just said she was the kind of woman to avoid."

"She is—for the long haul. I'm talking about one night."

"One night?"

"Not that kind of night."

"Okay, but remember, this is Wendy's best friend. Don't pull any of your tricks."

"Now, would I do a thing like that?"

"Only if you got half a chance."

"That's the problem with getting together with old friends. They know you too well. I promise I won't embarrass you." But that was all he promised.

Seth left him to go and talk to a waiter who had just joined them in the private dining room. Ethan loosened his shirt collar beneath his tie. He'd have been far more comfortable in his jeans and a sweatshirt, but he could survive a couple of nights with a silk noose around his neck for his old buddy.

Seth would have a noose around his neck forever, and

the guy couldn't wait. Poor sucker. But he really should cut his friend some slack, Ethan decided. Just because marriage hadn't worked for him didn't mean it couldn't work for Seth. He was definitely in love, and Wendy was a super woman.

The rest of the party had evidently entered the restaurant. It was hard not to miss the arrival of a group of giddy females. He recognized Alison's laughter—kind of lyrical and crinkly to the ear.

This weekend might not turn out to be nearly as dull as he'd feared.

ALISON SAT BETWEEN Barry Jackson and Ethan Granger. Barry was all but drooling over her. What a difference a nose made, or lack of so much nose. Ethan didn't appear to even be aware she was a female, which was unfortunate, because of the two men, Ethan was far more attractive.

He had nice, thick, raisin-brown hair with an unruly lock that kept falling over his forehead. She'd already resisted the urge a time or two to push it back in place for him. He felt for his napkin, bumping her arm as he did. "I'm sorry," he said, without turning his head.

"No problem. They have us squeezed around the table pretty tightly."

"It's Alison Fairchild, isn't it?" he asked, finally turning his head in her direction.

"Yes. How did you know? Did you recognize my voice?"

"I recognize your scent. What is it you're wearing?"

"It's called Passion."

"An intriguing name for a pleasing scent." He spread the napkin across his lap. "Could I ask a favor of you, Alison?"

"Of course."

"I acclimate better to my surroundings if I have some kind of image in my mind. Would you mind describing the dining room for me?"

She looked around. "The room is rectangular and there are windows across the back, though it's too dark outside to see anything tonight. We're all sitting at a long table covered in a white cloth with a scattering of rose petals and pink candles along the center. You're sitting at the end of the table, probably so that you have room for your guide dog to lie beside you."

"Yes, good old Longfellow. I can always count on him."

"That's an unusual name for a dog."

"Do you think so?"

He sounded offended. Probably overly sensitive. "A little unusual, but I like it. He's a very pretty dog."

"So people say. I like the feel of his hair between my fingers when I pet him and the coolness of his tongue when he licks my hand. You can tell a lot about a person or a dog by touching them."

His voice took on a seductive quality, and for a second she imagined his fingers tangling in her hair instead of Longfellow's. "Have you known Seth long?" she asked, deciding to move to a safer topic.

"We met in at summer camp when we were teenagers, and became fast friends. Seth made sure I did everything the seeing campers did. Well, almost everything. I stayed out of the touch football games. Never quite figured out where the ball was."

A sense of humor. She liked that about him. When the waiter brought out the food, she explained what was on his plate, describing the location of the prime rib, the potatoes and the green beans. "Would you like me to cut up your meat?"

"That would be most helpful."

Once she had, he experienced no difficulty forking his food and getting it to his mouth. It was amazing the way he did everything by touch and memory. He even managed his wine goblet without spilling a drop, though he did have to feel around to find his roll.

"Are you staying with Seth?" she asked.

"No. I have a room at the bed-and-breakfast where they're holding the reception."

"Twin Oaks. I love that place. Clint and Maureen Cooper are both so nice."

"Seth says they're brother and sister."

"They are. They inherited the farmhouse and decided to renovate it and turn it into an inn. Everyone who stays there once tends to come back again and again."

"I doubt I'll be doing that, but I will definitely miss those walnut griddle cakes Clint makes."

"Did you get a tour of the house? Maureen's done a wonderful job of decorating the place." Stupid remark, she knew it as soon as she'd made it. The man couldn't see antiques.

"Longfellow and I had the tour. We mostly concentrated on how to get around without knocking into any of the furnishings and knickknacks, though." His hand brushed her arm and he let it linger for a few seconds before he moved it.

A tremble of awareness skittered through her, surprising her. She was not usually that affected by a casual touch.

"You've told me about the room and the food," he said, fiddling with his napkin. "Tell me about you."

"There's not a lot to tell. I've lived in Cooper's Corner all my life, and I'm the postmistress."

"You seemed to get a lot of attention from the single men at the rehearsal tonight. My guess is you must be very pretty."

Heat climbed to her cheeks. No man had ever called her pretty before. Wouldn't you know the first guy who did would be blind? Still, it beat "Banana Nose" by a mile and a half.

"How tall are you?" Ethan asked.

Ah, that she could handle. "I'm five feet five."

He turned to her and put his left hand up to touch her hair. His fingers ran through the strands, then settled on her nearly bare shoulder. Her breath caught.

This was too bizarre. She'd just spent a fortune and used up three weeks' vacation time so that she could finally look decent, and she was getting turned on by a man who wouldn't notice if she had two noses. Worse, she had the crazy feeling he knew he was turning her on and was doing it on purpose.

"Your hair is very silky. Blond, isn't it?"

"Yes, but how can you tell the color just from feeling it?"

"A lucky guess."

Thankfully, he settled into eating and seemed to forget her until halfway through the meal, when his napkin slipped from his lap. He tried to catch it, but missed. Instead his hand landed across her left leg. A second later she felt his fingers brushing her exposed thigh. Only they didn't just brush. They stayed there.

His eyebrows rose. "Is that your leg?"

"Yes, and I'd thank you to remove your hand." Blind or not, he was going too far.

He slid his hand away. "Did you forget to wear your skirt?"

Outrage and embarrassment mingled with the leftover surge of awareness. She was certain her face was bloodred now. Ethan couldn't see it, but everyone else at the table could. "I have on a skirt," she snapped, keeping her voice to a whisper but not bothering to hide her irritation.

Without waiting for a reply, she pushed back from the table. It was time for a trip to the powder room. Wendy got up at the same time. They met at the door.

"I love your nose," Wendy whispered. "I wanted to say something earlier, but I could never catch you alone and I didn't want to make a big thing of it in front of everyone else."

Alison's anger cooled. "Do you really like it?"

"Of course. You look terrific. I just can't believe you didn't tell me you were going to have it done."

"I didn't tell anyone. I was afraid someone would try to talk me out of it, and I had already made up my mind to go for it."

"You made a wise decision. Did it hurt?"

"Not that much. Not at all after the first day or two. There was a lot of bruising and swelling, though."

"That explains your three weeks in New York." Wendy followed her into the ladies' room. "I notice you've been talking to Seth's friend Ethan. He's really good-looking, don't you think? Funny and sexy, too."

"I think he's a—" She bit her tongue. No point in saying he used his disability to grope females under the table. After all, now that she thought about it, it could have been an accident. The man was blind. "He seems nice enough."

"In that case, I need to ask a favor of you."

"Anything for the bride."

"Could you drive Ethan back to Twin Oaks after dinner? Seth had planned to take him, but we want to spend some time together, just the two of us. Our last night as lovers instead of a married couple."

"You and Seth will always be lovers."

"But you will drive Ethan back to Twin Oaks?"

"Of course." A tingle of apprehension danced along Alison's nerve endings. It had to be apprehension. It definitely wasn't anticipation. But the man was sexy, and he did know how to use those hands. She'd just have to make certain she kept him at arm's length. If his hands affected her like this, imagine what a good-night kiss might do.

"You look a little flushed, Allie. Are you certain you're all right?"

"I'm fine."

"Oh, and be careful with Ethan. Whatever you do, don't fall for him."

"I have no intention of falling for him. Why would you even think such a thing?"

"He's a man. You're a woman. Those things do happen. It sure happened to me."

"Then why are you warning me about Ethan? What's wrong with him?"

"I get the idea from Seth that he's strictly a love 'em and leave 'em kind of guy."

"That figures." *Arm's length,* Alison reminded herself as she touched up her lipstick and blotted the excess onto a tissue. Definitely arm's length. Only there wouldn't be an arm's length between them in her little car. She'd just have to make very sure he kept his hands to himself and that she kept her hormones in check. If she didn't…well, who knew what might happen.

CHAPTER TWO

ETHAN RAN HIS ARM across the back of the car seat, letting his fingers rest less than an inch from Alison's nearly bare shoulder. "Nice night for a ride."

Alison kept her eyes on the road. "It's not a particularly nice night. There are clouds rolling in from the west and there's been a steady flickering of lightning in the distance. It doesn't look good."

"Then it's a nice night for a *short* ride. You should be home long before the storm hits."

"It's not tonight I'm concerned about. It's the wedding tomorrow evening."

"Rain or not, it will be nice and dry inside the church."

"But the reception is supposed to be outside."

"That could dampen the enthusiasm a bit."

Alison's fear of letting Ethan get to her was making her react negatively to everything he said, behave as if she had no manners. She took a deep breath and let it out slowly. "I'm sure I'm worrying about nothing," she said, making her tone lighter. "Maureen will just move the party inside the B and B if there's inclement weather."

She turned off Oak Road into the curved, tree-lined drive that led to Twin Oaks. "Will you be staying in town long?"

"Just long enough for the wedding."

"That's too bad. Cooper's Corner is a wonderful place for relaxing."

"I'm not big on relaxing. What else does the area offer?"

"There are great trails for hiking and horseback riding. And lots of friendly people."

"So how has a nice, hometown lady like you avoided the marriage trap for so long?"

"Marriage is not a trap. It's a...a union of souls."

"Right. A union of souls. So why haven't you joined a union?"

"I just haven't met the right man yet."

"You must be awfully hard to please. What kind of man 'rings your bell'?" he asked teasingly.

"I'm not sure."

"Don't tell me it's never been rung."

Never been rung. The description fit all too well, but she wasn't going to admit that to Ethan. "That depends on what you mean by *rung*. I've met guys I was attracted to."

"You seemed to be enjoying the attention of a lot of guys tonight."

"Tonight's different."

"How so? It seemed pretty much like any other night to me, except for Wendy and Seth. It was big for them."

She rolled her right palm along the edge of the steering wheel while holding it steady with her left. "Have you ever heard the saying that today is the first day of the rest of your life?"

"Sure. It's pretty corny, but I guess it could work for some people."

"No. In my case, it's true. I'm starting over, going for the gusto, so to speak."

"What was wrong with your life before today?"

"I was...I don't know why I'm telling you this. It's nothing you'd be interested in."

"But I am interested. Besides, sometimes it's easier to talk to a stranger, especially one you won't be seeing after this weekend."

"That's true. And you're…"

"You can finish the sentence, Alison. You don't have to be afraid to acknowledge the fact that I'm visually impaired, or visually challenged, if you go with the popular theory that no one's really impaired and everyone faces challenges."

"I was just thinking how people always say that when one sense is lacking, the others make up for it. If that's true, you've probably already sensed that I'm trying out a new personality tonight."

"Oh, I get it. You're one of those women with multiple personalities that I read about in psych class."

"I certainly am not."

"Then I guess you'd better explain."

She slowed to a stop in front of the B and B. "The old me was…boring. All work and no play."

"All rules and no risks?"

"That's probably even more accurate. Now I want to experience life. That means I have to change a lot of things about myself. I know you can't see it, but the dress I'm wearing is totally out of character for me."

"The one with no skirt?"

"It has a skirt." She killed the engine and planned to do the same with this conversation. She'd tried being nice to him. It didn't work. "Do you need help getting inside?"

"No more than Longfellow and my cane can provide." He leaned in closer. "I know this may sound strange to you, but do you mind if I touch your face?"

Her grip tightened on the wheel, but she turned toward him. "Why would you do that?"

"Touch is how I see my world."

"Of course." She didn't like the prospect of being touched by Ethan, but she'd sound like some kind of heartless snob if she said no. If he told Wendy or Seth, they'd be appalled at her refusal. She released the wheel and reached across the space that separated them. Her hand trembled as she took his and placed in on her cheek.

He roamed the flesh with his fingertips, skimming her eyes, her cheeks, everywhere except her nose, before stopping at her lips. She was trembling, aroused. If she didn't stop him, he was going to kiss her. Or she was going to kiss him. She brushed his hand away. "I need to go now, Ethan. I really need to get home."

"Then I'll see you tomorrow?"

"Tomorrow?"

"The wedding."

"Right. The wedding."

"Thanks for the ride," he said as he picked up his cane and herded Longfellow out of the car.

She watched him walk to the door at Longfellow's side, his cane pecking along the edge of the walk, while her senses whirled like crazy. The touch of his fingers against her face had been incredible, like a kiss, only much more sensual.

Of all the things she'd expected tonight, reeling from a blind's man's touch had not been on the list. The one man who couldn't possibly have been impressed by her new nose, her sexy dress or her flawlessly applied makeup, and he was the one she was sitting here drooling over like a schoolgirl.

A love 'em and leave 'em kind of guy.

Wendy's words of caution flashed into her mind, and Alison had no trouble believing them. The guy might be visually impaired, but he was a smooth operator. He'd managed to catch her off guard and had kept her reacting to him all night. Here today, gone tomorrow—well, day after tomorrow. If she wasn't careful, she'd blow the weekend she'd been waiting for all her life on a man who used his impairment like an aphrodisiac.

Tonight, she'd played into his hands, literally and figuratively, but tomorrow night would be a different story entirely. She'd be pleasant, but aloof. She wouldn't give him a chance to use that touching routine on her again.

Still, a warm, gooey sensation that felt a lot like melted marshmallows on chocolate bubbled in her stomach as she drove home.

ALISON WOKE the next morning to the jangling ring of the telephone. Forcing her eyes open, she kicked off the covers and grabbed the receiver, managing a hoarse "Hello."

"So what's this I hear about a new nose?"

She didn't bother to bite back a groan. "Do you know what time it is, Madge?"

"Eight o'clock on a Saturday morning. You're usually up at six."

"Today I wasn't. I was awake half the night."

"Are you alone?"

"I'm in bed, Madge. Of course I'm alone."

"Hey, don't be so huffy. Mom said you had a new nose and were wearing a dress that left little to the imagination. I thought you might have gotten lucky."

"I didn't get my nose fixed so that I could pick up guys to sleep with."

"Maybe you should think about it. All nice surprises don't come through the mail, you know. So, tell me about your new nose. Are you absolutely gorgeous?"

"What did Mom say?"

"You can't go by what Mom says. She's a mom. I want to hear it from you."

Alison stretched so that she could catch a glimpse of herself in the mirror over the cherry dresser. "It looks good, Madge. Really good. Small. Much smaller. I love it."

"Great. I'm happy for you. I've always wondered why you didn't get that monstrosity cut down to size."

"You never said anything about surgery."

"That was because you never let on that it bothered you that much. All you did was go to work in that dowdy wardrobe of yours and spend your weekends running errands with Mom. What kind of nose do you need for that life?"

"I don't just run errands. I have a career."

"Hey, don't go postal on me."

"That's not funny."

"Sorry. I know postal workers are unsung heroes. I was only teasing, but I better come over and give you some pointers, since you have a new nose. Otherwise you'll fall for the first sweet-talking Romeo who lays a line on you."

Or a hand. The image of Ethan flashed across Alison's mind—the same one that had invaded her dreams and kept her awake half the night. "Don't worry. I know a rogue when I meet one." She threw her legs over the side of the bed, scooted her feet into a pair of fuzzy slippers and headed for the kitchen to start coffee, the portable phone still at her ear. "Mom says you lost your job."

"Yeah. Some guy got a little water on him. No big deal. The tips were lousy, anyway."

"How's the money situation?"

"I'll be all right, unless it takes more than a couple of weeks to find a job."

"It's never taken you any longer than that before."

"I know. It's just that I'm thinking I need a real job."

"Waitressing is a real job."

"The hours are long, though, and with this last job, I had no benefits. I need insurance coverage for Jake and me, and I need to start thinking about some kind of retirement options."

"You could go back into the secretarial field."

"My skills are rusty."

"So what are you considering?"

"I'm keeping my options open. In the meantime, I'm thinking about driving over and spending the weekend with you. Jake's school is closed for a few days because of some plumbing problems, so we can stay over until Monday if that's okay with you."

"Then come on. There's plenty of room, and I'd love to have you."

For a weekend. She hoped not a day longer. She loved her sister dearly, but everywhere that Madge went, chaos was sure to follow. Jake was an entirely different story. Alison had always thought her nephew was the most brilliant, funny and all-around wonderful kid in the world.

"In that case we'll be there sometime this afternoon," Madge said. "I know you'll be at Wendy's wedding tonight, so don't worry about us. We'll order pizza for dinner. Jake goes through withdrawal if he doesn't get his fill of pepperoni at least three times a week, anyway."

They talked a minute more while Alison filled the coffeepot with cool water and grounds, then flipped it on. After she hung up the phone, she walked outside to get the morning paper, thankful that the storm from last night had blown over without dropping rain on the already saturated lawn. It would be a great night for a wedding.

And tonight, she'd be on her toes, alert for any sensual assault Ethan Granger had in mind. By the time the coffee was ready, she'd already started a mental list of things to do today. Pick up groceries—things a fifteen-year-old boy might eat—and find out who in the devil Ron Pickering was and why he was going to Wendy and Seth's wedding as her mother's guest.

"I DON'T KNOW WHY you don't let me cover that gray for you," Lillian announced, the way she did every time Nora came to her salon just outside Cooper's Corner for a haircut. "It would take years off you, believe me."

Nora tilted her head to the side and stared into the mirror. "Do you think I need years taken off me?"

"It can't hurt."

Nora considered the comment and tried to picture what she'd look like minus the gray. She couldn't. She'd noticed the first telltale streaks the year Dale had died. They'd seemed fitting then, in tune with the way she'd felt. Lost. Overwhelmed with the task of raising two daughters on her own.

"How old are you now?" Lillian asked. "I know Madge is my age. So if she's thirty-five, you must be pushing…"

"I'm sixty," Nora answered, before Lillian had a chance to guess that she was older.

"Really. You look good for sixty." Lillian ran a finger down Nora's cheek. "Good skin, and none of those deep wrinkles some of my customers get. A little coloring on that gray and you could pass for fifty-five. A nice-looking fifty-five."

"I don't see why fifty-five would be a better age than sixty."

"Looking younger is always better. And it would impress that guy you were with at dinner last night."

"How did you know I was with a man last night?"

Lillian shook her finger teasingly at Nora. "A little bird told me. You should know there are no secrets kept from Lillian. When women come to the beauty shop, it's just like they're sitting in a confessional. They tell everything."

"He's just a friend."

"I didn't say he wasn't, but I bet he'd be even friendlier if you weren't gray."

"I'm not looking to impress a man." Still, if Alison had gotten a nose job, Nora thought, there was no reason she couldn't get her gray covered. And this had nothing whatsoever to do with Ron Pickering.

"If I do have it colored, are you certain you can make it look natural?"

"Absolutely. If you can't trust your hairdresser, who can you trust?"

Nora took a deep breath, feeling as if she might be about to jump from the edge of a steep cliff. "Okay, Lillian. I'm willing to give it a try, but I'm not at all sure I'm going to like it."

"You'll love it." Lillian smiled, looking a lot like the salesman had when Nora signed the contract on her first used car. He'd promised she was going to love it, too. And she had—until the front end dropped out of it two blocks from the lot.

"I'll be right back, Mrs. Fairchild. Just let me get you a smock and mix the color. By the time you leave here, you won't recognize yourself."

That statement was almost enough to make Nora back out. It had taken her sixty years to get to this point, and she liked who she was just fine. She had her own apartment with no one to know if she read a romance novel all night and slept until noon, or if she ate jelly doughnuts and milk for dinner just because that was what she wanted.

So why was she getting her gray covered after all these years? She didn't have a clue. It just seemed like the right time to do it.

ETHAN NURSED HIS COFFEE and a twinge of guilt. The coffee was hot. The guilt was downright chilly and totally out of character for him. He hadn't been completely honest with Alison, but then, when was he ever that honest with anyone? Living inside the carefully constructed walls of a fake identity was as much a part of his life as watching football—or carrying a gun.

He'd done this so long that sometimes he wondered if he hadn't lost his real self somewhere along the way, dropped it the way he did his assumed identities when he no longer needed them.

But the guilt wasn't about his secrets. It had more to do with the fact that he was playing a deceitful game with the maid of honor at his best friend's wedding. Asking her to describe herself, touching her shapely leg under the dinner table, running his fingers through her hair, caressing her face. If she hadn't thought he was blind, she would have let him have it—and almost had when he'd grabbed her leg. She was damn cute when she got all fired up like that.

The guilt slid to a back burner. He wasn't doing anything wrong. The FBI said he was a schoolteacher? Poof, he was a schoolteacher. They said he was blind? He was blind.

Besides, it might do Alison good to think she'd encountered a man who couldn't be swayed by her shapely body, full, sensual lips and flashing sapphire eyes—not to mention her cute little nose. A blind man could be just the reality check she needed as she began what was now the second day of her new life. She could experiment on him and not have to worry about getting rid of him when she was ready to move on.

He picked up the phone, dialed the first three digits of her number, then broke the connection. It was the second time he'd done that in the last half hour. Although he was sitting around bored out of his skull, he couldn't expect Alison to be doing the same.

A maid of honor probably had a million things to do the day of a wedding. Female things, like getting her toenails painted even though no one would see them, and having her hair pinned up in one of those fancy knots that tumbled down if you accidentally touched it.

He walked to the window and looked out over the countryside. The view was incredible. Rolling hills dotted by trees bursting to life in the warmth of spring. Farmhouses in the distance and the spire of the church where they'd attended the wedding rehearsal last night. The perfect day for being outside, and Clint had offered an overstuffed picnic basket for any guest wanting to go exploring around the property.

So why not call Alison? The worst she could say was no. He picked up the phone and this time dialed all seven digits in her number. The phone rang at least six times. He was just about to hang up when she answered.

"Hello."

"Hi. This is Ethan Granger." The only sound on the other end was heavy breathing. He refused to imagine what he might have interrupted. "You sound as if I might have caught you at a bad time. I can call back later."

"No. I was just coming in the back door and had to run to catch the phone. How can I help you?"

She'd obviously started on her list of pre-wedding activities. He wished he'd never made the call, but since he had, he might as well plunge ahead. "I was just thinking about what you said last night."

"What was that?"

"That it was too bad I couldn't stay in Cooper's Corner longer because there was so much to experience here. I thought if you had a couple of hours, you might be nice enough to share lunch with me and describe some of the countryside."

"Lunch?"

"Clint's offered to fix us a picnic basket."

Dead silence. He didn't know if she was considering accepting his invitation, or deciding how to politely tell him to buzz off. Cheating, he knew, but he decided to tip the odds in his favor. After all, who'd notice if her toenails didn't get painted?

"Maureen mentioned wildflowers and a picnic spot by a creek on the northern edge of the property. I'd love to visit it, but I can't drive, of course, and I can't really go exploring on my own. I do like getting outdoors, though. There's nothing like the sounds of a bubbling creek and the fragrant smells of wildflowers to inspire my imagination." Unless, of course, it was the thought of a gorgeous, sexy woman.

"I couldn't stay long."

Ah, she was weakening. "I'll be happy with whatever time you can spare."

"In that case, count me in. I have to put these groceries away and throw more laundry in the wash. I can be there at noon."

"Sounds perfect. I'll ask Clint for a basket for two." He hung up the phone, then reached down and gave Long-fellow a couple of pats and a good ear scratching. "Okay, buddy. I've got us a date. Now you have to make me look good. Nudge me closer to her at all the right times.''

Longfellow stared at him accusingly with his soulful brown eyes.

''Yeah. I know you're a professional, but so am I. This is serious stuff here. Play this just right and I might get my first kiss as a blind man.''

Longfellow emitted two sharp barks.

''Sorry, guy, but dog kisses don't count. Besides, this is for Alison as much as for me. She's starting her new life and needs the opportunity to practice her charms. And I'm willing to be used as her guinea pig.''

Only he was no fool. His need to see Alison again went a lot deeper than that. He'd felt the heavy pangs of serious attraction last night, the kind of feelings that would scare him to death if he lived in Cooper's Corner. But he didn't, and he'd be leaving in the morning. One picnic and one wedding reception with Alison were all that he'd have.

How much trouble could he possibly get into in one measly day and night?

It crossed his mind that the captain of the *Titanic* might have had that exact thought on the morning of his impact with the iceberg.

CHAPTER THREE

A SLIGHT BREEZE WHISPERED through the trees, and the fragrant perfume of honeysuckle and wildflowers titillated Alison's senses as she spread the picnic blanket on the ground. A few yards away, a mountain-fed stream gurgled and splashed over an uneven bed of rock. This was the last place she'd planned to be today, but when Ethan had called, her resolve from last night had taken a nosedive. The weather was too perfect, his voice too sexy, her will-power too out of practice.

"Why don't you sit here," she said, taking Ethan's hand and leading him. "I have the blanket spread out, close to the stream so you can hear the water babbling."

"How deep is the stream?"

"Only about twelve inches at this spot."

"Sounds like a perfect setting."

"It is." And he couldn't see it. The thought brought out her tender, nurturing side. "I'll tell you all about the scenery as we eat."

"Who could refuse a deal like that?" He stooped, touched the edge of the blanket and then positioned himself on the corner. Longfellow lay down beside him, contentedly sprawling in the sun now that his master was in place.

Ethan ran his hand along the curve of Longfellow's neck. "That's a smart boy. Get comfortable and let the beautiful woman do your job for you." Longfellow moved so as to make it easier for Ethan to scratch and spoil him.

Man and beast. The bond between them was touching, Alison thought, but at that moment Longfellow seemed more pet than guide dog. It had something to do with the way Ethan interacted with him, but it was nothing she could have explained in words.

Reaching over, she ran her fingers through Longfellow's long golden hair as well. "You must like dogs."

"Most of them. Loyal and friendly. Who else will lick you when you're down?"

She decided that comment was far better left untouched. "Wow, I think Clint outdid himself this time. Can you smell that fried chicken?" she asked as she took the lid from a plastic container.

"I can. I'll bet it's golden brown and crispy, too."

"It is." She found it fascinating that he thought in color.

Choosing a tempting chicken leg, she handed it to him, careful to put it in his hand. He bit into it with relish, and a scattering of crumbs tumbled down his shirt. He brushed them away. A learned response, she guessed, since he couldn't have seen the crumbs fall.

She leaned over to catch a few that he'd missed. Her hand was almost on his chest when she stopped. His shirt collar was open and the bronzed skin and a sprinkling of dark hair grabbed her attention, reached deep inside her and reminded her how long it had been since she'd touched a man with shoulders as broad as Ethan's. She pulled away and went back to the task of unpacking lunch. Touch was what had gotten her in trouble last night.

Ethan finished the leg in record time. "What else is in that basket?"

"Potato salad, packed on ice. Steamed green beans.

Pickles, olives…and what smells like Clint's fresh apple cake. Oh, and there's lemonade and a thermos of hot coffee to drink. What's your pleasure?''

A smile tipped his lips as he turned to face her. ''It would pleasure me most to put off eating for a few minutes. I'd like to walk over to that babbling brook, take off my shoes and feel the water splashing over my feet. Care to join me?''

''The water's cold.''

''But the day is warm. What kind of shoes are you wearing?''

She looked at her feet. The new Alison Fairchild should not have been caught dead in the mud-stained tennis shoes she had on, but with no one to see, it hadn't seemed worth changing into her new and far more feminine sandals. ''I'm wearing a pair of black, strappy sandals,'' she lied, describing the shoes she'd bought in New York just last week. A pang of guilt hit immediately. If she wasn't careful, her *new* nose might grow to the size of her last one.

''Sandals. Good choice,'' Ethan said, already slipping out of his loafers and socks. ''Put your feet over here, and I'll unbuckle them for you.''

His hands on her feet? No way. But his words confirmed her instincts from last night. The man might be visually impaired, but he knew exactly what he was doing where women were concerned. Now she was thankful she didn't have on the sandals. The temptation to let him unbuckle them might have been too great to resist.

''I'm perfectly capable of removing my own shoes,'' she said, yanking on the end of a shoelace.

''It was just a friendly offer.'' In one lithe motion, he got to his feet. Longfellow did, too.

She stared at Ethan's bare feet and felt a new wave of apprehension. Just normal male feet—large, manly. She'd never thought of bare feet as sexy before, but his were having a decidedly erotic effect on her.

"So, are we on?" he asked.

Not fully on, but she was getting there fast. "You'll have to be careful not to trip on the rocks," she warned, knowing somehow it wouldn't deter him.

"I'll have you to guide me. And if I fall, it won't be the first time."

"Okay. Just give me a few seconds to cover the food." She fit the lid back on the chicken and returned the potato salad to the ice. While she tugged off her socks, Ethan rolled up the legs of his jeans, exposing muscular calves, nicely tanned and peppered with dark hair.

He held out his hand without turning in her direction. She took it, aware of the slight pressure as his fingers wrapped around hers, aware of the feel of him, and now that she was so close, aware of the odor of him, musky and woodsy, and masculine to the core.

They walked across the carpet of grass until she stopped at the edge of the stream and rolled up her own pants. "The next step will put you into the water. It's clear and no more than six inches deep at the edge, but there are some sharp rocks on the bottom. I'll try to tell you where to step, but you'll need to put your feet down carefully, feel your way."

"Feeling is my speciality."

"So I've noticed. There's a big rock about two feet to the left of you and one about a foot to the right."

She slipped her right foot into the water and yanked it out immediately.

"What's wrong?" he asked, standing beside her, undaunted, with both feet planted in the stream.

"It's freezing."

"It only hurts for a second. After that it feels *sooo* good."

"You must be part polar bear."

"Not me. I'm all teddy bear."

Yeah, right. And she was Snow White. But she tried the water again, this time slowly, forcing herself not to react too quickly. It was still cold, but tolerable. She took a deep breath and guided him a few more steps, adjusting to the temperature by the second. "We're in the middle of the stream now. There's a school of minnows swimming around our feet. I think they like my toenail polish."

"Is it bright red?"

She lifted her foot out of the water. "More of a bronzy red. Do minnows like that color?"

"I don't know. I suspect men do, though." He turned toward her. "Feeling that cold water trickle over your feet makes your senses come alive, doesn't it?"

"So it appears."

He dropped her hand, made a cup with both of his and dipped it into the stream, letting the water filter through his fingers as he straightened again. He splashed what water remained in his hands onto his face. It ran down his cheeks and neck and clung as silvery highlights to the hairs just below the hollow of his neck.

She fought off a crazy urge to catch the droplets with her tongue, and waited for Ethan to take her hand again. Instead he turned toward her and found her face with his cold, wet fingertips. Her breath seemed to hang suspended as he trailed them across her eyelids and down her cheeks. This sensual onslaught was exactly what she'd been determined to avoid, but now that it had started, she couldn't bear to pull away.

"You seem tense. Does it bother you when I touch you?"

Bother her? Not unless you called turning her inside out a bother. "It's different."

"Different than what?"

"Than being with...other...men." Her throat seemed to close on her words and she had a difficult time getting them out. His fingers were on her neck now, his thumbs riding the tendons from her earlobes to the collar of her white shirt. "Most men look at women with their eyes, but they don't touch the way...you...do."

"Then maybe men who can see are the ones missing out." He leaned closer and touched his lips to hers, gently, yet she felt it clear down to her toes. The kiss deepened, and she wrapped her arms around his neck and kissed him back, holding on to him to keep her balance.

Here she was, standing in the middle of a cold stream, kissing a man who was practically a stranger, and she had the feeling she could do it all day—maybe for several days.

Finally he pulled away. "Are you hungry?" His voice was husky, echoing the desire that pummeled through her with a fierceness she'd never experienced before.

She dropped her hands from his neck. "You want to eat now?"

"If we don't, we'd better move to drier ground. Making love in a cold stream might have its limitations."

She sucked in a steadying breath as his words sank in. "I'm not going to make love with you."

"Then we definitely better eat."

Alison took a few steps toward shore, then remembered she had to lead him out of the water. She sloshed back through the stream. "Straight ahead," she said.

He veered to the right, collided with a boulder and almost fell seat first into the water. As soon as he quit teetering, she went back to tugging him along. Now that the kiss was over and her mind had returned to some minimal degree of functioning, she was anxious to get her shoes on, eat the picnic fare and get Ethan Granger back to Twin Oaks before he messed up her mind any more than he already had.

He was leaving town tomorrow, and the last thing she needed was to carry some torch for a ''love 'em and leave 'em kind of guy,'' especially now. The new Alison Fairchild hadn't even made her full debut.

As they ate the fantastic lunch Clint had prepared, she kept the tone light, and made certain there was no more touching other than the occasional brush of fingers as she handed Ethan food. Even that was distracting enough. To combat any sensual urges she might be tempted to give in to, she concentrated on her mother and her guest for tonight's wedding.

Ron Pickering. Alison had never even heard the name before, and she knew all her mother's friends—at least she'd thought she did. She couldn't imagine her mom with any man except her dad. They'd been so right together.

Not that it would bother her for her mother to have a date. It couldn't bother her. That would be absurd and selfish. After all, her father had been dead for fifteen years. But it wasn't safe for her mom to start dating at her age. She was far too naive and innocent. What did she know about men?

For that matter, what did Alison know about them? She glanced over at Ethan, who was finishing off a chunk of fresh apple cake. She didn't know much, but she did know when a man was trouble. And the blind schoolteacher with the hard, lean body, the fantastic hands and the ability to leave her breathless with a kiss was big-time trouble.

NORA TWISTED TO THE RIGHT and then to the left, staring into the mirror in her bedroom and eyeing the lines of the green dress she'd been wearing to weddings and parties for the last five years. It seemed to fit a little tighter than it had the last time she'd worn it, but it was still a perfectly good dress. Besides, Ron Pickering hadn't seen it before. It would be new to him.

There she went again, acting as if this was a real date when it was no such thing, no more than last night's dinner had been, though Ron had insisted on paying the tab.

A date. Now that would be something. The only man she'd ever really dated had been Dale Fairchild. Dated him all through college and married him the week after they'd graduated.

Ron had been the best man at their wedding. After that, he'd dropped from their lives except for a Christmas card every now and then or a note to let them know he'd gotten married, or that Eleanor had given birth to one of their three sons, or to tell them he'd bought a house in the hills north of San Francisco.

She still couldn't imagine why he was passing though Cooper's Corner. It wasn't really a passing-through sort of town. But he was, and she'd not only agreed to go to dinner with him but had invited him to the wedding. It had been a stupid, impulsive act, and she was already regretting it. Dinner was pleasant, but that should have been it.

She tugged a couple of times on the dress until she got it to hang right. The dress would do fine. She wasn't sure about the hair. She didn't even look like herself.

The doorbell rang. She kicked off the sturdy-heeled pumps she'd been trying on with the dress and slipped her feet back into her comfortable loafers. A second later she was peeking through her peephole and into the face of her youngest daughter. She swung open the door. "Alison, where have you been? Madge called here a good two hours ago looking for you."

"I had lunch with a friend." She dropped her handbag on the sofa and stared at Nora. "You had your hair colored."

"Can you tell?"

"Can I tell? You were practically solid gray last night when I was here. Today, you don't have one gray hair showing."

"Lillian's tried to talk me into it for years. I finally gave in and let her do it. This shade of brown is pretty much my natural color. Do you think it makes me look too young?"

Alison stared a minute longer. "Sixty is a lot younger than it used to be."

"My arthritis doesn't know that."

"I'm just surprised you didn't tell me last night you were thinking of having your hair tinted."

"I wasn't thinking of it last night. Besides, you didn't ask my opinion on your nose job."

"Touché." Alison ran her fingers through Nora's hair, fluffing it as she did. "Lillian must have used a good conditioner on it. It's soft."

"You don't like it, do you."

Alison managed a half smile. "Actually, it looks quite nice."

"Thank you, dear. Now, what are you doing here again today, especially when you haven't even seen Madge or Jake yet?"

"I wanted to see you." She glanced toward the kitchen. "Why don't we make a pot of coffee?"

"You know I don't drink coffee in the afternoon."

"But I do, and I need a cup."

Something in Alison's voice suggested she was not here

for coffee or to spread cheer but to lecture. Worse, Nora had the sneaking and disturbing suspicion that the topic on her daughter's mind might be Ron.

Nora led the way to the kitchen, started a fresh brew and took a couple of mugs from the cupboard. Perhaps a half cup wouldn't hurt her. She'd be up later than usual tonight. She took her time pouring half-and-half from the plastic carton into her crystal cream pitcher. Neither of them took sugar. Finally, when she could put off the inevitable no longer, she joined Alison at the table.

"What is it you want to talk about?"

"Your guest for the wedding tonight."

"What about him?"

"Who is Ron Pickering?"

"Actually, he was a friend of your father's. You probably heard your dad mention him before."

"Not that I recall. Does he live in Cooper's Corner?"

"No. He lives in California and has for years. Your dad met him when he was in college in Boston. He was the best man at our wedding. You've seen his picture."

"So why is he in Cooper's Corner now?"

"He's just passing through. He called and said he'd be in town this weekend, and I invited him to go to the wedding as my guest."

Nora walked back to the counter and filled the mugs with coffee, grateful to have something to do with her hands. She wasn't surprised at Alison's questions. The two of them had always had this problem with role reversal. Anyone hearing them would have thought Alison was the mother and Nora the daughter.

"Why isn't Ron's wife with him?"

"She's in a cemetery plot. Otherwise I'd have asked her to join us."

Alison sighed. "Okay, I'm sorry. I know I'm probably

coming on a little strong, but times are different now than they were when you and Dad were dating. There are a lot of men out there preying on widows. You can't be too careful.''

"I've been a widow for fifteen years, dear. So far no man's been preying on me, and I'm quite sure Ron isn't, either.''

"When was the last time you talked to him?''

"At dinner last night.''

"You're seeing him two nights in a row?''

Nora went for evasive. "He and your father were good friends. He and Eleanor sent that beautiful spray of red and white gladiolas to Dale's funeral.''

"Did they come to the funeral?''

"No. I haven't seen Ron since the day your dad and I married.''

Alison leaned her elbows on the table and sipped her coffee. "You haven't seen him in all those years and he just calls from out of the blue and asks to see you. That seems a little strange, don't you think?''

"Would you rather I not see him?''

"Yes.'' She set the coffee down and flattened her hands on the table. "I mean, no, of course not. There's no reason you can't go out with a man. I just worry about you.''

"Your sister, Madge, worries because I don't date. You worry if I do. And neither of you should waste your time worrying about me at all. Not that this is a date, because it isn't.''

"Whatever you call it, it's fine with me. Go to the wedding with Ron and have a good time. Just be careful, that's all.''

"I don't think Ron is going to expect to stop and neck, if that's what you're worried about.'' Nora stood and patted the roundness of her stomach. She was a good thirty pounds overweight and she knew it. "He'd have to be blind to want to do a lot of feeling around on me."

Alison sat up straighter. "Speaking of that, did you know that Seth's best man is blind?"

"I heard that just as I was leaving the beauty shop today. Maggie Porter was in there getting her nails done for the wedding tonight. She said he was blind but incredibly handsome and sexy. Did you think the same about him?"

"I didn't notice."

Alison finished her coffee, carried her mug to the sink and rinsed it out. "I guess I better get home and check on Chaosville."

"Be nice to Madge. She's having a rough time of it."

"I'm always nice to Madge."

Nora walked Alison to the door and gave her a hug. "I know it's going to be different seeing me with a man who's not your father, dear, but it's been fifteen years."

"I know, Mom. Dad would be the first to tell you to go. And I want you to go, too. It's just that…"

"I know how you much you loved your father, Alison. I loved him, too. And even if I dated every night from now until I'm eighty, no one would take your father's place in my heart."

"I know. It's just that…well, Dad was Dad."

"And we all loved him very much."

"But all men aren't like he was. It's a jungle out there, and you never know what kind of beast you might run into."

"Cooper's Corner is a fairly tame jungle." She kissed Alison on the cheek. "Don't worry about me. I'll be fine. Just go out there and enjoy your new nose. I heard Maggie talking about that, too," she said, eager to change the subject to something besides her upcoming evening with Ron.

"What did she say?"

"It's not what she said, it's the way she said it. She's green with envy." Nora reached up and touched the tip of Alison's nose. "It's even starting to grow on me."

"Let's just hope it doesn't *grow* on *me*."

They were both laughing when Alison left. She'd probably assuaged Alison's fears about going to the wedding with Ron tonight, Nora thought. Now only one of them was nervous.

ALISON STOPPED BEHIND Madge's van, which was blocking the door to the garage. There was a new dent in the rear, just above the right taillight, and a layer of thick red mud splattered the back end. She jumped back just in time to dodge the manned skateboard that was barreling up her driveway.

"Hi, Aunt Alison." The front wheels of the skateboard left the pavement as Jake popped a wheelie before jumping off, leaving the missile to sail into the grass.

"Hi, yourself," she said when he'd landed. "Are there speed limits for those things?"

"I never go faster than the speed of light." He gave her a bear hug, then stood back and stared at her. "Wow. Some nose job."

"Thanks, pal." She beamed, knowing he meant it. If he hadn't liked it, he would have said that, too.

"Did it hurt when the doctor lobbed it off?"

"I didn't feel a thing. I had some pain when the anesthetic wore off, but not too much. You couldn't tell it by the bruises and swelling, though. My face looked as if someone had used it for a punching bag. Someone big."

"You look hot now." He stuffed his hands in his pocket. "Guess Mom told you about losing her job."

"She told me, but don't worry. She'll find another soon."

"I just hope she doesn't start talking about moving to Boston the way she usually does when she loses a job. Woodstown High's baseball team has a chance of going all the way to state this year, and Coach says I'm the best pitcher on the team."

"Then I'm going to have to get up to Woodstown High and make some games."

"That'd be cool. I'm a mean, keen pitchin' machine."

Alison put her arm about Jake's shoulders as they started inside. He'd always been small for his age, and at fifteen, he could have easily passed for twelve, except that he was supersmart, even for fifteen.

Jake pushed open the back door and Alison followed him inside. A slice of cold pepperoni pizza sat on the cardboard delivery box in the middle of the table, surrounded by a shaker of cracked pepper and an open package of chocolate chip cookies. A half-empty pitcher of iced tea rested on the counter beside a wadded-up paper towel, and there was a smear of tomato sauce across the counter.

Jake walked to the foot of the staircase, cupped his hand at his mouth and yelled, "Mom, Aunt Alison's home."

A few seconds later, Madge came bounding down the steps in her bare feet, her short blond hair bouncing around her cheeks. Petite as she was, and dressed in a pair of denim cutoffs and a red T-shirt, she could have passed for Jake's sister.

"Turn around quick, Alison. I don't want a peek at your new killer nose until I'm close enough to get a real look." She stopped halfway down the stairs and closed her eyes. "I mean it. Turn around and don't turn back until I say."

"You're making too much of this," Alison protested, but she did as Madge said, turning to face the kitchen, her gaze glued on the chaos there.

"Give us a drumroll, Jake."

Jake obliged with enthusiasm.

"Now, slowly turn around," Madge directed. "I want to get the full effect."

Alison propped her hands on her hips and tried for a vampish runway walk, careful to skirt Madge and Jake's luggage, which had been dropped in the living room. Finally, she turned to face her sister. "What's the verdict?"

"Wow! Double wow! You don't even look like you."

"Was I that bad before?"

"You were nothing like this. So now that you're gorgeous, you've got to get out of that post office more. You can't find a husband hiding behind the mail chutes."

"I don't hide. I work."

"Same thing. If you didn't have that wedding tonight, I'd take you out on the town myself, see to just what kind of trouble we could get you into."

"I'm not interested in trouble and you shouldn't talk that way in front of Jake. He might believe you."

"I'm not a kid anymore, Aunt Alison. We already had a lesson on all that man-woman stuff in school. I got an A in sex education."

"That's my boy," Madge said, reaching over to tousle his slightly shaggy brown hair. She smiled at him conspiratorially. "But don't tell your Aunt Alison what you know. She thinks men are only a return address on a postage-due envelope."

Alison didn't dispute her sister's words. Actually, before last night, that statement hadn't been too far from the truth.

Before Ethan Granger had let his fingers trace the outline of her face and send tremors of sensual awareness skittering up her spine.

Before he'd kissed her.

"I know what you're thinking," Madge said.

Alison sincerely hoped she didn't.

"Don't give it another thought. Jake is going to carry the suitcases upstairs and put them in our rooms—aren't you, Jake?"

"Oh, can't it wait? They're not in the way. Tell her, Aunt Alison."

"They are in the middle of the room," she replied. "I'm just not sure why there are so many of them."

"Just in case we plan to stay longer than the weekend," Madge said. She turned to Jake. "Upstairs now!"

Jake shrugged his shoulders and rolled his eyes but went to perform the task.

"And I'm going to restore the kitchen to the same unhealthy and unreasonable state of cleanness it was in when we arrived," Madge announced.

Alison linked her arm with her sister's. "The kitchen can wait. We haven't had a chance to talk about you yet."

"It's the same old story, just different sidebars. Even crappy joints find me dispensable. The topic is not fit conversation for a day when we're celebrating my little sister's transformation."

The negativism that crept into Madge's voice seemed totally out of place. Chaos and calamity went with Madge like maple syrup with pancakes, but in spite of everything, she usually danced through life with the enthusiasm of a rock and roll star.

"We could take a glass of iced tea out to the back deck."

Madge shook her head. "We'll do that tomorrow, and I'll tell you all about the jerk who got exactly what he deserved."

"So you didn't spill the water?"

"Dumped, spilled, what's the difference. The effect was the same. Cooled him off real fast. Bet he'll think twice before he runs his hand under another waitress's skirt. You should have seen his face. It was worth ten jobs."

Madge started laughing, and Alison joined in. Chaos and all, it was good to have Madge around—as long as she wasn't staying too long.

"If you're sure you don't want to talk, I think I'll go upstairs and take a nice, long bubble bath before I have to start getting dressed for the wedding. It's been a long day."

A long day, and it promised to be an even longer night unless she learned how to handle the advances of Ethan Granger. Alison knew that being alone with the man and his defense-destroying touch was dangerous. The only solution was to ignore him completely, not let those sensuous hands anywhere near her.

He was leaving tomorrow, and she hadn't sunk all that money into a new nose just to sit around and grieve for some guy who'd be miles away, probably touching someone else's nose and killing her with kisses.

But she was still thinking about Ethan when she relaxed in the tub of hot water and frothy, fragrant bubbles. Eyes closed, head resting on the bath pillow, she trailed her fingers across her face the way Ethan had done. Simple, yet so devastatingly erotic, it had felt like foreplay.

But if just his touch had been that arousing, what would

it be like to actually make love with him? To lie beside him naked and feel his hard body pressed against hers?

Her heart did a ridiculous flip-flop, and her insides turned to mush. Holding her nose, she slid all the way under the water, determined to wash the images from her mind. When she came up for air, she knew it was useless. It would take all of her willpower to stay away from him tonight.

CHAPTER FOUR

ETHAN DROPPED A FEW ice cubes into a glass, poured a couple of fingers of brandy from the decanter that rested on the polished antique secretary, and added a splash of water. He wasn't normally much of a drinker, but if he had to parade around the rest of the night in this monkey suit, he'd need a little fortification.

Still, the weekend hadn't been the dud he'd expected when Seth had persuaded him to come to Cooper's Corner and serve as his best man. In fact, the wedding had been nice enough—as weddings went. They made Ethan nervous, but Seth had acted like a man being escorted to heaven instead of one being locked into a lifetime of "honey do's" and rug rats.

Now all that remained of Ethan's duties was going downstairs and joining in the reception revelries. Tomorrow he'd be on a plane back to New Orleans and, he hoped, a teaching job in an inner-city school where the threats of violence and the undercurrents of gang rivalries were reaching dangerous levels. He'd be there already if bureaucracy hadn't gummed up the works.

He sipped his drink, walked to the window and looked out. A string of cars lined the curved drive, and waiters in white coats were setting up a carving station and carrying platters of hors d'oeuvres across the lawn to waiting tables. And somewhere down there, Alison Fairchild had probably forgotten the kisses that had left him punch-drunk this afternoon, and was busily planning her next conquest.

She'd bought herself a new look and she was out to get a man. It was as plain as the nose on her face—pun intended. She'd be the belle of the ball tonight, have guys standing in line to dance with her and take her home. It wouldn't be easy foiling her plans, but he loved a challenge, the more difficult the better. Hell, he was FBI.

BY THE TIME ALISON freshened up in Twin Oaks' charming powder room and made it out to the west lawn, the party was in full swing. The bed-and-breakfast always reeked of the romance of a bygone era, but tonight the magic was even more pronounced. It was as if Cupid himself had shown up to add to the ambience. Not only had the beauty of the ceremony warmed the coldest hearts, but Maureen and Clint had provided the usual enchanting amenities.

Inside, candles in wall sconces cast a golden glow throughout the spacious gathering room, and huge crystal vases were filled with fragrant, cascading blossoms. Outside, strings of tiny white lights draped the trees and turned the grounds into a fairyland.

A few people lingered inside, but most had found their way outdoors, where long tables covered in white linen overflowed with delectable foods, decadent chocolate truffles, champagne and fruit punch. Clint had even set up a portable dance floor on a grassy area to the rear of the rambling farmhouse, and a four-piece combo provided music beneath a full moon and a blanket of dazzling stars.

A perfect setting to follow a perfect wedding.

Alison stood a few yards from the back door and surveyed the area, hoping to catch a glimpse of her mother so that she could go and meet the infamous Ron Pickering. It would be difficult to spot them, since a huge percentage of Cooper's Corner residents were in attendance. Wendy's parents were standing near the dance floor, surrounded by well-wishers. Gina was a teacher and Howard a reading consultant at the local school, and they knew practically everyone in town.

Phyllis and Philo Cooper were stationed near the champagne fountain. Phyllis was talking a mile a minute, no doubt catching everyone up with what was going on in her life and the lives of her fellow townsfolk. If you shopped in the Cooper's general store, you were fair game. Phyllis didn't consider herself a gossip but more of a town crier. Alison wondered what she was saying about her new nose. Not that it mattered. It would be old news after tonight.

Dr. Dorn and his wife, Martha, were holding hands at a table in the center of the action. In their mid-eighties and still in love, they were an inspiration to everyone.

Practially the whole town was accounted for, but there was still no sign of her mother and Mr. Pickering. They'd been at the wedding. Alison had spied them sitting together near the back of the church as she'd walked down the aisle, and her stomach had tightened. They weren't sitting close, but it just didn't seem right to see her mother with another man.

Alison knew her reaction was childish and selfish, and she had to get past it. Still, she was concerned about her mom. Nora had been cherished and protected when her husband was alive, and she'd had no real experience with men since. It would be easy for a man to take advantage of her, to lead her on and then leave her heartbroken and disillusioned. Alison couldn't bear the thought of anyone hurting her.

She scanned the area around the dance floor again, this

time spotting Ethan engaged in an animated discussion with Maggie Porter. Her breath caught. He looked positively scrumptious in the gray tuxedo.

"Maggie was right. He is quite a hunk."

Alison turned at the sound of her mother's voice. She was a few feet behind Alison, her *date* walking at her side. "Who's a hunk?"

"Seth's best man, the hunk you're staring at," Nora said, flashing a knowing smile. "Besides looking great, he has a warm handshake, and that always speaks well of a man."

"When did you meet him?"

"Seth introduced him to Ron and me back at the church." She turned from Alison to the man standing at her side. "And speaking of introductions, I want you to meet Ron Pickering. Ron, this is my youngest daughter, Alison, the postmistress."

"And you're every bit as pretty as your mother said." Ron stuck out his hand. "I feel like I know you, after seeing you grow from a baby to adulthood in the pictures."

"What pictures were those?"

"The family picture on the Christmas card Nora sent every year."

"Not every year, Ron. There were lots of years we had no idea where you were."

Alison didn't like the way this virtual stranger made it sound as if they were all old friends. For that matter, she didn't like the way he looked at her mother, or the intimate tone he used when he spoke her name. Alison's first instinct was that Ron Pickering couldn't be trusted, and her first instincts were often right.

She nodded as her mother talked about how beautiful the wedding had been, but mostly, she studied Ron, looking for things about him not to like. His ears were a little big, but there was no way she could fault him for that, not after years of being called "Banana Nose" for a body part she had no control over.

His hair was gray, thin and receding, deep wrinkles had set in around his eyes, and he had a little paunch at the waistline—all signs that he was probably as old as her mom, but nothing to indicate any major character flaws. Those would be more difficult to ferret out.

Nora touched Alison's arm. "Look, Wendy and Seth are about to share their first dance as husband and wife. Let's go closer, so no one will step in front of us and spoil our view. They make such a lovely couple."

"You two go ahead," Alison said. "I think I'm going to grab a bite to eat." She watched them walk away. Ron took her mother's arm and whispered something in her ear, and Nora's laughter carried over the music. Her mother liked him. Alison could tell. That uneasy feeling assailed her once more. It should be her father here, laughing and growing old with the woman he'd loved so dearly.

She swallowed hard and tried to concentrate on being pleased that her mother was enjoying herself. Alison was making the first stab at progress when she spotted Kevin Bosco swaggering across the lawn in her direction, looking every bit as handsome as he had last night when she'd bumped into him at the rehearsal. Good. He was just the diversion she needed.

"I wondered where you were," Kevin said, stopping at her side. "I've been looking all over for you."

"I was inside for a while."

"As long as someone else wasn't taking up all your time. I ran into Barry a minute ago, and he said you played nursemaid to Seth's blind friend last night—spent the evening telling him where he was and what he was eating. Said you even drove him home.''

''That was last night,'' she crooned, barely resisting the urge to turn and see if Ethan was still entertaining Maggie. ''This is tonight.''

A waiter passed by with a tray of filled champagne flutes. Kevin took two and placed one in Alison's hand. ''To old friends,'' he said, ''and a night to remember.''

She clinked her glass with his. Moonlight, music and Kevin. This was the night she'd been waiting for all her life, and she wasn't going to let anything ruin it for her.

Not her mother, who'd walked off arm in arm with a man whose intentions Alison didn't trust. Not Madge, who was likely spilling red wine on Alison's new carpet or scattering her clothes and belongings all over the house. And definitely not Ethan Granger, who was no doubt plotting how and when to trail his hot little fingers over Maggie's face.

''A night to remember,'' Alison said, repeating Kevin's toast. ''Now let's party.''

MAUREEN COOPER STROLLED the grounds of Twin Oaks, stopping to talk to everyone and making sure the serving trays stayed full and the guests happy. Wedding receptions were her favorite occasions at the bed-and-breakfast, probably because the tears were always ones of joy—at least almost always—and the newlyweds glowed with happiness and great expectations.

She stared at Wendy and Seth, who were talking with friends at the edge of the dance floor. Their love for each other was almost tangible. She'd thought she'd had that kind of love once.

A cool breeze brushed Maureen's face, tossing strands of her long hair against her cheeks. Pushing the troubling thoughts aside, she tucked the flying hair behind her ears and let her gaze settle on Alison Fairchild, amazed at the transformation that had come over her.

It wasn't just the nose that was different, though there was no mistaking the fact that she'd had plastic surgery. It was the makeup, the hair, the walk, the voice—all a hundred times more provocative than they'd been the last time Maureen had seen Alison. She was dancing with Kevin Bosco now, and he was smiling like a guy who'd just realized he had the winning lottery ticket.

But as much as Alison appeared to be enjoying Kevin's company, Maureen had an idea it was mostly for show. Kevin was attractive enough, but Maureen had seen Alison and Ethan Granger when they'd returned from their picnic, and she was convinced the two of them had shared more than Clint's chicken and potato salad today. And whatever they'd sampled had only whetted their appetite for more. They might avoid each other for a while, but she had a sneaking suspicion that before the night was over, the two of them would be together.

Romance. When it was right, it could be the most beautiful experience in the world. When it went sour, it could tear the heart right out of you.

"I NEVER KNEW you were such a great dancer."

"Thank you." Alison refrained from pointing out to Kevin that he would have known ten years ago if he'd ever asked her to dance. He twirled her around, and she grew giddy from the movement and the two glasses of champagne she'd drunk.

She'd spent most of the last hour dancing, but not always with Kevin. At least a half-dozen single guys who'd barely spoken to her when they'd run into her at the post office had appeared at her elbow and asked her to dance.

Everyone had come around except Ethan Granger. Apparently he'd seen—or felt—enough of her. Not that she minded. Even if he'd asked, she had no intention of dancing with him. Flirting with Kevin was fun, like taking a first drive in a red convertible.

Involvement with Ethan was titillating, dizzying, like breaking the speed limit in that same automobile and then seeing the cliff edge straight ahead. One moment of thrill followed by the realization that she was in for disaster. The man had probably practiced that erotic face-feel routine on half the female population in his acquaintance. The kiss, too. No man learned to kiss like that without lots of practice.

She peered over Kevin's shoulder as they danced, spotting Ethan on the lawn, talking to Wendy. If Alison didn't know better, she would think he was looking right at her. Wendy definitely was. She put up her hand and gave a little wave.

A second later, Wendy and Ethan stepped onto the dance floor, leaving Longfellow on the lawn, watching his master as if he thought Wendy might be about to abduct him. They wove through the cluster of gyrating bodies, heading directly toward Alison and Kevin.

Kevin's mouth was at her ear, his breath hot on her cheek. "Are you cold?"

"No. I'm fine."

"You're shaking."

Damn. She was. She made a conscious effort to slow her pulse and steady her nerves as she watched Wendy whisper something in Ethan's ear. Ethan nodded, then attempted to tap Kevin on the shoulder. The knuckle rap actually hit a spot in the middle of his back. Kevin whirled around.

"Sorry about cutting in," Ethan said, "but as best man,

I feel it's only appropriate that I get one dance with the maid of honor.''

Kevin frowned. "I guess that's up to Alison."

She barely hesitated before nodding in acceptance. She might have a new nose and a new outlook on life, but one look at Ethan and her willpower had melted like a pat of butter in a hot pan.

"One dance," Kevin said, reluctantly letting go of her hand.

"I guess that's up to Alison," Ethan said, mimicking Kevin's words and tone, but adding his own mischievous grin.

Wendy took Alison's right hand and placed it in Ethan's left, then tossed an arm over Kevin's shoulder and led him off the dance floor, talking and laughing as she did, an apparent attempt to charm him out of his wounded pride.

Ethan slid his right arm around Alison's waist. His touch set off a wave of heat that rushed through her body with the force of a forest fire. What was Wendy thinking? She'd warned Alison to be wary of Ethan and then she'd practically pushed her into his arms. Was Wendy so much in love with Seth that she had no clue Ethan was the sexiest man who'd ever set foot inside the city limits of Cooper's Corner?

The music stopped before they'd taken their first step. Alison breathed a little easier. "Guess it wasn't meant to be," she said, wishing she sounded less breathless.

"You don't expect me to give up that easily." With his fingers splayed across the back of her waist, he pulled her closer. "Not after I found the courage to get this far."

"Courage?"

"I'm not much of a dancer," he admitted. "It's one of the few situations in which I can't depend on Longfellow to guide me. In fact, the only way I can handle myself on a dance floor is if I hold my partner very, very close.''

The music started, a slow, hauntingly romantic tune, and Ethan swayed for a second to the beat before pulling her so close that it would have been impossible to fit a fingernail file between their bodies.

Her mind seemed to lose contact with reality, and she had difficulty making her feet move, much less follow the right steps. His body was pressed against hers and she was drunk on emotions she couldn't begin to understand.

Gained a nose, lost her mind. The surgeon had never mentioned insanity as a side effect, unless it had been on one of the release forms she'd signed, typed in such small print she'd missed it altogether.

"Just relax," Ethan whispered, his mouth at her ear.

"I am relaxed. Why wouldn't I be?"

"I don't know. Maybe you're afraid you might like dancing with me."

"I haven't given it a thought one way or the other." She took a deep breath and wished she was a better liar. Closing her eyes, she rested her head against his shoulder, aware of the hard planes of his chest, the brush of his thigh against hers, the feel of his hand on her lower back. She gave up fighting the attraction and lost herself in the dance the way she'd lost herself in his kiss that afternoon, so completely she didn't even realize when the music stopped, barely noticed when their bodies quit swaying. Ethan continued to hold her close.

"If we leave now, we could probably escape your jealous lover."

"Kevin's not my lover."

"He plans to be."

"How would you know that?"

"I can sense those things. That's why I'm willing to

go out on a limb here to protect you. I say we cut out of here now.''

''Where is it you want to go?''

''To my room.''

Reality returned like a swift kick. ''If you think I'm going to go up to your room and—and...''

''And make love?''

''Right. I mean, wrong. I'm not.''

''I was only going to ask you to go up and help me find the envelope with Seth and Wendy's plane tickets in it. If I don't locate it, they'll have a hard time getting to Hawaii tomorrow. But making love would be nice, too.''

''And that's how you'd protect me from Kevin? No thanks.'' She jerked from his grasp, but he caught her wrist before she could get away.

''Okay, cancel the making love. Actually, that was your suggestion, anyway. Just come with me to help find the envelope. I had it this afternoon, but apparently I mislaid it. I sometimes have difficulty finding things in an unfamiliar environment.''

''Ask Maggie Porter. I'm sure she'll help you out.''

''You're the maid of honor.''

''What does that have to do with this?''

''It's as much your responsibility as mine to make sure everything goes off without a hitch. Helping me find the plane tickets is the least you can do for the newlyweds.''

When he put it like that, he didn't leave her a lot of choice. ''I'll go with you and help you search for the tickets under one condition.''

''You name it.''

''No touching of any kind.''

''Does that include kissing?''

''Especially kissing.''

''I promise I won't do anything you don't want me to

do.'' He put his right hand over his heart. ''Scout's honor.''

''How do I know you were ever a Scout?''

''Guess you'll just have to trust me on that one.''

That would take a big leap of faith. She didn't even trust herself when he was around. But she couldn't ignore his plea for help. After all, he couldn't see to search the out-of-the-way spaces in the room. The envelope with the tickets could have fallen to the floor in plain sight, and he wouldn't be able to see them.

''Okay, Ethan. I'll help you look for the tickets, but that's all I'm doing in your room.''

''Absolutely. What kind of guy do you take me for?''

''I'll take the Fifth on that question.''

LONGFELLOW STOPPED outside the door to Ethan's room, the perfect guide. ''Good dog.'' Ethan reached down and stroked the back of his head before reaching in his pocket for the large brass door key.

Alison stepped closer. ''Would you like me to unlock the door?''

''Not necessary.'' Following the procedures he'd been taught, he looked straight ahead and located the doorknob, then the keyhole by touch. Not wanting to be exact, he clinked the key against the metal plate before letting it slide into place.

It wasn't so important that he not make a mistake with Alison, but once he was back in New Orleans, a tiny telling error could jeopardize the success of the operation and even his life. *Act blind, talk blind, think blind.* Those were his training goals. That, and to learn everything he could about the workings of the drug-dealing gang that was gaining a deadly foothold in one of New Orleans's inner-city schools. Threatening staff and faculty. A disaster in the works.

The reality of the situation would consume his mind as soon as he was back in the Crescent City, but it all seemed a world away from the serene environment of Twin Oaks and Cooper's Corner. He'd never fit into this kind of peaceful existence on a permanent basis, but it was amazing—and surprising—how much he was enjoying his visit.

Alison stepped past him as he swung the door open, and the sweet, fragrant scent of her perfume jolted his senses. Even if he had been blind he would have noticed and reacted to that. She flicked on the overhead light.

Staring at her and marveling at the way her presence brightened his room, he felt a twinge of guilt at the means he'd used to get her up here. But if he hadn't lured her away from the dance floor, she'd be dazzling some other guy.

He loosened the dreaded bow tie and unbuttoned the top two buttons of the starched, pleated shirt. "Hope you don't mind my making myself comfortable."

"Just as long as you don't start removing your clothes."

"I thought our only rule was that I'm not supposed to touch you."

"I'm a woman. I reserve the right to change the rules by the minute."

He was counting on that.

"I love this room," she said, turning slowly so that her gaze could take in every inch of space. "It's so inviting. If I tried to combine the fabrics, colors and different furniture styles like this, I'd end up with a mismatched hodgepodge that would frighten guests away. Maureen has such a talent for decorating."

"I don't know about the visual effect, but I know it's comfortable for me and Longfellow." He hadn't paid a lot of attention to the decorating scheme before Alison had arrived, but it was definitely to his liking now.

She was dressed like all the other female attendants in the wedding, but the deep blue color of the satiny dress, the spaghetti straps that revealed her creamy shoulders, and the tight fitted waist did a lot more for her than it did for any of the others. The only problem was that the skirt fell to her ankles, hiding her gorgeous legs.

"Do you have any idea where you might have put the envelope?" she asked, walking over to a mahogany chest and running her fingers along the grapes and vines carved into the dark wood.

"Not a clue."

"When was the last time you saw it?"

"I had it in my hands this morning before I went downstairs to breakfast. I must have put it down somewhere when the smell of griddle cakes and maple syrup got to be too much to resist. I haven't had it since."

"I don't understand why you ever had the plane tickets. It seems to me that Seth would have taken care of those himself."

As indeed he had. Ethan tried to think of a good answer to Alison's question. None came to mind. "Guess he just had so much on his plate that he didn't want to take a chance on forgetting them."

"They're not leaving until tomorrow."

"*Early* tomorrow. They're going to the airport directly from Twin Oaks."

"Still, wouldn't Seth have kept the tickets in his possession?"

"I'm ordinarily very dependable, and Seth was rushing

around trying to finish packing and finalize some special honeymoon plans.''

It was a weak story, but she seemed to be buying it. The problem now was how Ethan was going to get out of spending the night looking for an envelope that didn't exist.

She walked about the room, searching on top of all the furniture. ''Do you mind if I look inside the drawers?''

''Be my guest.''

She opened the first one, then pulled away, her face turning the shade of a rich cabernet. He had to work hard to keep from smiling as she stared at his neat stack of shorts as if she'd never seen men's underwear before. The woman was obviously a lot more naive than she seemed.

His imagination flew into overdrive. If folded shorts in a drawer made her blush, imagine how she'd react to a pair covering a man's private parts. At that thought, his private parts gave a little twinge.

She closed the drawer with a lot more force than necessary as he walked over to stand beside her. ''I've pretty much checked the drawers,'' he told her. ''I ran my hands all the way to the bottom and felt everything thoroughly.'' He brushed her shoulder with his hand, casually, as if it were accidental.

She took a deep breath and stepped away from him. ''If the tickets aren't in a drawer, they must have fallen under or behind something.''

''That's possible.''

She stooped and looked beneath the chest, her round behind sticking almost straight up. ''Tickets can't just disappear into thin air,'' she said, straightening up again and smoothing the front of her dress. ''Are you certain you didn't take them out of this room?''

''I don't think so. Let me think about it a minute.'' He

walked to the window and opened it, letting the music waft into the room. "I had the tickets with me. I decided to go to breakfast. I put the tickets…"

"Keep thinking. Where did you put the tickets?" She walked over and leaned against the window frame, so close their bodies were almost touching.

He exhaled a slow, steady stream of air, playing his part to the hilt. "My briefcase. I slipped them into the side pocket. I can't believe I forgot doing that."

"Case solved," she said. "Though you'd better double-check that they're really there."

Ethan shook his head. "No. I know for a fact that's where they are."

"Guess it's time for me to get back to the party, then."

But he didn't want her to go, and she was making no move toward leaving. Instead she was looking at him with those big blue eyes. The music changed to a slow, rhythmic ballad about a man and a woman and a kiss.

"You don't have to go," he said.

"There's no lost envelope to find. Why would I stay?" Her voice was soft, tingly, a little shaky.

He reached out to touch her, then pulled away. "It's tough being a Scout. But if you changed the rules, we could have one last dance, right here in the room."

She bit her bottom lip and narrowed her eyes, as if fearing she was about to make a big mistake.

"What harm can come from a dance?" he urged. "A goodbye dance between the maid of honor and the best man. It's traditional."

"I've never heard of that custom."

"Really. It's big where I come from. It's said to be good luck for the newlyweds."

"One last dance," she said, looking at him from under

her dark lashes, "and then I really have to go. And this is just for luck for Seth and Wendy."

"Naturally." Ethan held out his hand. She took it, then stepped into his arms. One last dance, but if he was lucky, it would last all night long.

CHAPTER FIVE ˜

ALISON'S RESOLVE to stay on the defensive weakened the second she stepped into Ethan's arms—and it had been none too strong before. The slightest touch and she seemed to lose the ability to think logically. Instead her emotions took over, twisting her insides and making it difficult to breathe.

It made no sense at all. She barely knew Ethan, and what she did know about him wouldn't explain an attraction so strong it possessed her like some love-crazed demon.

"I'm glad you stayed," Ethan whispered, his breath warm on her cheek.

"I shouldn't have."

"I can't imagine why not."

Right now neither could she. The music stopped. He held her close and nuzzled his lips in her hair. She ached to stretch up and put her mouth to his, to taste him the way she had this afternoon. To feel their breath mingle and their tongues tango. But if she did, she'd never find the strength to walk out that door.

"I need to go," she whispered, her voice strained, as if she were forcing it through a sieve.

He touched his lips to her earlobe. "I really wish you wouldn't."

She went weak, hungry to experience all the new sensations whirling inside her. But staying went against every grain of common sense she possessed. She was eager to explore all her feelings, yet was still afraid of this man. He'd come with a warning and seemed to be playing a game that only he knew the rules to. "Why, Ethan? Why do you want me here?"

"You're talking to a man, Alison. We never understand emotions. All I know is that I want to be with you."

"That's not enough of a reason."

Slipping a rough thumb beneath her chin, he tilted her face toward his. "Then maybe this will be." He touched his mouth to hers gently, coaxing.

"You don't play fair."

"Who does?"

He kissed her hard then and she kissed him back, over and over, sometimes deep and wet, other times quick and breathless. One of his hands roamed her back, the other tangled in her hair, and all the while she was sinking deeper into a passion that obliterated her caution as if it had never been.

Her heart knocked around in her chest like a crazed jumping bean as Ethan picked her up and carried her toward the bed. They were nearly there when someone's knuckles rapped hard against the door.

Ethan put his finger to his lips. "Don't make a sound. Maybe they'll go away."

The knocking grew louder. "Ethan, are you in there?"

"It's Seth," Alison whispered. "You have to answer him. He may want his airplane tickets."

Ethan grimaced. "He doesn't need them until tomorrow morning."

"You can't just ignore him." She wiggled from his grasp and straightened her dress as best she could as she padded toward the door in her stocking feet. She didn't remember kicking off her pumps, but then who'd expect her to when kissing Ethan?

"Oops. I'm sorry." Seth's gaze went from Alison to Ethan. "I didn't mean to interrupt anything. You should have told me to go away."

"Right," Ethan agreed. "So go away."

"You're not interrupting anything," Alison argued, aware from the look Seth was giving her that it was a wasted lie. Her hair was probably a mess and her lipstick couldn't have survived the latest onslaught.

"So why aren't you with your bride?" Ethan asked.

"I doubted I'd get to see you in the morning and I wanted to thank you for giving up one of your busy weekends to get me through the happy occasion."

"Hey, what are friends for?"

"And I'll be glad to return the favor anytime you tie the knot."

"Not going to happen."

The two men shook hands and Seth turned to Alison. "Wendy and I both appreciate all you've done, Allie, especially me. Wendy would have gone nuts trying to plan all of this without your help."

"My pleasure, but I think you may still need some help."

"No way. I can handle the honeymoon all by myself."

"Once you get there." She touched Seth's arm before he could slip away. "Aren't you forgetting something?"

"Can't thing of anything."

"Ethan has your airplane tickets in his briefcase. You won't get very far without them."

Seth looked at her as if she were a bit daft. "The tickets are in my room, tucked away in the outside pocket of my suitcase. I've checked them half a dozen times since I put them in there last night."

"Oh, is that so?"

She turned back to Ethan, her insides crackling again. But this time the heat was not connected to passion. Ethan dropped to the edge of the bed, the palms of his hands wrapped around his temples like a vise. Caught in the act.

Seth wisely made his exit as Alison stamped across the room, retrieved her shoes and slid her feet into them. "You just never give up, do you?" she demanded, hands on her hips. "Life is just one big seduction scene to you."

"I can explain…."

"Oh, go *feel* yourself," she muttered, for want of anything better to hurl at him. There were probably a multitude of four-letter words she could have used with justification, but she used them about as often as she robbed a bank or jumped from a speeding car.

She slammed the door behind her with a vengeance, hoping it rattled Ethan's brain. The sound echoed around her as she hurried down the stairs. The new Alison might be open to new experiences, but she was just as naive as the old one had been. That was obviously one more thing she needed to change, but she'd do it.

Lesson one: Blind or not, if a man looked like trouble, smelled like trouble and acted like trouble, he probably was. But tomorrow Ethan would be out of Cooper's Corner and her life forever. Tomorrow couldn't come too soon.

NORA WALKED BESIDE RON up the brick walk that led from the parking lot to her apartment. In some ways it seemed strange to have him beside her. In other ways, it seemed as natural as breathing or talking.

"I had a good time this weekend," he said as they reached the door.

"So did I."

"It's hard to believe I was so nervous before I got here. I had your number half dialed twice Friday morning to back out."

Nora stopped fumbling in her purse for the key and looked at Ron. He appeared older in the glare of the porch light, the lines in his face deeper and his hair lighter. She probably did, too, but that didn't seem to bother Ron.

"I can't imagine you being afraid to do anything, Ron Pickering. What was it the guys called you in college? Reckless Ron?"

"That was only on the football field."

"And when you were driving around town in that old Plymouth."

"Now, that was a dandy car."

"I should say. The first time Dale ever kissed me was in the back seat of that car. We were out at the overlook, watching for falling stars. Let's see, you were with that blond bombshell. What was her name?"

"I have no clue."

"Oh, sure you do. Emma…Anna…Emily. That was it. Emily Lou. I don't remember her last name, though."

"That was a long time ago."

Nora patted her stomach. "Quite a few years and a good thirty pounds."

"You still look good."

"For an old woman?"

"You're not old."

"I'm sixty." At that moment she was glad she'd let Lillian cover the gray.

"I'm sixty-three, and we still managed to hit a few hot licks on the dance floor tonight."

"We didn't do too badly considering how long it's been since I've danced."

"We didn't do badly at all."

She fit her key into the lock.

"I'd like to see you again, Nora."

"In another thirty-seven years?"

"I was thinking maybe we shouldn't wait that long. How about next weekend?"

"I thought you were only passing through town."

"I am, but I can pass through next week, as well. I'm living just south of Boston now, in the home my parents had. I didn't have the heart to sell it, so I rented it out when Dad died. I moved back a couple of months ago."

"You moved back for good?"

"There wasn't a lot for me in California after Eleanor died. The kids are scattered all over the world, and they can visit me as easily in Boston as in California."

"Next weekend." She mulled the idea over in her mind. She'd enjoyed the last couple of days, but she hadn't expected anything further. "You're not talking about a date, are you?"

"I'm talking about a nice dinner and some pleasant conversation. I guess that would qualify as a date."

Nora stood in the glare of the porch light with a balding man who wasn't her husband who'd just asked her for a real date. The moment should feel awkward. She should be nervous. She was—a little—but she wanted to see him again. He was a piece of her past, and she didn't want to say goodbye. "Dinner sounds good, Ron. Conversation sounds even better."

He took her hand. "I'll call you."

"If you want. If you change your mind, I'll understand."

He took her hand and squeezed it. "I won't change my mind." And then he was gone, not looking half-bad from the back as he walked to his car. Nora stepped inside her apartment, stopped at the mirror over the mantle and stared at the woman in the glass. Not a gray hair in sight.

She wasn't sure if it was the new hair color or the pleasant evening she'd had with Ron Pickering, but she felt younger than she had in years. She didn't expect anything to come of a date with him. Nonetheless, it was nice to be appreciated by a man again. And he had said she looked good. Probably his eyesight was going.

"ARE YOU STILL ALIVE in here?"

Alison managed to open one eye. The sun was pouring though the slatted blinds at the window. Madge was standing over her with a tray of toast, jam and coffee.

"What time is it?" Alison muttered through the husky dregs of sleep.

"Eight-thirty. You never sleep this late. It must have been a helluva wedding reception. I didn't even hear you come in last night."

Alison rolled over and raised herself up on her elbows. "I hope you didn't wake me just to tell me I got in late last night."

"Nope. I woke you up to hear all the details. Were you and your nose the hit of the evening?"

"Wendy and Seth were the hit of the wedding. My nose and I were just a side item." She reached for the coffee and took a long sip, hoping the caffeine would kick in quickly.

"You were a stunning side item. And speaking of stunning, Mom said the best man was quite a hunk. She said the two of you did some serious belly rubbing on the dance floor."

"Mom did not say that!"

"Not in those words, but the gist of the message was

the same. So tell me about this mystery man. Did the two of you make magic?''

Magic. It had seemed that way—until Seth broke up the magician's routine. She rolled her head and stretched her neck. "The two of us didn't make anything. And the only reason we danced so closely was because that's the way he keeps his bearings on the dance floor—or so he claimed.''

"Sounds seductive.''

"Try nauseating.'' She picked up a slice of buttered toast from the tray and took a bite. At least chewing would give her a valid excuse to avoid answering Madge's barrage of questions for a minute or two. After storming out of Ethan's room, she had returned to the reception and danced with Kevin until midnight, when the band put away their instruments and the last guests went home.

So why hadn't it been thoughts of Kevin, rather than memories of Ethan's kisses, that teased her senses when she'd finally collapsed into bed? She chewed, swallowed and washed the toast down with more coffee.

"At any rate, you must have enjoyed yourself to stay out so late.''

"I did. It was a beautiful wedding, and Wendy and Seth looked so happy together.''

"That's what Mom said. I invited her over for lunch today. I hope you don't mind.''

"Are you cooking?''

"No. I knew you'd want to do that. Besides, I did breakfast.''

"Toast?''

"And coffee,'' Madge added, dropping down to sit cross-legged on the side of Alison's bed. "You're the domestic one, not me. You should have a husband and a houseful of kids.''

"First I should have a date."

"Wear those new outfits in your closet and keep swaying those hips like you were yesterday, and you'll have
more dates than you can handle."

"How do you know what's in my closet?"

"I snooped, of course. Thought you might have something I could wear."

"You never change."

"But I'm thinking maybe I should." Madge was still
in her pajamas, blue flannel with white polar bears skid-
ding across chunks of ice.

"Is that why you're up before noon on a Sunday morning?"

"Partly. I have a lot on my mind."

"Such as?"

"I started thinking last night. Here you are, getting a
new nose and a new personality…"

"All I got was a new nose. The surgeon didn't do personalities."

"Joke all you want, but you're different and it's not
just the nose. Your haircut is a lot more stylish, you're
wearing makeup, and you have cute little sweaters and
short fitted skirts in your closet. And that stretchy metallic
pantsuit is to die for."

So Madge had her figured out. That didn't surprise Alison at all. They'd always been opposites, but still close.
"I do feel different," she admitted. "It's hard to explain,
but it's kind of like that time Daddy took us shopping at
FAO Swartz and told us we could have anything we
wanted up to a hundred dollars."

"I remember," Madge said. "I grabbed that Barbie
doll in the red sequined dress and carried it around for
hours while you tried to decide what you wanted."

"And I ended up choosing the dress-up kit so I could

pretend to be a fairy princess. I think I still have that outfit somewhere. Anyway, I finally feel like that princess." She smoothed the sheets. "Corny, huh? So, tell me what's on your mind?"

"I feel kind of left out, as if the world's rushing off and leaving me behind. I've felt that way a little ever since Jimmy died, but all of a sudden it seems worse."

"Do you still miss him after all these years?"

"Sometimes. At other times I have difficulty putting a face to the memories. I just wish he'd lived longer, that he'd had a chance to know his son." She fingered the tie on her ponytail. "But he didn't, and that's life."

"It's life, but it's okay to talk about it and to miss him."

"I know, but grieving's not me. I don't analyze my actions the way you do, Alison. I just jump in and pay the price later, kind of like dumping the ice water. But maybe it's time I start thinking. If you can change your looks and your whole personality, and Mom can get her hair colored and start dating again at sixty, maybe it's time I do something more with my life."

"What kind of changes are you talking about?"

"I'm not certain, but I'm not getting any younger. Jake's fifteen. I think maybe I need to learn a skill, think about a career."

Alison had broached this topic with Madge several times in the past, and her sister had always gotten up and walked away. Madge did not respond well to what she called family pressure to conform. Alison decided to play the devil's advocate this time.

"Liking what you do is important."

"Boy, do I know that. Stick me in that post office of yours all day listening to women complain about the price of postage stamps or the fact that their mail got bent, and I'd go batty in a week.''

Alison bristled, then swallowed the momentary irritation with another sip of coffee. This was Madge she was talking to. She didn't have a clue what Alison really did. ''I like my job.''

''You would.'' Madge wiggled her toes, then slid them under the edge of the covers. ''I'd love to go into business for myself.''

''Doing what?''

''Something fun where I'd meet lots of interesting people.''

''People, or guys?''

''Guys are people, Alison. They're the sex with hair on their chest and rippling muscles and other useful and fascinating body parts. You must have noticed. Why else would you get a nose job?''

Alison ignored the rhetorical question as she nibbled the last of her toast. Somehow she couldn't see her sister being disciplined enough to have her own business, not to mention the fact that she had zero capital for investment. ''Being in business for yourself has advantages, but if you work for the right company you can get some important benefits, like health insurance and a retirement plan.''

''Yeah. I'm just considering all my options at this point. I'm giving this serious thought, though. It's time I turned my life around.''

''I'll be glad to help in any way I can.''

''I appreciate that, and I may need you. Now, tell me about the wedding last night and start with the best man. I've never danced with a blind man. Did he just ooze testosterone and sensuality when he held you so close?''

The emotions from the night before rekindled like a

glowing campfire catching a gust of wind. Alison's mind and body reeled as if Ethan were holding her again, kissing her senseless, his hands searing her flesh.

Madge clapped her hands in sheer glee. "He did get to you. Knocked my practical little sister for a genuine loop. I can see it in your eyes. Did you kiss him?"

"Why would you think that?"

"Your face is bloodred, right down to your new nose. Are you going to see him again?"

"No. He's leaving town today. And even if he wasn't, I wouldn't see him. He's a jerk and only interested in one thing."

"That can be a real good quality in a man, Alison. Especially if the one thing he's interested in is you." Madge slid off the bed and stuffed her feet back into a pair of slippers that looked like deranged rabbits. "Time to refill my coffee cup and peruse the classified section of the Sunday paper, see if I get any ideas for new career choices." She disappeared out the door, then briefly stuck her head back in. "Alison and Ethan behind a tree, k-i-s-s-i-n-g," she chanted, as if they were kids again.

Alison kicked off the covers as the taste of Ethan seemed to settle on her lips and a slow burn began deep inside her. She had indeed kissed Ethan Granger. The man was a jerk, but, boy, could he kiss!

With luck, he and his hot lips were on a plane to New Orleans by now.

"WHAT DO YOU MEAN, my flight has been canceled?"

The woman behind the counter smiled benignly, no doubt thinking his question was too stupid to deserve an answer. She was right. He knew exactly what having your flight canceled meant. It meant a giant headache while trying to get squeezed onto the next flight, or else sitting in the airport half the day in a chair designed to help soldiers endure enemy torture.

"I'm very sorry, sir. There were mechanical problems, but I'm sure I can get you into New Orleans today." She typed frantically on her computer, shaking her head as each new schedule appeared. "I can confirm a seat on the 4:00 p.m. flight, but there's a good chance you can go standby before that."

"If that's the best you can do, I guess I'll take it."

She started typing again, not even bothering to give him the airline's standard patronizing smile, since she assumed he couldn't see it, anyway.

If he didn't catch a standby seat, that meant four wasted hours he could have spent in Cooper's Corner. Of course, after that fiasco last night, it would have taken some heavy-duty apologizing to get Alison to see him again. Which was too damn bad, because he couldn't remember when he'd been with a woman who'd affected him the way she did. She wanted to know why he liked her. He'd like to know the same thing. All he knew was that she made him feel totally alive, and that was a nice feeling after the last assignment he'd had.

He'd seen a teenage boy shot down while walking home from school. It had left Ethan devastated, ready to resign from the bureau and find a job that didn't involve guns or killing or dealing with the scum of the earth. In the end he'd stayed, and agreed to take the assignment of a blind schoolteacher, hoping this time he could make sure no one got killed. Threats of school violence seldom warranted interference by the FBI, but when the source of the problem was big-time drug dealers vying for position, the bureau occasionally got a ticket to the show.

Ethan found a quiet corner and dialed his supervisor's number on his cell phone. Thomas Lee Haversack spent every Sunday alone since his wife had left him. He pretended to hate having his guys call and disturb his solitude. They didn't buy it.

"What the devil do you want, Ethan?"

"Is that any way to answer your phone?"

"It is on Sunday. Can't a man get a day off to read his paper in peace without having you guys harass him? Besides, I thought you were off in some idyllic countryside inn at a wedding."

"I was. I'm at the airport in Boston now, on standby. They canceled my flight to New Orleans."

"Well, there's no hurry to get back there. They're still not ready to put you in the classroom."

"When will they be ready?"

"Could be a week. Could be two."

"I thought we had all the details worked out."

"We do. Apparently the school board doesn't."

"What's the holdup, when two kids were beaten to a pulp last week and a teacher attacked in his home the week before?"

"They still want our involvement. They're just not ready yet."

"So what do I do, sit in that crummy apartment and wait until they call us?"

"And keep practicing at being a blind man."

"Any reason I have to practice in New Orleans?"

"You have an apartment there. Your identity is already established."

"It's established in Cooper's Corner, too."

"Don't start this. I gave you a weekend. That was pushing it, as far as I'm concerned. You're on assignment in New Orleans."

"And if I wasn't blind, I could be out on the streets

gathering facts. But I am, so what's the use of wasting my time sitting around waiting?''

Ethan put his well-honed powers of persuasion to work. By the time he'd finished the call, his mind was going ninety to nothing, with a whole new realm of possibilities.

Picking up his carry-on bag and tossing the strap over his shoulder, he headed back to the ticket counter, Longfellow at his side and his cane clicking away on the tile floor.

BY MONDAY MORNING, Alison was more than ready to go back to work. Any semblance of order had vanished from her house. Neither Madge nor Jake considered the table as a place to eat, so plates, glasses and silverware turned up in the darnedest places. She'd just missed tripping over one of Jake's shoes on her way to the kitchen this morning, and she'd had to move his skateboard from behind her car before she could back out of the driveway.

But she loved them both dearly, and the truth was she'd miss them—a little—when they left. It had been a good weekend to have them around. They'd helped to keep her mind off Ethan Granger. The first weekend of her new life, and she'd spent her Sunday afternoon daydreaming about a devilishly sexy man with no conscience.

She unlocked the door of the post office and stood for a few seconds, letting the quiet and order seep into her system. The mail sorters were on duty in the back, but the rest of the building was dark and peaceful—and empty.

She was always the first of the regular day shift to show up, and usually the last to leave. Madge might make fun of her job, but Alison loved it. Getting people's mail to them on time and in good condition through rain, hail, sleet and snow was important to the country and to the economy.

Gee, she was full of herself today, she decided as she opened the door and slipped inside her neat-as-a-pin office. Maybe it was Madge's comments yesterday that had her defending her choice of careers. More likely it was watching Wendy say "I do" and begin her new life as Seth's wife. They'd have children, be a family, have someone to share all the ups and downs with.

No matter how much Alison loved her job, she also wanted a husband, babies, dirty diapers and driving car pools. She wanted some nice, dependable man who'd stay around and grow old with her. The kind of relationship her mom and dad had enjoyed.

And with that thought, came a pinprick of uneasiness. Her mom had joined the crew at Alison's house for lunch yesterday and gone on and on about how much she'd enjoyed attending the wedding with Ron Pickering. You'd have thought she was a teenager talking about her first real date.

It had to be some kind of crazy stage women went through at sixty. Ron Pickering probably knew all about that stage, and had waited for the opportune time to show up and weasel his way into Nora's life. Her mother might smell roses, but Alison smelled a skunk.

The phone on her desk rang, and she shoved the thoughts of her personal life to the back corners of her mind as she switched into the role of postmistress. Well, most of her personal life made it to the back corners. Ethan still lurked around the fringes.

ETHAN PUSHED OPEN the spotlessly clean glass door of the Cooper's Corner post office at ten minutes before ten, Longfellow at his side. The place was humming. A line of people waited to buy stamps or mail packages. A man in a blue flannel suit was emptying his post office box and a little gray-haired lady was standing at a table pressing adhesive-backed stamps on a stack of postcards.

Ethan let Longfellow lead him to a spot at the end of the line. Alison's name was printed boldly over a door on the far side of the post office, but since he supposedly couldn't see that, he'd have to ask for directions.

The woman in front of him stared at him for a minute. "You must be here to buy stamps."

"What makes you think that?"

"You don't have anything in your hand to mail."

"Actually, I'm here to see the postmistress."

"Then you don't have to waste your time standing in line. Alison's office is right over there." She took his hand. "Come with me."

A nice friendly town, just like Seth and Alison had said. Ethan and Longfellow followed the woman and waited while she knocked on the door.

"Come in."

Alison's voice crept under his skin. It was a pleasant but tingly feeling, like the cascade of hot water when he stepped into the shower on a cold morning.

The lady turned the knob and pushed the door open. "There's a man here to see you."

"Fine. Show him in."

Ethan walked to the door and watched recognition sparkle in Alison's gorgeous blue eyes for the briefest of moments before she exhaled a slow stream of air, then clamped her full red lips into a tight line.

"What are you doing here?"

"Nice to see you again, too, Alison." He closed the door behind him as he entered her office, almost catching Longfellow's tail. Guess he could use a little more practice at the blind bit. Right now he also needed all the charm he could muster, and a lot of luck, if he was going to pull off what he had planned.

It was a long shot. But he had nothing to lose; and time with Alison Fairchild to gain.

CHAPTER SIX

ALISON STARED at Ethan, trying to regain the feeling of competence and control she'd possessed before he'd stepped inside her office. It was impossible.

"Aren't you going to ask me to have a seat?"

"I was hoping you wouldn't be staying." She stood, walked over and guided him to a chair, reminding herself she had nothing to worry about. Ethan was just a man, albeit one with a cane and a guide dog and the ability to touch more sensually than most men did when making love. But it was the middle of the morning and they were in her office, not in his bedroom or an isolated picnic spot.

She stooped to stroke the dog's head, feeling much more at ease with the beautiful retriever than with his master. "Good morning, Longfellow." He wagged his tail in appreciation. "Now," she said, walking back to her chair as Ethan settled in his. "What can I do for you?"

"For starters, you could talk to me in as friendly a tone as you do with Longfellow."

"Longfellow didn't lure me to his room under false pretenses."

"That wasn't my fault."

"It wasn't your fault?"

"Right. Would you have come any other way?"

"Definitely not."

"I rest my case. Besides, I only lured you there. You

stayed willingly even after I admitted the tickets were safely stored in my briefcase.''

''Which they weren't.''

''Nonetheless, we danced and kissed, and you liked it as much as I did—well, maybe not that much, but you liked it. Admit it. It's no crime.''

She hadn't *liked* it. She'd loved it. And just sitting across from him and talking about it gave her that same crazy, jittery sensation in the pit of her stomach that had got her in trouble in the first place. She could all but taste his lips and feel his large, sensual hands caressing her skin.

She blushed like mad. Thankfully, Ethan couldn't see that. She hesitated until she made sure she could keep her voice steady and detached, convinced he'd recognize any weakness in her tone.

''Did you stay in town just so you could come by my office and remind me of my foolish mistake? If so, you've done that, and I have work to do.''

''Actually, I came by to make you a proposition.''

She swallowed hard, past the lump that clogged her throat. ''What kind of proposition?''

''I had a change in plans. I thought I had a teaching job waiting for me in New Orleans. Now it seems there's some hangup with the paperwork.''

''I thought you already had a job.''

''I was teaching at a high school in Waco, Texas, but they had to make some midyear cuts and I was low man on the seniority pole. I had planned to take the rest of the school year off, but found I missed teaching.''

''So you decided to move from Texas to Louisiana?''

''Why not? There was a job opening for a history teacher in New Orleans and I'd never been there, so I applied. But since I have a little time before I report to work, I've decided to follow your suggestion and stay in Cooper's Corner long enough to explore the area.''

''That's great. I'm sure Maureen and Clint can give you advice on how to make the most of your time.''

''They're very accommodating. In fact, Maureen's the one who suggested I come in and talk to you this morning. I had wanted to stay with them, but the rooms at Twin Oaks are all booked, and she thought you could help me out.''

''I really don't see how.''

''Maureen says you live alone in a huge, rambling house with more space than you can possibly use. She thought that, under the circumstances, you'd be willing to let me stay there awhile. I'd pay you, of course. Kind of like a temporary bed-and-breakfast.''

''I don't take in lodgers.''

''I realize that. Forget the bed-and-breakfast analogy. Think of it as sharing your home with the best man in your good friend's wedding.''

''How long are you talking about?''

''I'm not sure. A few days, possibly even a couple of weeks.''

She could see it now. Ethan Granger sitting across the table from her at breakfast. Sleeping under her roof. Stretched out on her sofa when she came home from work in the evening.

Tremors skittered up her spine like letters flying through the routing chute. ''It's out of the question, Ethan.'' Drat. Her voice gave her away this time. It was husky, her words punctuated by short, puffy breaths.

''It would be strictly a business deal,'' he answered her. ''We could go back to the no-touch rule.''

And it would last about as long as it had the other night. ''It wouldn't work,'' she insisted. ''There is no way we can live in the same house for any extended period of time.''

"Then how about letting me stay there just until I can make other arrangements? I won't be a minute's trouble. Hey, I can even help you with meals. I can scramble eggs, though I sometimes overcook them. And those boxed dinners—the ones where you add water and simmer—I'm a whiz at those. I can't grill steaks, but I can buy them.''

Steaks on the grill. She'd make a salad and slather a loaf of fresh, crusty bread with butter. They'd sit on the patio, sipping a glass of wine while the steaks turned brown on the outside, a tempting pink deep in the center. He'd refill her glass. Their fingers would touch. She shook her head.

The phone on her desk jangled. She picked up the receiver. "Good morning. Alison Fairchild speaking.''

"And this is your big sister on the line with terrific news.''

"You got a job?''

"Grander than that. I have secured the opportunity to improve my life and income-producing ability.''

"Care to explain?'' Alison waited for the grandiose scheme, dreading to hear what Madge had come up with this time. The last time she'd been this excited, she'd taken a job trying to sell overpriced vacation-package deals. She'd stayed with it a month and sold a total of one, which netted her twenty dollars.''

"I'm going back to school. Not college or anything, but I've signed up for a special program.''

"What kind of program?''

"A *free* six-week, five-days-a-week, six-hours-a-day course to develop and/or enhance word processing and secretarial skills. It will allow women who've been out of the workforce for an extended period of time to update their skills so that they can—wait a second. I lost my place.''

Alison could hear the rustle of newspaper.

''Secure good-paying positions in the business world. Sounds perfect, right?''

''It sounds great, Madge.''

''Glad you agree, because I called this morning and enrolled. I haven't been officially approved, but I've been granted temporary status. The woman seemed certain I'd be accepted on the basis of being an unemployed single mother.''

''Where is this program and when do you start?''

''New Ashford, and I start tomorrow. There is one little catch, though.''

''If it's finances, I can help some. That is, if you're serious enough to stick with this.''

''I'm serious, and I have it all worked out so it won't cost much. Since the program's being offered in New Ashford, I thought Jake and I could just stay with you. I'll put my little bit of furniture in storage. That way I won't need to pay rent. And if you buy groceries, we're all set. You, me and Jake, all living together for six weeks. It'll be a blast.''

A blast. A chaotic, clamorous, clangorous blast. ''What about Jake's school?''

''He can finish out the year here in the regional high school.''

''How does he feel about that?''

''He was upset at first, but he understands how important this is. Besides, the schools here are great.''

''Why don't you just keep your apartment. I'll help with the rent. I can take some money out of my savings account.''

''No, I don't want to be a burden. You've worked hard

for that money and you're too generous with Jake and me as it is.''

''Really, Madge, if you're serious about this training, then I'd like to help.''

''You will be helping, just not by paying my rent. Besides, I may not even be staying in Woodstown after the training. They have a job placement service and I might end up anywhere. I could even end up here in Cooper's Corner. Heaven forbid that I'd get stuck in a small town like this forever, but it would be nice to have Jake finish out high school here.''

''So you'll just commute to New Ashford every day.''

''What's a couple of hours a day in the grand scheme of things? And just think how much fun we'll have living together. Just like one big, happy family.''

Fun? Alison groaned, quietly, so Madge wouldn't hear.

''Gotta run, Allie. Jake and I will drive back to the apartment today, collect some more clothes, make plans to store the furniture and be back here by bedtime. Unless you don't want us here.''

Not want a demolition crew setting up quarters in her living room? Or land mines being planted on the staircase and in the driveway? But Alison had trouble saying no to telemarketing callers, and she sure couldn't refuse a request for help from her sister. ''Of course I don't mind your moving in, Madge. After all, we're family.''

She hung up the phone and stared at Ethan, still sitting patiently in the chair across from her, looking fantastic and way too sure of himself. Ethan Granger and Madge. The two thorns in what should have been the crowning moment of her life. One turned her on faster and hotter than an atomic explosion. The other drove her to near madness. Actually, they both did that.

''You're very quiet,'' Ethan said, crossing one foot

over his knee, a clear sign he wasn't about to just give up on the moving-in idea and walk away. "I hope the phone call wasn't bad news."

"No." No worse than having him stop in this morning and drop a preposterous proposal in her lap. As if she'd dare risk staying alone with him in her house...

Only now they wouldn't be alone. It would be Alison, Madge, Jake and Ethan, a tad different from the little love nest he likely had pictured in his mind. She wouldn't wish Madge on her worst enemy, not for an extended stay. Would she dare do that to Ethan of the sensual hands and made-up stories of lost plane tickets?

Absolutely.

"You know, Ethan, I do have a really large house, and now that I think about it, it would be most ungracious of me not to rent a room to Seth's best man."

His face lit up, his smoky-gray eyes growing bright as a smile curved his lips. Her heart danced a little in her chest, but this time the traitorous attraction didn't worry her as much. There would be no chance for him to unleash his sensual, seductive powers on her with company and chaos all around.

"You don't know what this means to me, Alison."

"I think I do, Ethan." She knew and she loved it. "Just consider yourself part of the *family*."

"Is it okay if I move in tonight?"

"Why not? I get home about five-thirty. I'll need time to prepare your room, though."

"How about eight?"

"Great." Even if Madge wasn't home by then, Alison could get him settled and retire to her own room. "How will you get there?"

"Clint said he'd bring me after dinner. He drove me into town this morning and dropped me off here while he ran a couple of errands. But don't worry about me. He'll be back soon and Longfellow and I can wait in the sunshine until he returns.''

Her insides were more than a little shaky as she watched Longfellow lead Ethan past the short line of people waiting for service, and into the outer area where the post office boxes were located. Even from this distance he sent a sizzle of awareness through her system. She hoped she had not just made a major mistake.

I'm counting on you, Madge. If I ever needed chaperon services, I need them now.

THAT ANNOYING TWINGE of chagrin hit again as Ethan repacked his bags. It wasn't caused by his attraction to Alison. That was one of those things a man didn't have a lot of control over. Every now and then you met a woman and things just clicked.

The regret was strictly because he couldn't be totally honest with her. He stuffed the last of his shaving gear into the blue duffel and zipped it shut. He wasn't exactly lying to Alison. For the moment, he was Ethan Granger, blind schoolteacher. Six months from now he'd be someone else. That was the game, and he was a player.

He took one last look around the room, then washed his hands at the old-fashioned pedestal sink and dried them before going downstairs to join Maureen and Clint at their family dinner. After that, it was on to the Fairchild household. Twinge of guilt or not, he couldn't wait.

"YOU'RE RENTING A ROOM to some gorgeous hunk?" Madge sputtered, spewing a few crumbs of chocolate chip cookie from her mouth. "And I thought I was the one with big news."

"I'm renting a room to a friend of Seth's. It has nothing to do with the way he looks, and it's only for a few days."

"Mom said the man was very nice looking."

"Have you ever heard Mom say anyone was ugly?"

"So is this Ethan Granger ugly?"

"No." She picked up the throw from the sofa and folded it neatly before draping it over the back. "He's nice looking, if you like the long, lean, rugged type."

"And who doesn't?" Madge stretched her short legs across the sofa, catching the edge of the neatly folded throw with her big toe and pulling it over her feet. "Are you certain your nose was all you had operated on when you went to New York?"

"My nose has nothing to do with this."

"Well, I can't remember you ever doing anything this daring before. But don't get me wrong. I'm all for it. It's about time you started flaunting your charms."

"I'm not flaunting and I don't see what's daring about renting a room to a friend of a friend. I certainly have enough of them. Even with you and Jake here, there are two extra bedrooms."

"Sure he's not planning on sneaking into yours when the lights go out? Or maybe you're planning to sneak into his."

Alison spun around, hopefully fast enough so Madge couldn't see the blush burning her cheeks. That very scenario had flitted through her mind on the drive home tonight. Ethan coming to her room in the darkness, climbing into bed beside her and touching her all over with his hot, exploring hands. She'd practically run a stop sign.

The doorbell rang, followed a split second later by the phone. Madge jumped up to answer the door, leaving Alison to get the phone, once she found it. When Madge was around, the cordless might be anywhere. Following the ring, Alison finally located it under an open magazine in the seat of the antique rocker.

"Hello."

"Hi, there."

"Kevin?"

"Yeah. Did I catch you at a bad time?"

"No, of course not." She strained her neck to see around the corner. All she saw was Longfellow's tail, but Madge was obviously introducing herself. She could hear her girlish voice blending with Ethan's masculine one.

"It was great being with you at the wedding," Kevin said.

"Thanks. I enjoyed seeing you again, too."

"Almost like old times, huh?"

Not like any old times she remembered, but why bring up the fact that in high school Kevin hadn't known she existed unless he needed help with his algebra homework? "Like old times," she lied. "Except that we're adults now."

"No doubt about that."

Madge, Ethan and Longfellow stepped into the room. Her hand was already up to greet Ethan when she realized the effort would be wasted. His sightless eyes stared straight ahead as Madge led him to the overstuffed chair near the fireplace. Madge was laughing at something, no doubt one of Ethan's charming, witty comments.

"…Wednesday night?"

"I'm sorry, Kevin. What about Wednesday night?"

"I must have caught you at a bad time. It sounds as if you're having a party."

"No party. Madge is here, and…a friend. So what about Wednesday night?"

"I thought we might try out that new coffeehouse in New Ashford. They have a classical guitarist who plays from eight until ten on Wednesday nights, and I hear he's really good.''

A date. Her first invitation in months. *The* Kevin Bosco was asking the former Alison Uglychild out for coffee.

''I know it's late to ask, so if you have other plans, it's not a problem.''

Other plans on a Wednesday night? Let's see. Surely cleaning the upstairs bathrooms did not constitute other plans. She was about to say so when Jake came bounding down the steps.

''Hey, swell dog!'' He made a beeline for Longfellow, who immediately tensed.

Ethan rested a hand on the animal and talked to him in a soothing voice, letting him know Jake wasn't a threat. Then he gave Jake the go-ahead to pet him.

''Listen, Alison. Why don't I call you some other time? You obviously have a lot going on there.''

''No. Wednesday night is great.''

''Pick you up at seven-thirty?''

''Seven-thirty,'' she agreed. She barely heard his parting comment over Jake's excited chatter. He and Longfellow had apparently already hit it off, and Ethan was right there in the mix with them. This was not working out the way she'd planned. Ethan was supposed to be cowering from the chaos. Instead, he was adding to it and giving every indication of loving it.

''Who was on the phone?'' Madge asked.

''Kevin Bosco.''

''Nice.'' She turned back to Ethan. ''I just can't believe you're a history teacher. How in the world do you manage a roomful of high school students when you can't see what they're doing?''

''I sic Longfellow on them. One bite for not doing their homework, a pound of flesh for disrupting class.''

Jake found the tongue-in-cheek remark uproariously funny.

Returning the phone to the wall cradle where it belonged, Alison crossed the room toward the threesome who had invaded her quiet, orderly home and taken over. Ethan Granger might have been a king holding court, the way Madge and Jake were looking at him and hanging on his every word. Masculine, intelligent, funny and—who was she kidding—an absolute hunk.

This was her big moment—the one that made the price of the plastic surgery worthwhile. Her first real date in a year, and with Kevin Bosco of all people. Yet she knew the slow, rising heat inside her was fueled by Ethan.

And the man would be sleeping a few doors down the hall. Heaven help her.

BY WEDNESDAY NIGHT, Alison was really glad she was going out with Kevin and getting away from the constant temptation of Ethan. Fortunately, they hadn't been alone again, but even with the house rocking with activity, she got that funny, fluttering feeling inside every time they crossed paths.

She checked her appearance in the full-length mirror one last time. The face, the dress, the shoes, the hairstyle—they still amazed her, sometimes even startled her when she passed a mirror and caught a glimpse of herself. At times it was as if her spirit had been relocated in someone else's body, kind of like falling asleep a caterpillar and waking up a butterfly.

Even stranger was the fact that she was beginning to feel different inside. Though she felt immodest even thinking it, she'd actually started to believe she was the cute and confident woman smiling back at her from the mirror. A lifetime of inhibitions brought on by believing she was ugly had started slipping away.

She'd decided that was the real reason she was reacting so strongly to Ethan. It was all part of the changes going on inside her, the unfamiliarity with having men attracted to her. It made her more susceptible to his magnetism. Having found an explanation for her weakness gave her some small degree of satisfaction and renewed her determination to resist him.

Tousling her hair a little to reinforce that careless, casual look she'd spent a half hour perfecting, she turned her back to the mirror and practically danced down the stairs in her new high-heeled sandals. The family room was empty, but the smell of her mother's pot roast simmering on the range assured her that the Fairchild entourage with Ethan in tow had not gone far.

Nora had volunteered to come over and cook dinner for the family tonight, claiming she had to make certain they were feeding her grandson right. But Alison knew Ethan was the real draw. Her mother couldn't resist seeing how the charming, good-looking blind schoolteacher fit in Chaosville.

Alison stepped to the storm door that led to the back porch and peered out. The sun had already dropped below the horizon, painting the undersides of the clouds in broad strokes of gold. Normally it was her favorite time of day, her quiet time after a bustling afternoon at the post office. This week the only quiet times came after everyone was in bed at night.

Longfellow hunched at the edge of the driveway, watching his master but staying out of the way while Jake was apparently teaching Ethan how to toss a basketball through the hoop that hung from the front of the garage.

She watched for a few minutes, captivated by the way

Jake and Ethan interacted like old friends in spite of the years that separated them. Amazingly enough, Ethan made a basket every now and then, relying solely on Jake's verbal direction. When he did, Longfellow howled his approval and Madge and Nora cheered from the squeaking porch swing.

Alison pushed open the door and joined them on the wide, covered porch.

"Another new dress?" her mother asked, her gaze fixed on the hemline.

"It is. Do you like it?"

"It's nice, but short."

"For heaven's sake, Mom," Madge chimed in. "Give her a break. It only seems short because she's kept her legs hidden beneath those long, shapeless skirts and baggy trousers for so long."

Nora shook her head. "Alison's always been a conservative dresser, the way I am."

"On you, it's tasteful, Mother. Alison's twenty-eight. On her it's dumpy and a waste of a great figure." Madge was never one to mince words.

Jake dribbled the ball down the drive, then turned in their direction. "Hey, Aunt Alison, come out and play some basketball. I finally found someone you can beat, but you better hurry. A little more practice and he'll skunk you."

"Not tonight."

"You afraid of a little competition?" This time it was Ethan offering the challenge.

"I'm not afraid. I just don't want to show you up."

"I'll take my chances as long as Jake here is coaching me."

"Yeah, Aunt Alison. You and Ethan in a game of one-on-one." He dribbled the ball under Ethan's nose.

Without even looking in Jake's direction, Ethan reached out and got a hand between Jake and the ball, stealing it from him. He held it up, tried to spin it on his finger and actually succeeded for a second. "One-on-one, Alison," he taunted. "Come on and take me, if you think you can."

"Don't let him get away with that," Madge heckled. "Show him what you're made of."

The problem was, Alison realized, he already knew what she was made of from their previous games of one-on-one in his room at Twin Oaks and down by the stream.

Jake retrieved the ball Ethan had dropped, shot it once, then handed it back to Ethan. Ethan put the ball in the air, missing the basket entirely. "Air ball," Madge called good-naturedly from the porch swing.

"I'm throwing up air balls and still Alison's afraid to take me on."

"It's not that," Madge said. "She's all dressed for her date with Mr. Heartthrob."

"Ah, so that's it," Ethan said. "I understand now. She doesn't want to get all hot and sweaty before the big date."

That did it. Alison marched down the steps toward the driveway. She'd been shooting baskets with Jake ever since he was big enough to hold a ball. Even in her heels, she could sink a few. Besides, she'd never been able to walk away from a challenge.

"You're on," she said, sidling up beside Ethan. "No fighting for the ball, though. I wouldn't want to hurt you. We'll just shoot and keep score."

"But fighting for the ball is half the fun," he protested. "You're not afraid of being bested by a blind man, are you?"

"Fear isn't a factor. Those are my rules. Take them or leave them."

Ethan shrugged. "Is she always this bossy, Jake?"

"Pretty much."

"Alison Fairchild, you are surely not going to play basketball in those shoes," her mother protested from the porch. "You'll fall and break your neck."

Alison waved her arguments off. "I'm not playing a real game. I'm only sinking a few baskets to show Ethan I'm not afraid to take him on. I'll beat him in no time."

Ethan dribbled the ball awkwardly, his empty gaze directed straight ahead. He missed the ball and it rolled away from him. Alison caught it before it continued down the drive and into the street. A glimmer of tenderness surfaced, the way it always did when she was confronted with his determination to ignore his disability. But this time she refused to be taken in.

"Ladies first," Ethan said.

She squared herself up in front of the basket, bounced the ball a couple of times, then tossed it toward the hoop. It hit the ring and bounced off.

"She missed," Jake said. "You're in the game, Ethan." He handed Ethan the ball and tugged him into position. "The goal is right in front of you, same distance as when we were practicing. Put an arch on it the way I showed you."

"Gotcha, partner."

She wasn't sure how her nephew, the one she had spoiled rotten ever since he was born, was suddenly part of the opposition, but he clearly was not only Ethan's coach but his biggest fan. She watched as Ethan released the ball without once looking at it.

It hit the ring, rolled around it, then fell on the outside.

"So close," Jake said. "Another half inch and you'd have had it.

The spectators on the porch swing let out a collective

sigh of disappointment. *Her* family on Ethan's side. Of course, they saw him as handicapped by his lack of sight. They had no idea what talents he possessed with his hands and his lips. A flicker of heat crept up Alison's spine, distracting her just enough that she was caught unaware when Jake threw the ball to her.

She reached out to grab it and stepped off the edge of the paved driveway. The heel of her right shoe sank in the wet earth and she stumbled. She tried to catch herself but went down anyway, her arm twisting behind her. Her skirt flew up and moisture from the damp ground soaked into her panties.

At that moment, Kevin pulled into the driveway in his bright red sports car.

CHAPTER SEVEN

ALISON SHUDDERED. Her first date in a year, and here she was sitting on the ground in wet underwear.

"Are you all right?" Ethan asked, taking a couple of steps in her direction. Fortunately, he couldn't see her unladylike position, though Kevin was staring as he climbed from beneath the steering wheel of the low-slung vehicle.

"I'm fine. I just slipped and fell. No harm done."

Jake turned to admire the car. "You should see that set of wheels, Ethan."

"Not bad," Madge agreed, leaving the porch swing to come and check on Alison. "If you're too injured to keep your date with the sports car jock, I can always go for you," she teased.

"I am not injured and I'm not canceling my date. Now if you hovering vultures will just stand back, I'll get up." She tried, but the heel of her shoe was still buried in the muddy earth.

She veered forward, falling against Ethan, who had not stepped back as she'd ordered. He caught her and steadied her, holding her much too close. Kevin had joined them on the driveway and stood staring at Alison in Ethan's arms.

She pushed away, tugging her skirt back in place. "Hello, Kevin. Whatever this looks like, it isn't. I tripped and fell."

"Are you all right?" he asked, staring at the smear of mud that zigzagged up her right leg.

"I'm fine, but I need to go inside and clean up a bit."

"Sure. We have plenty of time." He took her arm as she started toward the back steps. Kevin was attractive and sexy. So why the hell didn't her insides heat up and crackle like a pinecone in a forest fire when he touched her? Nonetheless, she was going on this date and she'd have fun if it killed her.

"Are you sure you're all right, dear?" Nora asked. "You're holding your right arm as if it hurts."

Alison grimaced. Her mother would pick now to become so observant. In spite of her assertions that she was fine, Alison's wrist had started to smart. Evidently she'd twisted it when she fell on it.

"It's nothing to worry about," she said, hoping to reassure her mother.

"Playing basketball in high-heeled shoes," Nora muttered under her breath, just loud enough for Alison to hear as she walked past. "It's the nose surgery. I think they gave her too much medication when they put her to sleep. My calm, sensible daughter has taken complete leave of her senses."

At that moment, Alison was not entirely convinced that her mother wasn't right.

"HAVE YOU EVER BEEN scared of anybody, Ethan?"

Ethan stretched his long legs in front of him on the sofa and wished he could turn to look Jake in the eye. Never making eye contact had turned out to be one of the toughest parts of playing the role of a blind man. "Everybody's been scared before."

"I bet Aunt Alison hasn't." Jake continued to sort through a stack of collector baseball cards he'd been fooling with for the last half hour. "She's tough as nails—for a woman. Smart, too. That's what my mom says. Did you know that she's in charge of all the mail in Cooper's Corner?"

"That's what I heard. Being postmistress is a big job, but tough, smart people are afraid sometimes, too." Ethan considered his answer carefully. The question of fear had seemingly sprung from nowhere, but Ethan had sensed from the tone of Jake's voice that the subject had been preying on the boy's mind. He'd likely saved it until his grandmother had left and his mother had gone upstairs to read, leaving the two of them alone.

"Fear isn't necessarily a bad thing, Jake. Sometimes a healthy dose of fear is the best means of survival."

"It doesn't make you feel like much of a man, though."

"I get the feeling we're not talking in generalities here. You can level with me, man to man."

"Oh, it's just some stuff going on at school. You know how some guys like to bully younger students, especially if they're bigger than you are."

And most of the students were probably bigger than Jake. Ethan's experience and research kicked in. He knew all too well how a few students could make life miserable for their victims. He also knew that sometimes it was carried to dangerous levels. "Are you having trouble with someone at your high school?"

"A little bit. I guess it doesn't matter, though. I have to change schools now, anyway."

"Sounds like it might be a good time for a change."

"It's the worst possible time—like the end of my life."

"Changing schools isn't easy, but surely it's not that bad."

"Yeah, man. This time it is. I finally found something I love that I'm good at—I mean *really* good at."

Ethan understood that feeling all too well. It had taken him a lot longer than high school to reach that point. "Is basketball where you found your niche?"

"No, I'm too short for that. It's baseball. I'm the star pitcher of the Woodstown Warriors. Coach says that with my pitching and the heavy hitters we've got this year, we might just go all the way to state."

"That does sound impressive."

"Except that now I've got to give it up. Coach Reynolds is going to be so pissed. I hate to even call him and let him know I won't be coming back to school. But it's not just him. I'm letting down everybody."

"Did you talk to your mom about this?"

"I tried, but she doesn't understand. I guess baseball's a man thing. And I don't want to be the one to make her give up her classes. She needs a break. It's hard on her—you know, being a single parent at all."

"I guess it would be."

"Do you know anything about collector baseball cards?"

"I know what they are."

"Well, I know you can't see the pictures, but if you're interested, I can tell you about my collection. I've got all the big names, even some that were playing back when you were a kid."

"I thought I heard the rustle of cards. It sounds as if you're sitting on the floor."

"I am. Wanna join me?"

"Sure." Listening to Jake talk about baseball was a hell of a lot better entertainment than imagining Alison and Kevin out together. Besides, the talk of bullies and fear had Ethan a little worried. Jake was a good kid, but even good kids could get caught up in problems that were out of their control. If they talked awhile longer, Jake might open up and tell him the whole story.

Jake took his arm and led him to a spot on the floor. Ethan checked the time on his braille watch as he fit himself between two stacks of cards. Ten minutes after ten, and Alison still wasn't back. Just how much time did it take to drink a cup of coffee and listen to some guy hit a few chords on a guitar?

Ethan tried to force thoughts of her to the back of his mind as Jake began quoting batting averages and win-loss records. He failed miserably. The woman was doing strange things to his brain.

But it was only temporary. That's the way his life had always been.

Old memories crept into his mind, ones he thought he'd buried years before. The constant moving from place to place. A series of new stepfathers. So many schools that they ran together in his mind. Here today, somewhere else tomorrow.

Short term. That was him.

THE *NEW* ALISON'S first foray into the world of dating was a disaster. In all fairness, it wasn't totally Kevin's fault. He tried to make conversation and had brought up the name of every person they'd both known in high school. They went through that list in about thirty minutes. After that, it was tough to find a common ground for discussion. Alison's mind kept drifting back to the house and the fun the family was probably having without her, and adding to her distraction was the fact that her wrist ached.

Kevin worked for a law firm in Boston that specialized in corporate law. He described several of his cases in detail and expected her to be as interested in the legal problems faced by multibillion-dollar corporations as she was. It was clear he considered his occupation much more fascinating than hers, because he didn't ask her one question about her own work.

By the time they reached her driveway again, Alison was sure he'd like to reach across her, push open the passenger door, shove her to the curb and speed away from what was probably the most boring night he'd spent in a long time. Unfortunately, she was mistaken. He killed the engine and turned to face her, apparently in no hurry to escape.

"I had a nice time tonight, Alison."

"I did, too," she lied.

"It must be tough for you being stuck here in Cooper's Corner," Kevin said, "still living in the same house you grew up in."

"I'm not stuck. I love Cooper's Corner and the house. It's been in my mother's family for almost a hundred years. It has character and a history. I've never really thought of living anywhere else." This time she spoke the total truth.

"I couldn't do it, not after living in Boston. When I come home for a visit I feel as if my days move in slow motion. Everywhere you go you see the same people, doing the same things, asking you the same questions. I like being on the happening edge, in the hub of things."

She didn't disagree with him about Cooper's Corner. The pace was slower than in a large city, and the people didn't change all that much from year to year. The choices were simpler. If she needed groceries, she went to Cooper's Corner General Store. If she wanted a burger, she drove to the Burger Barn. If she got tired of her own cooking, she went to Tubb's Café. Not a lot of decisions, but she never felt bored or stifled, and she'd never really thought of moving away.

"It's not as if I never leave Cooper's Corner," she said. "I make frequent weekend trips to Boston and New York, and I travel on vacation. But Cooper's Corner is a great place to live and raise a family," she offered. "Good schools. Safe streets. Friendly neighbors."

"I don't plan on having a family for a long, long time. I want my career on a solid footing first." He snaked his arm across the back of the seat. "Don't get me wrong," he said. "I'm not complaining about being in Cooper's Corner this week. Running into you has made it a lot more interesting."

"Thanks."

He bent over and kissed her. This was where she was supposed to get gooseflesh, start trembling with anticipation and passion. Nothing happened. Perhaps it was the aspirin she'd taken with her cappuccino and sandwich.

There was nothing wrong with Kevin's technique. His lips hit hers just right. His hand was on the back of her neck, and his lips were parted as his tongue probed her mouth. She reminded herself this was Kevin Bosco she was kissing, hoping that would impress her libido enough to stir a little arousal. Her libido continued to consider the experience rather blah. Finally, she pulled away. "I really should go in, Kevin."

"I don't suppose it would do to invite me in for a nightcap, with your sister and her kid staying here?"

"Wouldn't be a good idea."

"I'd like to see you again."

That surprised her. Could it be that the infamous Kevin Bosco didn't suspect that he hadn't "rung her bell," as Ethan would say? Ethan. Damn. It was probably his fault

Kevin's kiss was such a non-event. If he hadn't gotten to her first, she might have found it exciting.

"How about dinner and a movie on Saturday night?" Kevin said, his hand still lingering on her neck.

She considered the invitation, but hesitated to accept or decline. "Why do you want to go out with me, Kevin?"

"You're an intelligent and very lovely woman."

"But why now, after all these years?"

"You seem different."

"You mean I *look* different?"

"That's part of it, but it's more than the nose job. You're dynamic, sexy and super attractive. You have a style about you you've never had before."

"Thanks, Kevin." The new image was exactly what she'd set out to achieve, so it shouldn't gall her to think that the old Alison wouldn't have gotten to first base with Kevin. It did annoy her, though. She couldn't deny that.

He walked her to the door. "You didn't answer me about Saturday night," he said, propping a hand against the jamb and leaning in close.

The thought of another date with Kevin didn't appeal to her at all, but she should give him a chance. Besides, it would beat staying home with Ethan and being assaulted by his nonstop charm. "Dinner and a movie. I'd like that."

"Great. I'll call you and we'll decide on a time."

She said good-night and pushed the door open, hurrying in before he felt compelled to kiss her again. The house was quiet for the first time in days. Apparently everyone had gone to bed early. Great. That meant she wouldn't have to lie and say that she and Kevin had shared a wonderful evening.

She set her handbag on the table in the foyer and

stepped out of her heels. Cradling her right wrist in her left hand, she stepped into the family room.

"It's about time you made it home."

She stared at Ethan, who was sitting on the couch in the semidarkness. "What kind of greeting is that?"

He stood and took a few steps in her direction, apparently moving toward the sound of her voice. "I was worried about you."

"You were worried about me?"

"Sure. You were out with that big-city hustler who's trying to get you into the sack."

"For a teacher, your vocabulary could stand some improvement."

"I teach history, not English."

"Whatever. You can put your mind at ease. Kevin was a perfect gentleman. Even if he hadn't been, I don't see how you can fault him after the way you lured me to your room at Twin Oaks Saturday night."

"My motives were pure."

"And I suppose that's the reason you waited up for me tonight, to demonstrate your pure motives?"

"Actually I felt a little responsible for cajoling you into a game you weren't dressed for. How's your wrist?"

"Sore."

"I was afraid it might be. Come sit on the couch and let me get you some ice for it. That will keep the swelling down."

"You don't have to do that."

"I know. But I'd like to, and it won't kill you to let someone take care of you for a change."

"You're right. It won't kill me." It would feel good, and she was letting her fear of responding sensually to Ethan turn her into a jerk.

She sighed in thankful resignation, dropped to the

couch and let him prop the throw pillows behind her back. He moved tentatively, felt his way around her, but his hands were gentle and the pillows were still warm from his body. They even smelled of him, clean and woodsy.

"I'll get the ice." He commanded Longfellow to stay, and headed for the kitchen without dog or cane.

Alison was amazed that he'd already familiarized himself so well with the layout of the house, though his steps were slow and he still used his hands to guide him through doors and around large pieces of furniture.

"You need some aspirin," he said from the kitchen. "That'll help the swelling and the pain and let you get some sleep. Want to tell me where it is, or do you have a stronger pain reliever?"

"Aspirin's fine. I have some in my handbag."

She closed her eyes, feeling pampered and a little guilty that she'd been so hard on Ethan. She'd only agreed to rent him a room because she'd thought Madge would drive him crazy. Now she wondered if anything fazed the guy.

"Where do I find a bowl for the ice?"

"In the cabinet to the left of the sink, second shelf."

Alison could hear him moving around the kitchen until he found the right cupboard. The sound of the door opening was followed by the clanking of dishes. His ability to find his way intrigued her, and she wondered if he'd been born blind or if he'd faced the loss of his eyesight in later life. She wasn't sure which would be worse—to have never seen the beauty of sunsets and mountain ranges, or to have to adjust to such a loss when you knew how much you were missing.

He returned a few minutes later and sat beside her while he fashioned a pouch out of a terry dish towel he'd found in the kitchen. Once he'd filled it with ice, he fitted it around her swollen wrist. His hands brushed her skin as he worked, but this time his touch was efficient, not seductive.

Still, his nearness made her insides tremble. There was no way she could be around him without feeling something. She'd just have to accept that and deal with it.

"How's that?" he asked, still adjusting the towel.

"Perfect."

"Good. Now, where's the handbag?"

"On the table in the foyer. You'll have to be careful, though. There's a pile of cards on the floor."

"Yeah, I know right where they are. They're Jake's baseball cards. He described them to me and gave me the noteworthy statistics. He's got quite a collection."

"He should. He's been adding to it for years. He has collector books filled with those cards."

"So he said. These are his latest additions, the ones he hasn't had time to categorize yet. That boy does love baseball." He walked to the foyer, retrieved her handbag, then got a glass of water from the kitchen.

"It's a shame Jake's not going to get to finish the year out at his old school and play on the varsity team," Ethan said, returning to the couch.

"Madge said he was handling the prospect of switching schools well."

"Outwardly, maybe."

"Why do you say that?"

"He talked to me about how much he'd looked forward to pitching this season. Being part of the team seems to mean a lot to him."

"I'm sure it does. Maybe I'll talk to Madge again. It's just that this is the first time in years she's been so motivated to make a positive change in her life. She tends to jump from one thing to another, never giving herself a chance to be successful in any position. She loves Jake, though, and she's a great mother.''

Alison rummaged in the handbag, found the aspirin and shook two into her hand.

''Do you want something besides water? A soft drink? Some juice?''

''No, the water's fine.'' She took the glass from him, acutely aware that it was the first time in a long time that someone had catered to her, except after her surgery, of course. Even then, she hadn't needed a lot of help. Her friend Cassandra had only taken off one day from work to drive Alison to the outpatient surgery and back to the apartment again. Alison was used to being the take-charge, self-sufficient daughter. Why not? She'd never had the distraction of a love life to worry about.

''You make a good nurse,'' she said, once she'd swallowed the aspirin.

''Does that surprise you?''

''A little.''

''Because I'm a man or because I'm blind?''

She thought about her answer. ''Probably both. To tell you the truth, I don't know a lot about men or blindness. I know about post office regulations and getting the mail through on time.''

''Then we're even. The only thing I know about the mail is how to send checks to pay my bills. And no man understands women.''

''Were you born blind?''

''No. I was born with a degenerative eye disease. It wasn't diagnosed until I was twelve, when my sight started deteriorating. By age fifteen, I was considered legally blind, though I could still see to get around. By the time I graduated high school, my world consisted mostly of light and shadows.''

"Do you still see light and shadows?"

"I can tell if the lights in a room are on or off, and I know if someone shines a bright light in my eyes. That's pretty much it."

"It must have been a terrible blow for you to learn you were going blind at such a vulnerable age."

"It was, but there was nothing I could do but live with it."

And that was it. She didn't press further. It was obvious he didn't want to talk about how devastating the experience must have been. Still, knowing what he'd gone through—what he was still going through—made the fact that he was so tender and caring tonight far more meaningful, almost poignant.

"Why did you wait up for me when the rest of the family went to bed, Ethan?"

"I had an idea your wrist was hurting a lot more than you let on. You were just too stubborn to admit you needed to stay home, or else the coffee date was awfully important to you."

"I am a bit stubborn at times."

"That's what your mother and sister said. 'Put a mule to shame'—I think that's how they phrased it."

"It's one of their favorite expressions. Of course, I'm just like my mother. I don't suppose she told you I got the obstinacy trait from her."

"No, but Madge did."

"Good old Madge. What else did she say about me?"

"That she's glad you finally got your nose fixed and she hopes it means you're going to get out of the house and have a little fun for a change. She thinks you're…"

"A dud?"

He smiled. "I think that is the word she used. But she

has high hopes for you now that you have your new nose to flaunt.''

"I don't flaunt."

"That's debatable."

"What else did Madge say about me?"

"She thinks you like me. Warned me that if I waited up for you, you'd probably try to seduce me."

"Seduce you? I would never even think of such a thing, and if you..." The heat crept back to Alison's cheeks. When she looked up, she saw the mischievous smile on Ethan's face and realized he was teasing her. "Madge said no such thing. She knows better."

"Okay, that was my idea. But when I felt your wrist and realized it was a little swollen, I figured you were probably in no shape to seduce or be seduced."

"Even if my wrist were in perfect shape, nothing would have happened. I don't flaunt and I definitely don't seduce."

"Sure you do. You might not mean to, but you turn me on all the time, and I can't even see those sexy little dresses everyone is talking about, or those expressive eyes. Or your shapely body, for that matter. You must have seduced Kevin at the wedding the other night. He wasted no time in asking you out."

She swallowed hard. This conversation was quickly getting out of hand, and if she didn't put a stop to it, it might lead in directions she didn't want to go.

"Are you always this bold, Ethan?"

"I think of it as honest. But, yeah, what you see is what you get with me. I don't do flowery speeches or spend a lot of time beating around the bush. I leave that to those fancy-talking guys."

He might not use flowery speeches, but he had some pretty practiced hand movements. She wasn't going to mention them now, however. "For the record, I like you fine, Ethan, when you're not groping. It's just my feelings toward you are like those for a friend."

"So, what you're saying is you kiss all your friends the way we kissed at Twin Oaks the other night?"

"I don't kiss... I mean, my friends... No, of course not." He had her flustered and he knew it. Damn, what was it with her? His hands, his lips, his conversation, even the scent of him messed up her mind.

"I appreciate the ice and the pillows, but I'm very tired, Ethan. I'd really like to just go to bed and get some sleep."

"Probably a great idea. Do you want me to help you out of that dress?"

"Absolutely not."

"Don't get so uptight. I can't see anything."

She pointed to the stairs, then realized he couldn't see that, either. "Go to bed, Ethan. I'll be fine."

"I'll walk upstairs with you and carry the rest of the ice in case you want to make a cold compress during the night."

They walked up the stairs together, Longfellow at Ethan's side. She stopped when she reached her door. Ethan stopped, too. She took the bowl of ice from him with her left hand, cradling it against her stomach. One spot of cold in a body that had grown increasingly warm as they'd neared her bedroom.

"Sure you don't need some help getting into bed?"

His voice was husky, his face too close to hers. The only fact she was certain of was that if she invited him into her bedroom, even her swollen painful and wrist wouldn't keep them from making love. "I'm sure I can get undressed by myself."

"Party pooper." He found her face with his hand,

cupped her chin, then leaned over and gave her a fast but totally thorough kiss on the lips before stepping away. Somehow she managed not to kiss him back, though she wanted to so badly she had to force her lips to stay closed.

"If you need anything, I'll be right down the hall. I'll sleep with my door open so I can hear you if you call."

"I won't call. I'll be fine." And even if she wasn't fine, she wouldn't call Ethan. There was no way she'd face him and his kisses in the middle of the night. As it was, it was going to take every ounce of willpower she possessed to keep her distance from him for as long as he lived under the same roof.

She stepped into her room and closed the door, then leaned against it. Her body was still reeling from his kiss and the desire that rocked though her.

It would be tough, but keep her distance she would. This was the beginning of a new life for her. She would not have it sabotaged by a man looking for a little vacation entertainment.

Only Ethan didn't seem at all the selfish operator she'd imagined him to be. Tonight he'd been so sweet and thoughtful.

Unless...

Unless sweet and thoughtful were just two more weapons in his arsenal for this seduction campaign. Now that would be really playing dirty. She had a good mind to call Seth right now, disturb his honeymoon and tell him just what she thought of his best man. Machiavellian to the core.

She walked over to the dresser, set the bowl of ice on a coaster and stared into the mirror. The woman who looked back at her not only had a cute little nose, she had stars in her eyes, hung there by a man who was sleeping just down the hall with his door open, waiting for her call.

But she wouldn't call. Old love 'em and leave 'em Ethan would be sleeping alone tonight. Unfortunately, so would she.

"SO, LONGFELLOW, old boy, what do you think of our Miss Fairchild?" Ethan scratched a spot behind Longfellow's ear as he dropped to the side of the bed. Longfellow was curled up in his dog bed, no doubt wishing his master would curl up in his and cut out the conversation.

"She's all woman, that's for sure." Ethan poked his feet under the covers and pulled the blanket up beneath his chin. "I'd have sworn that first night that she was a practiced femme fatale, but she isn't. She's so inexperienced and innocent that even when I'm kissing her I'm thinking she might just break in half like a fragile, porcelain doll if I squeeze too hard."

Longfellow's tail thumped against the side of his wicker bed.

"So you noticed that, too. Well, what do we do about it, buddy? You're supposed to be both my best friend and my caretaker. You should have a few answers. Am I biting off more than I can chew? Am I going to be able to just walk away when this is over? But then, I have to, don't I?"

Longfellow burrowed his nose under his own blanket and closed his eyes.

"So my trials and tribulations bore you, do they?"

Ethan closed his eyes, knowing it was a wasted effort. He wasn't likely to fall asleep anytime soon, not when his body was still buzzing from the time spent with Alison. Fitting the ice pack around her wrist. Kissing her at her bedroom door. It had been a long time since he'd been with a woman, but not so long that he didn't remember what it was supposed to feel like.

Granted, he was getting rusty in the romance department, but as best he could remember, it had never felt quite like this before. He'd have to be very careful. If he let himself start caring too much, it would all go up in smoke.

And guess who'd get buried under the pile of rubble? It wouldn't be the vivacious blonde with the townful of men chasing after her, Kevin Bosco leading the pack.

Still, it was Alison's body he imagined snuggled against his when he pulled the spare pillow against his chest and wrapped himself around it. Soft as a kitten. Kind of purred like one, too, when she caught her breath between kisses. Probably did the same thing when she kissed Kevin Bosco tonight.

Ethan pounded a fist into the pillow. "Tell you what, Longfellow. Never trust a female."

Longfellow barked once. Ethan took that for agreement. They both knew he was already in way over his head.

CHAPTER EIGHT

ETHAN SLEPT LITTLE after tending Alison's wrist and seeing her to her door, but Thursday afternoon found him more confused than tired. Playing the role of blind man was much more difficult in Cooper's Corner than it had been in training, or even when he'd moved to New Orleans and settled in his own apartment. Longfellow, the cane, staring straight ahead with an empty gaze were all part of his new identity. But the ruse just didn't work in a family setting, not when everyone else seemed to lack any kind of pretense.

Most of all he hated lying to Alison, especially when she'd asked questions last night about his blindness. Coming here had been a mistake. He knew it with a certainty that he never seemed to have about anything connected with his personal life.

Personal life. Who was he kidding? He had no personal life. He should clear out of Cooper's Corner today, go back to his lonely little apartment in New Orleans and wait for the school board to okay his position. He belonged there, had a job to do.

So why didn't he leave? Good question. He didn't have a good answer. All he knew was that he liked being here. He loved watching Alison adjust to her new image, and was constantly amazed that she hadn't realized her zest for life was far more attractive than her new nose.

She was upstairs now, devouring a new John Grisham

novel. At least that's what she'd been doing the last time he'd checked on her. She'd gone into work this morning, but had left before noon to have the doctor check her wrist. Nothing was broken, but it was a nasty sprain, and the doctor had given her a sling to wear for a few days, and had suggested she go home and give the arm a rest. Resting was not one of Alison's strong suits.

Ethan stretched out, slipped off his moccasins and propped his stocking feet on the coffee table. Jake was sprawled on the floor watching a Cubs game. It was the perfect opportunity for Ethan to practice the skills he'd need in his next assignment—pretend to see nothing while taking in everything.

Jake turned toward Ethan. "How come you're not teaching this semester?"

"I lost one job and took my time finding another. I'm waiting for a position to come through. They should be calling me any day."

"Where will you work?"

"In New Orleans."

"Cool. That's supposed to be a fun city."

"That's what they tell me."

"How do you handle grading papers and all that stuff?"

"I team teach with another teacher. I lecture. She checks homework and grades papers."

"You're a history teacher, huh? Wish you were a math teacher. I could use a little help with my algebra. Do you miss teaching?"

"Not since I came to Cooper's Corner. There's never a dull moment in the Fairchild residence."

"Yeah. I like it here, but I miss playing baseball. If I were home I'd be at ball practice right now. We have a big game on Monday. Well, the Woodstown Warriors have a big game. I won't be pitching.''

''Have you told the coach yet that you won't be back?''

''Not yet. I tried to call him again this morning, but no one answered at school. The plumbing's still messed up. When it's fixed, I have to get my things, check out of Woodstown and then I'll enroll in the district high school here.''

''If I could drive, I'd take you over and let you tell him in person.''

''That would be great. Or if I was just a little older, I'd have my license and could drive myself. In fact, if I had my driver's license, that would solve everything. I could just drop Mom off in New Ashford and drive myself on to school.''

''How much farther is it?''

''Another forty-five minutes. I wouldn't care, though. It would be worth getting up at daybreak if I could play ball. I've been working on this curveball that drops to the outside just before it crosses the plate.''

''You said there were some troublemakers at Woodstown. At least this way you'll be rid of them.''

''They didn't really bother me. And what's a little teasing, anyway, compared to letting down your whole team, and not getting to pitch?''

Poor kid. All he wanted to do was play ball, and now he'd had his dream season yanked out from under him. Ethan shifted his weight as his muscles tightened. He'd love to be able to drive Jake over to talk to his coach in person.

This assignment was giving him an appreciation of what life must be like for people with impaired vision. Those who were truly blind would never experience so many of the simple pleasures that he took for granted, such as climbing behind the wheel of a car and driving wherever he wanted to go.

"Is there a chance you can make the team at Cooper's Corner?" he asked, trying to help Jake find a solution.

"About as much chance as I have to pitch for the Red Sox. No one ever starts you if you move midseason. I think it might even be against the rules."

"Could be."

"I'll be all right."

"I'm sure you will." Still, it bothered Ethan to see Jake have to drop out. He'd learned a lot about adolescents in the two years since they'd assigned him to the school violence team. Peer pressure was frequently overwhelming, and kids' egos bruised easily. They hid their feelings well, but that didn't mean their disappointments didn't eat away at them. Life for teenagers was frequently not the carefree time spent eating pizza and listening to rap music that most people thought it was. Like right now. Jake had turned his attention back to the game, but Ethan was certain he was still upset that he wouldn't be on anyone's pitching mound this year.

"Oh, man, that wasn't a strike! It was low and outside. That ump is blind." Jake groaned. "Sorry, Ethan. I didn't mean anything by that remark."

"No offense taken. I've been thinking of applying for a job as an umpire. Either that or a pilot. Think anyone would get upset if I stepped into the cockpit with my sunglasses on and Longfellow at my side?"

Jake laughed, and Ethan stood and stretched, suddenly too restless to sit. This wasn't his family. Jake wasn't his responsibility. He had just two-stepped his way into their lives and had no right interfering, yet he was almost certain Madge didn't realize how upset Jake was about changing schools.

"Do you need something?" Jake asked. "If you do, I'll get it for you."

"I just thought I'd go upstairs and check on your aunt. She's awfully quiet up there."

Jake smiled. "You like her, don't you?"

"What's not to like?"

"Nothing. She's cool. Well, actually, she's hot now. I know you can't see what she looks like, but take my word for it, she's good-looking—for an aunt."

"You wouldn't be putting me on, would you?"

"Heck, no."

Concentrating on moving the way he'd been taught, with slow steps, eyes straight ahead, cane checking for obstacles in his path, Ethan and Longfellow hit the staircase. He couldn't do a thing about Jake, so he might as well turn his attention to Alison.

After all, she was good-looking—for an aunt.

THE DOOR TO ALISON'S ROOM was shut, probably a sign that she didn't want to be disturbed. She was a difficult woman to understand, and seemed to operate on a dozen different levels at once. The efficient postmistress, the dependable daughter and sister, the adoring aunt, the seductive temptress just beginning to test her powers on the opposite sex.

He knocked on her door. No answer. She was probably asleep, but he'd better check on her all the same. He eased the door open and peeked inside.

The bathroom door was ajar. He caught a glimpse of her in the steamy mirror of the vanity. Naked. Rubbing a green terry towel over her long, shapely legs. He gulped for breath as the sight hit him with the same impact as if he'd been run over by a cement truck.

"Is that you, Ethan?"

"Yeah." He couldn't have gotten out more if his life had depended on it.

"I'll be with you in a second."

She stepped through the door, a white robe pulled over her shoulders but open enough so he could see the tempting triangle of hair at the apex of her thighs and the pink tips of her erect nipples. He knew there was no way he could stand there and pull off the blind routine. One glimpse at the bulge in his jeans and she'd know he could see it all.

He turned away, weak with wanting. "I was just checking to see if you needed anything," he said, knowing his voice sounded like a kid lying about a broken window when the bat was in his hands and the ball in plain sight.

"I'm fine."

"That's good." He kept his gaze directed toward the door. "I'll get out and give you some privacy."

She didn't say anything, but even with his back to her, he could sense the tension that heated the space between them. Once outside, he leaned against the wall, his breathing still choppy, his body racked with a passion that denied all reason.

What he wanted was inside that room, yet here he was, stalking away in the opposite direction, cane in hand, guide dog at his side. He wondered if the FBI knew what their latest brainchild had cost him. One day he might just tell them. He could all but hear their raucous laughter now.

"Come on, Longfellow, old boy. You can nap in my room while I take a cold shower. A *very* cold shower."

NORA STOOD in the department store dressing room on Friday afternoon and stared at her reflection. The blue cotton dress she'd tried on had a simple rounded neck and was slightly gathered at the waist. It would look great with the necklace and earrings Alison had given her for Christmas three years ago. And the fit was good. The three pounds she had lost this week made a difference.

Not that she'd been on an actual diet. She had no reason to diet. She was just concentrating on developing healthier eating habits. Women her age should do that. And she wasn't buying this dress for her date with Ron. She wasn't buying it for any particular reason except that she could use another nice outfit.

She turned slowly, looking at it from all angles. It was an attractive, functional dress, and she'd have lots of opportunities to wear it. The young saleslady stepped up to the cubicle. Nora could see her feet under the door.

"How does the dress fit?"

"I'm not sure. Would you take a look and give me an honest opinion?"

"Certainly."

Nora opened the door. "Do you think it's too young looking for me? I'm sixty, and I don't want people to think I'm trying to dress like my daughters."

"Sixty isn't old. My grandmother is seventy-two and she just started dating a man in his eighties. They go everywhere together, even out dancing."

"You're kidding."

"No way. The woman has more energy than I do. Besides, you look good for sixty, and the dress looks great on you. It's a classic style. You can dress it up or down. Go to dinner or to a fancy affair with just a change of accessories. You could even wear it dancing if you had the right shoes."

"You don't mind that your grandmother dates?"

"Why would I? Live and let live, that's what I say. I hope I'm having that much fun when I get to be her age."

"Does your mother feel that way, too?"

"My mom's been married three times herself. She can't afford to say anything about what Grandma does."

"I guess not."

Nora ran her fingers along her hips, riding the sheen of the fabric. The dress was fine, but she didn't really need it. She didn't need to go out with Ron, either. Dating after all these years of being alone with her memories of Dale was just too complicated. All she had to do was call Ron and cancel. He'd understand, probably even be grateful.

"Shall I ring the dress up for you?" the salesclerk asked.

Nora stared at the dress one last time. It did look good on her, and the memories had survived for years. They wouldn't vanish if she and Ron went to dinner once. "I'll take it," she said, astonishing herself.

Now all she had to do was go over to Alison's tonight for dinner and find a way to tell her two daughters that she was going on a bona fide date when even the word made her nervous.

Alison walking around with a new nose and a very sexy man living under her roof, Madge finally making a move to upgrade her marketable skills, and Nora going on a date. Change was definitely in the wind. Or else someone had spiked Cooper's Corner's water supply with a bit of magic dust.

Who knew what might happen next?

ALISON SAT at the kitchen table watching Madge and Ethan prepare dinner—spaghetti sauce from a jar, pasta, salad and steamed green beans. Ethan's job was to stir the spaghetti sauce, and he managed that quite nicely. Madge had tied a crisp white apron over his plaid shirt and jeans, and he looked every bit the consummate chef—*gorgeous* consummate chef.

Actually, he'd looked good in every role she'd seen him in so far. From shooting baskets with Jake to fitting an ice pack over her swollen wrist—which was well on the mend now, thanks to the pampering she'd gotten over the last two days.

"You might want to turn the heat down under this sauce," Ethan said. "It's starting to sputter."

Alison jumped up to go to his rescue just as the mixture came to a rolling boil and red sauce splattered out of the pot and onto the top of her range.

Madge beat her to it. "Step back, Ethan. Let a pro handle this." She took the pot and moved it to the back of the stove. The overflow rolled onto the element, and the smell of burning tomatoes filled the air.

"You're supposed to simmer spaghetti sauce," Alison said, grabbing a dishcloth and dabbing at the sticky mess.

"That takes too long. The stuff has already been simmered in…" She stopped to read the label "…in the kitchen of some Italian grandmother who has a lot more time to cook than I do. All it needs is to be hot, which it is now."

"Hot and splattered."

"Hey, it'll come out in the wash. Now you go sit back down and rest that arm. Ethan and I cooked dinner last night without your help and we can manage again."

Alison sighed and dropped back into her chair. "Last night we had canned vegetable soup."

"Heated and poured into bowls," Madge said. "That qualifies as cooking in my book."

"And grilled cheese sandwiches," Ethan reminded her.

"See?" Madge said. "We know our way around a kitchen." She opened the door of the refrigerator and peered inside. "Now, where do you keep your grated Parmesan?"

"In the meat and cheese tray, where it's been kept ever since you grew up here. The grater is in the bottom cabinet under the silverware drawer, where it's been…"

"I know," Madge said. "Ever since I lived here. But I thought you might have moved into the new millennium and started buying Parmesan in a shaker can the way the rest of the world does."

"I'm glad you haven't," Ethan said, finding his way to the table, Longfellow at his side. "Nothing beats fresh grated cheese. Well, almost nothing."

"Okay, I have the cheese," Madge announced. "Now, is anyone going to ask me about my day?"

"How was your day, Madge?" Ethan asked.

"I did my first spreadsheet on the computer, got all the information tucked away in those neat little boxes. It looked very professional, if I do say so myself. The instructor says I'm a natural. I'm not sure he's totally unbiased, though. I think he has the hots for me. Unfortunately, he's a nerdy little toad with no sense of humor, and he's old enough to be my father."

"Way to go, Madge," Alison said, lifting her almost empty iced tea glass in salute. "For managing the spreadsheet," she added. "Not for getting the instructor hot. I know you're a natural at that."

"Me? I'm not the one who has the phone ringing day and night. Let's see now, how many times has Kevin Bosco called in the last two days?"

"At least a dozen that I know of," Ethan answered.

Alison kicked him lightly under the table. "That is a gross exaggeration."

"More like an understatement," he said, ignoring the painless kick.

Madge held a head of romaine under the faucet, splattering water in every direction. "The *new* Alison Fairchild is an overnight temptress."

"Temptress was my first impression of her," Ethan agreed, nodding his head. "She carried me off to an isolated spot for a picnic and knocked my socks off."

"Hey, I didn't know you guys had dated. A picnic, no less. So, did you neck?"

A slow flush crept up Alison's skin as she remembered the picnic and the kisses with a mixture of embarrassment and titillation.

"Define necking," Ethan said.

"We didn't neck!" Alison protested. "Not according to anyone's definition."

"But she did knock my socks off."

Alison scooted back from the table. "You pulled your own socks off, and then you talked me out of mine and into the icy stream."

He threw up his hands as if shocked. "Don't tell me you had socks on with those cute little strappy black sandals."

Caught in her own lie. "I was speaking figuratively."

"So why didn't you guys tell me you had a past?" Madge asked, tearing lettuce for the salad with reckless abandon.

"We have no past," Alison protested.

"Definitely not," Ethan teased. "We're all present—with a possibility for the future. If I could just see well enough to locate her bedroom. It's tough being a blind man in a rambling old house."

"Wouldn't do you any good if you found it," Madge said. "She has a strong lock on the door. I know. I used to try to sneak into her room and borrow her CDs—without asking, of course. I could never get to them."

"That's because once they fell into your hands, they disappeared entirely."

"I did have a habit of losing things in my room. My poor gerbil once vanished for days."

"He was well-fed, though," Alison said. "He found your stash of junk food."

"My survival pack. You know, I don't think Mother ever knew I had that."

"I used to keep chocolate chip cookies hidden under my pillow," Ethan said. "Until the night I woke up in a bed of ants. Nasty little creatures, those ants."

"Better than mice. I found one of those once," Madge said, obviously enjoying the exchange of horror stories. "I think he was after my Twinkies."

Ethan stretched his long legs under the table and slouched comfortably in his chair. "So, Madge, how does Jake feel about switching schools so late in the year?" he said, changing the subject almost seamlessly.

"He's disappointed, but he's all right with it."

"That's good. I've had students who found that to be a rather traumatic experience."

"Jake's too well balanced to let something like changing schools throw him."

"Bet he'll miss pitching for the Woodstown Warriors, though," Jake said, not letting the subject go. "Baseball's pretty much his life right now."

"It's the first thing he's really been good at. He was too small for soccer and football and way too short for basketball. But driving him all the way to Woodstown would add another hour and a half to my day. That's too far when the high school for this district is terrific."

"He's your son. You know him better than I do, but I think this baseball thing is a lot more important to him than he's admitting." Ethan's usual teasing tone had grown deadly serious. "I know it would make it tough on you, but if there's any way at all to work it out so he could play the rest of the season, I think it would be worth it. He's told me several times how much he wishes he could pitch for the Warriors this season."

Madge wiped her hands on her apron. "You're really worried about Jake, aren't you?"

"I'm concerned."

Alison was amazed by Ethan's compassion and insight, though a little hurt that her nephew had gone to Ethan instead of her with his problems. Jake probably needed a man in his life more than they'd realized. "I'll help financially if you want to keep the apartment in Woodstown," she offered again. "I would help out with the driving if I could, but my hours at the post office make that impossible."

Madge nodded, but her expression reflected her concern. "I think maybe I should call Jake in and get him involved in this conversation."

"I can leave," Ethan offered.

"I'd rather you stay. Jake seems to be more honest with you than he is with me about this. You stay, too, Alison. This kind of involves all of us."

Alison nodded and waited until Madge left to go find Jake before she reached across the table and placed her hands on top of Ethan's.

"A woman's touch," he said, smiling. "What did I do to deserve this?"

"Jumped in on Jake's behalf."

"We men have to stick together."

"You know, for a blind man, you see some things pretty clearly."

"And some I miss completely." He toyed with her

hands. "Is that what frightens you about me, Alison? Is my being blind the turnoff?"

The turnoff? There were no turnoffs with Ethan Granger, though she wished for them constantly. Everything he did and everything he said was a turn-on of magnificent proportions. But she was frightened of him. Scared to death that she was going to start caring too much. Afraid of the way it would hurt when he packed his suitcases and walked away from her and Cooper's Corner forever.

"It's not you, Ethan. It's…the situation."

"The situation as I see it is that the two of us make fireworks every time we touch."

"Fireworks are beautiful and exciting, but one glittering display and they're all over."

"One explosive, awesome, breathtaking moment is more than a lot of people ever get, Alison. Think about that before you throw our chance at it away."

His words ignited a need inside her, so intense she could barely suck air into her lungs. Fortunately she didn't have to answer. Madge and Jake came through the kitchen door, arm in arm, Jake looking as if he were being hauled before a firing squad with itchy fingers.

Madge and Jake stared at the table, and Alison finally realized that her hands were still linked with Ethan's. She jerked them away and managed a shaky smile.

"What's this about?" Jake asked.

"Baseball," Ethan said. "Turns out it's not just a man thing."

Madge stooped a little so that she could look Jake in the eye. "How important is playing at Woodstown this season? Give me the truth. Don't spare my feelings."

He stared at his mom and then at Ethan.

Ethan seemed to sense his hesitancy. "Probably a good time to tell her what you told me, Jake."

Jake shuffled his feet and stared at the floor. "It's real important, Mom. The team needs me, and I want to play really bad. But I know you need to take those classes."

Madge slipped an arm about Jake's shoulder. "The classes are important to me, but not nearly as important as you are. I think if we put our heads together, a smart bunch of people like us can surely come up with something that works for both of us."

Jake grinned, a broad smile that showed all his teeth.

And Alison realized that she had never liked a man more than she liked Ethan Granger at that minute. Fiery tingles of awareness aside, she just plain liked having him in her kitchen and on Jake's side.

One explosive, awesome, breathtaking moment is more than a lot of people ever get. Ethan's words echoed in her mind. She'd certainly never had that before, and there was no guarantee she'd ever feel the way she felt about Ethan for any other man, no matter how many guys she dated. Was she really ready to throw such an opportunity away, when all she had to do to claim it was walk down the hall and climb into his bed?

She guessed it all came down to whether Alison Fairchild had actually changed or if she was still too frightened to take a risk. She'd have to decide soon.

CHAPTER NINE

"Guess what, Grandma?"

Nora stared at her handsome grandson across the dining room table. He was growing up much too fast. It seemed like only yesterday she'd rocked him to sleep in her arms. But then everything was starting to seem like only yesterday. "I'm terrible at guessing," she said. "But whatever it is, I'd say it's good."

"I don't have to change schools. I'm going to play baseball for Woodstown." He reared back and raised his arm as if he were about to toss her a ball. "You've got to come see me pitch."

"I'd love to see you pitch." She was pleased for him. Still, she'd hoped Madge was ready to move on with her life. She'd seemed to be in a holding pattern ever since she'd lost her husband so many years before. Nora looked at Madge. "You're not quitting your classes, are you?"

"Nope. Keeping the classes. Giving up sleep." She leaned over and tousled her son's hair. "No sacrifice's too great for the future major league pitching ace."

Nora lifted her eyebrows. "Oh?"

"Mom's dropping me off at school before she goes to class in the mornings," Jake explained. "On the days I don't have practice or a game, I'm going to stay with my friend Ben. On the other days, Mom can just pick me up at the baseball diamond."

Nora tried to imagine her oldest daughter getting up at

the crack of dawn to make such a long commute, but the image wouldn't quite jell in her mind. She chided herself for being so negative. It wasn't as if Madge had never carried through on *anything*. She'd stuck with being a mom, and Jake was one terrific teenager.

"That's great," Nora said, determined to stay positive about all of this. School was only for two more months. Madge could do it.

"Yeah, Ethan talked to Mom about it and she agreed. And Aunt Alison said that one day she'd come over and watch me pitch. And if Ethan's still here, he can come with her. He can't really see me pitch, but he said he'd like to come and hear the sound of my pitches walloping into the catcher's mitt as I strike the other team out."

Alison and Ethan. Together. An interesting possibility, though not likely. Alison was having too much fun attracting men like Kevin Bosco. "So how is your visit to Cooper's Corner so far, Ethan?" Nora asked. "Have you had a chance to get out and experience the town?"

Ethan wiped his mouth on his napkin before he answered. "Mostly I've just experienced the Fairchild family. That's been fascinating in itself. But I'm hoping Alison will show me around a little this weekend."

"Another picnic?" Madge asked. "Without your socks?"

"Definitely without my socks."

"If you stayed out of cold streams, you wouldn't have to worry about your socks," Alison said, tossing her hair and firing off a very seductive, un-Alisonlike look. Maybe she'd judged the situation too quickly, Nora decided.

Dale used to call looks like that a come-on. Nora had used them on him all the time, and he'd always succumbed. At the thought of Dale, guilt swelled inside her. Stupid, unwarranted guilt, she knew, but that didn't alter its effect. They'd had the perfect marriage, the perfect life—not that they hadn't had a few spats. An occasional good, healthy argument kept both partners alert, and making up kept the fires of passion alive. A perfect marriage, yet she'd had Ron Pickering on her mind almost constantly this week.

She had trouble keeping up with the conversation that continued throughout dinner. Her mind was occupied with thoughts of her date tomorrow night. What would Ron expect of her? Would things grow awkward?

Or would they get along splendidly the way they had last weekend? Would he want to kiss her? Would she want to kiss him? She didn't even know how to kiss anymore, and she couldn't ask her daughters about it. Maybe she should just cancel.

"There's coffee," Madge said, "and Oreos for dessert if anyone wants them."

Alison reached over and squeezed Nora's shoulder. "You've barely touched your food, Mother. You're not sick, are you?"

Nora scanned the table. Everyone else was finished and she hadn't even tasted her pasta. It was probably for the best. The way her stomach was churning tonight, food would only give her indigestion. And her stomach would likely keep churning until she confessed to her daughters that she was going on an actual date tomorrow night. Madge would be fine with it. Alison would lecture and make Nora worry even more.

"I'm fine," she said, "just not hungry. But I do have something I'd like to talk to you and Madge about."

"Then why don't the three of you take your coffee and go relax in the family room," Ethan suggested. "Jake and I will wash dishes."

"Oh, man," Jake protested. "Don't ever offer. It's bad enough when they make you."

"Not so bad for me," Ethan teased. "You'll have to do most of the work."

"And think of the male bonding you'll enjoy," Alison interjected. "You can talk batting averages, sliders, curves, fastballs. All that technical stuff women don't appreciate."

Jake grinned. Nora grimaced. She could put off the inevitable no longer. She was going out with Ron Pickering, and as soon as she said it out loud in front of people, it would become more real, like pregnancy once you put on a maternity frock. She poured herself a cup of coffee and walked to the family room, preparing herself mentally for the game of twenty questions that was sure to follow.

ALISON'S INSIDES WERE shaky as she took a seat on the edge of the big cushioned sofa. Something was wrong with her mother. She hadn't been herself all week. Half the time her mind seemed to be somewhere else, the way it had tonight at dinner.

Nora had always had a healthy appetite. Tonight she hadn't even dabbed her fork into her spaghetti. She must be sick and keeping it from them. That would be just like her, suffering alone instead of worrying her daughters, until she'd reached the point when she couldn't keep her secret any longer.

"So what's up, Mom?" Madge said, plunging right in where Alison feared to tread. "Now that you've gotten your hair colored, I suppose you plan to sign up for one of those singles' cruises to some exotic port."

"Certainly not. And it's not something horrible either, Alison, so wipe that stricken look off your face."

Alison breathed a little easier. "So what is the news?"

"It's not exactly news, but I think you might like to know about my plans for tomorrow evening."

"I do," Madge said, "especially since I have none. Give me a vicarious thrill."

"It's just that...well..." Nora sighed and swallowed hard before starting again. "I'm going to dinner tomorrow night with Ron Pickering."

The words slammed into Alison as if she'd been slapped hard across the face. Her mother was...her mother. She'd never shown the least bit of interest in men, not since Alison's father had died. They'd been so close, best friends, holding hands and in love right to the end. Now this Romeo showed up, and her mother had apparently forgotten all of that.

"That's great, Mom," Madge said. "You should go out and have a good time, but you're not serious about this guy, are you?"

Nora frowned. "The flu is serious at my age. Arthritis is serious. Not a dinner date."

Madge pulled her feet into the chair with her. "Then I'm all for it."

Nora stared at Alison, obviously waiting for her response. Alison shifted and tried to think of something halfway honest she could say without seeming totally negative. "What do you really know about this man?" she asked, wishing she sounded less like a prosecuting attorney and more like a daughter.

"He was the best man at our wedding."

"That was thirty-eight years ago. People change in thirty-eight years."

"I certainly hope so, dear. If he hasn't matured a lot during that time, I doubt we'll have much in common."

"I don't see what you'll have in common with him now except that he knew Dad, and I can't imagine he's coming back to Cooper's Corner just to talk about old times. And where's he coming from? I thought he lived in California."

"He did. It seems he's moved back to Boston."

Alison shook her head in exasperation. "You're turning into someone I don't know anymore, Mother, and I don't think the change is good for you. All that brown hair, dancing with this Ron Pickering guy at the wedding reception, and now this. It's not like you. Not at all like you."

"Okay, hold on here," Madge interrupted. "Are you saying you're this upset because our steady-as-a-rock mother has finally made a few changes to her life after fifteen years of being a widow?"

"I'm just saying the changes are coming too fast."

"Fast? Hell-*o!* Have you noticed yourself lately? You've changed so much in the last week, I almost called the FBI and reported that you've been taken over by some alien being."

"I have a new nose and some new clothes. That's all."

Madge and Nora both burst into laughter.

"You've changed a lot more than that," her mother said. "You don't even walk or talk the same."

"You're wearing makeup," Madge added. "Even mascara and blush. And you bat those baby blues as if you had sand in them. You've got poor Ethan reeling and he can't even see your new nose or your new clothes. He just knows you're *hot.*"

Alison felt the heat rush to her cheeks.

"And that's another thing," Nora said. "You blush a lot more often. I wonder what in the world is going on in that mind of yours."

"Give a girl a tissue and she can blow her nose. Give her a new nose and she becomes a siren," Madge teased.

Alison knew they were telling the truth. Since the nose job, she felt like a new person, attractive and confident.

"We're not upset with you for changing, Alison, though I still haven't quite forgiven you for having surgery without telling me first," Nora said. "The change looks good on you. The nose does, too," she admitted, "even though there was nothing wrong with the old one."

"Okay, Mom. I get the message. Just be cautious. Remember, men are not always exactly what they seem."

"Let's not get started on that subject," Madge said. "We could be here all night if I start spouting my experiences with disreputable men."

Nora walked over, dropped to the sofa beside Alison and took her hand. "I don't think this is really about mistrust or Ron. I think it's about my being with a man besides your dad. Am I right, Alison?"

Alison sighed, and held tight to her mother's hand. She had always been a terrible liar, even when she tried to fool herself. "You and Dad were so perfect together. Holding hands and in love right to the end. I can't seem to picture you with anyone else but him."

"I know, sweetie. I'm having trouble with that, too. But even if I start seeing Ron on a regular basis, it won't change what I had with your father. Ours was a very special love, and it will always live in my heart. But I can't stop living. Your father would be the first person to tell me that."

Alison put her arm around her mother's shoulders. "You're right, of course. You should see Ron, and you should have a good time. It just might take a little while for me to get used to it."

"I'll understand."

Silence enveloped them, but it wasn't an awkward silence, more of a chance to let them deal with their own feelings and emotions. Alison knew it was right for her mother to move on, and in time she would get used to it.

Finally Nora spoke. "Why don't you tell us about your classes, Madge?"

Alison left the conversation to Madge and her mother. She'd heard about the classes every night and couldn't remember Madge ever being this excited about anything related to work or school.

Her mind drifted to Ethan. All Ethans. The rogue who'd lured her to his room under false pretenses and then tried to seduce her. The guy who'd befriended Jake and realized that missing out on the baseball season would break his heart. The man who fit into her family almost better than she did, who'd stayed up Wednesday night while she was out on a date so he could tend her sprained wrist. The man Madge said was hot for the former Alison Uglychild without even knowing what she looked like.

The man who was leaving town in the next few days. Old love 'em and leave 'em Ethan.

She stayed in the family room for a few more minutes, then excused herself and went to bed. Ethan Granger might heat her insides to the boiling point with a kiss, but he was not for her. She wanted the kind of love her mother had enjoyed with her dad.

THE FAIRCHILD HOUSE was finally quiet. Ethan and Jake had been the last ones up. They'd caught the end of a West Coast baseball game on television after a rousing family game of Cranium, in which Ethan had to curb his competitive spirit or else risk blowing his cover of being blind. Now even Jake had gone to bed, leaving Ethan and Longfellow to savor the quiet. Longfellow had promptly curled up beside the cold hearth and fallen asleep.

And upstairs in a big four-poster brass bed, Alison was

sleeping all alone. Ethan tried to imagine her in something slinky and silk, but the image that seared into his mind was one in which she was wrapped in a fluffy green towel and a smile.

There had to be a limit as to how much temptation a man could take without falling at a woman's feet and begging for mercy. He figured it was about three more days at best, so he had to work fast if he wanted to save face.

He'd been here almost a week now, and nothing had gone according to plan. It wasn't that he didn't like Jake, Madge and Nora. He did. He liked them a lot. But his plan had been to get to know Alison better. He'd envisioned the two of them alone in the rambling old house, lingering in bed on lazy weekend mornings, making love for hours, then exploring the countryside. She was ready to start her new life, like a kid in a candy store who couldn't wait to wrap her tongue around one of those all-day suckers—as soon as she decided which one to choose.

Ethan got to his feet. Longfellow poked his head from between his paws and stretched his back legs until they disappeared under the edge of the couch, then rose to his haunches, ready to get up if Ethan needed him. ''Always alert and on the job, aren't you, old boy? The FBI could use a few more agents with your work ethic. And your intelligence, too. You've probably already figured out I'm a fake.''

Thankfully, no one else had. That had been the one rule the FBI had insisted on. No one he came in contact with except his co-workers at the agency and his trainers could know that he wasn't actually blind. It would negate the intensiveness of the training and affect his ability to carry off his assignment if he were not totally immersed in his role.

Seth and Wendy were the only ones who knew the truth, and it had taken lots of persuasion to obtain that clearance. The FBI wasn't particularly fond of having their undercover agents appear in the weddings of pre-assignment friends. They would never have approved it if he'd already begun the assignment.

Ethan walked to the foot of the stairs and looked up, listening. All was quiet. Satisfied that everyone was asleep, he went to the bookshelf and pulled down a photograph album from the top shelf. He'd noticed it earlier today, but of course couldn't say anything.

He stopped on the first page and studied an old photo of Alison. She was just a kid in it, probably no more then ten. Scrawny, but cute. Long blond hair fell past her shoulders, and she was dressed in jeans, an oversize sweatshirt, a faded baseball cap and tennis shoes.

Squinting, he tried to get a better look at the infamous nose. It was noticeably large for her face, but not nearly what he'd expected from Alison's description. Still, he was certain it was big enough to get her teased. Kids were merciless at that age. He skimmed the rest of the album, then chose another from the shelf. This one had more recent pictures, mostly of Jake, but a few of Madge, Nora and Alison.

The difference between the way she looked now and the way she looked in the photographs was striking, but it wasn't only the newly sculpted nose. In the photos Alison was wearing conservative, tailored clothing—professional looking, but lacking pizzazz. Nowhere was there even a glimpse of her terrific legs. No sign of the teasing, seductive smile that drove him over the edge, either.

It was as if she'd spent her life up to now as a bud. But, man oh man, when she'd finally blossomed, she'd done a bang-up job of it. As Jake would say, she was awesome. And her looks were only part of the attraction. The album almost slipped from his hand as he remembered the effect her kisses had on him. He caught it just before it crashed to the floor and woke up the whole house.

But if mere kisses did that to him, what would it would be like making love to Alison? His imagination ran wild at the prospect, creating a storm of desire that sent his pulse soaring and had him aching for release.

But no matter how badly he wanted her, no matter how hot the sparks that flew when they were together, he'd be sleeping alone tonight. "Just you and me again, Longfellow. You know, if you really want to help me, you should forget about keeping me from stepping into the path of cars or bumping my shins on the furniture, and go to work on Alison. Nudge her in my direction every chance you get. Let's get serious about this best friend stuff. You know, you scratch my back and I'll scratch behind your ears."

Longfellow looked at him with his soulful brown eyes.

"Okay, I'll throw in a doggie treat, too, but only if you get me all the way into the bedroom. I'll take it from there."

He replaced the albums on the shelf, then climbed the steps slowly, Longfellow at his side. The door to Alison's room was shut tight. Still, he paused there for a minute, wondering just what she'd do if he knocked and asked to come in for a good-night kiss. Probably evict him, toss his clothes on the lawn and leave him to sleep on the cold, wet grass. He headed toward his own room.

It was probably for the best. Already, he was letting dangerous thoughts creep into his mind. Imagining what it would be like to come home from an assignment and find Alison waiting for him. Imagining the two of them cooking in her kitchen and playing basketball in the back-yard with their son.

And here he was, dreaming again when he knew damn good and well it would never work. He could never sur-vive the pain of sinking down roots, only to have them yanked out and destroyed again. It wasn't Alison. It was just the way things were.

His job was the one certain thing in his life, the only thing he'd ever been good at, the one place he'd made his own. And it was no kind of life for a man with a wife. Sure, every now and then some agents managed to do it—combine married life with moving from one identity to another, from one location to another—but more often than not they failed. And Ethan couldn't take that risk again. He couldn't do that to himself or to Alison.

Still, he'd never wanted a woman more.

CHAPTER TEN

ALISON WOKE the next morning to an impatient rapping on her door. Her first thought was that it was Ethan, mainly because he seemed to be the first thing on her mind every morning these days. She jerked the sheet up to her neck before it hit her that if it was Ethan, covering herself was a wasted effort. Not that it mattered, anyway. She had on her flannel pj's, and they hid more than most of her clothes did these days.

She steeled herself to say no to whatever Ethan had in mind. "Can't a person sleep on her day off?"

"C'mon, Aunt Alison, it's ten past eight."

"And since when did you become the alarm clock on a Saturday morning?" She rubbed her eyes and sat up in bed. "Come on in, Jake."

He pushed through the door, a tray in hand. "I brought you coffee."

Jake was a super kid—for a teenager—but she couldn't remember him being this thoughtful before. "And whose idea was this?"

He smiled sheepishly. "Ethan's."

"I knew it. You two are cooking up something. Confess."

"It's not a scheme, at least not a bad one. The Woodstown school carnival is this weekend, and Ethan and I thought you might want to go."

"Why didn't you mention it before now?"

"I didn't want to hang out there when I thought I was going to have to drop off the team. It would have been a drag to go around telling everybody goodbye all afternoon. But now I'm not leaving. And all my friends are going today, practically the whole team."

She stuck out her arm. "I'm wounded and taking it easy."

Jake moved in close to examine her wrist. She had to admit it didn't look like much of an injury anymore. The bruises were fading and the swelling had all but disappeared. Still, it was the best excuse she had. Jake stared at her with that dejected look that always got to her.

"Maybe your mother can drive you," she suggested.

"She's got to study for a test, and Grandma said last night that she has plans for today. Probably getting ready for her date tonight."

"How do you know about that?"

"Mom told me. Some guy she used to know a long time ago is taking her to dinner."

"How do you feel about your grandmother going out with a man?"

"Kinda cool. So, will you please drive us to the carnival, Aunt Alison? I'll weed your flower garden next week."

"You really want to go, don't you?"

"Sure. Ben Smith went last night. He says they have this new ride called Mega Drop that's just like falling from a six-story building, except you never hit the ground. Awesome, man. Just awesome. Ethan says he'd like to go to. I know he can't see much of what's going on, but it would beat hanging around here all day."

It would beat hanging around here. And if she drove them to the carnival, she wouldn't have to be alone with Ethan for even a second. She took a long sip of her coffee.

"I could probably win you one of those big teddy bears. I've got a great pitching arm. You'd have to front me the money. I've only got a few dollars saved up and I'll have to use that for the rides."

"Guess it would be tough for you to miss something as awesome as falling from a six-story building."

"A major bummer."

"I thought so. Probably scar you for life."

"Then you'll drive us?"

"How can I refuse? But I'm holding you to your promise, and my flower garden's a jungle."

"All right!" He tore out of the room as if he'd been shot from that handmade peashooter he'd had in the yard yesterday, then came back to give her a quick hug before thundering down the stairs, yelling, "Hey, Ethan, we're on!"

His shout echoed through the house as Alison climbed from the bed and padded to the bathroom to douse her face with cold water and brush her teeth. She stared into the mirror and wiggled her nose. Still there. Still perfect. Still blending in with the rest of her face.

"Looking good, Alison Fairchild. Looking good." Feeling good, too, she realized reluctantly. As much as she hated to admit it, the prospect of going to the carnival with Jake and Ethan was far more exciting than the thought of her date with Kevin that evening.

THE CARNIVAL WAS HELD behind the high school football field on a patch of grass and dirt bordered by a creek and a stretch of forest. Alison searched for a parking space, locating one between two SUVs. After everyone had climbed from the car, she took a few dollars from her wallet and stuffed them in her pocket, then locked her handbag and jacket in the trunk. A Jeep full of guys passed as she was removing her key from the trunk lock. One of them gave a loud wolf whistle.

"Wow, Aunt Alison, that guy was whistling at you," Jake commented.

"Guys know a fox when they see one," Ethan said.

"Yeah, but she wasn't even facing them."

"Is that so? Guess she must look pretty good from the back today."

"Yeah," Jake said, giving her the once-over. "For an aunt."

He took off ahead of them. Ethan and Longfellow matched their pace to Alison's, which was far from slow. "So what are you wearing today?" Ethan said, looking straight ahead and marking his path with his cane. "Never mind. Let me guess."

"That's not necessary."

"But I want to. Judging from that whistle, I'd say you're wearing a straight denim skirt, about the length of that little thing you had on at the wedding rehearsal."

"When you groped my leg under the table?"

"It was a very nice leg."

She blushed. Damn. Why was it he could always make her blush, when no one else in the world could unless talking to her about him? "Compliments don't make up for groping," she said, determined not to fall into his tantalizing trap today.

"Groping is a matter of perception."

"Groping is a matter of latching on to my leg under the dinner table."

"So, am I right about the skirt?"

"You're absolutely wrong. I have on a pair of oversize sweatpants." A blatant lie. She had on a pair of snug-fitting jeans and a sweater.

"Is it okay if I check to see if you're lying?"

"Absolutely not."

"Is this another one of those no-touching days?"

"Every day from now until the end of time is a no-touching day between us, Ethan. This is a no-touching relationship. You abuse the privilege."

"So you're punishing me?"

"I didn't say that."

"Then what are you doing?"

"Protecting myself."

"From what? Enjoying life? I thought that was what you were ready to do."

"It is, just not with you."

"That makes no sense. I like you. You like me. We have got to be the best kissing team since…"

"Since Tracy and Hepburn?"

"Who the hell are they?"

Obviously the man was not into old movies. "It doesn't matter."

"Then don't throw them into the middle of our argument."

"We're not having an argument."

"I say we are, and I'm ready to kiss and make up."

Jake stopped and turned back, scanning the clusters of people strolling to the gate until he found them. "Hey, you guys, come on. We're missing the fun."

"Indeed we are," Alison agreed. She picked up her pace, then slowed when she saw a woman staring at her as if she were some kind of bitch for marching off and leaving a blind man on his own to maneuver a path dotted with potholes.

"Sounds as if there are quite a few people here," Ethan said. "Tell me about Woodstown."

"What would you like to know?"

"General information. Rural? Urban? Small? Medium-size?"

"It's a mixture of rural and urban. There are truck and dairy farms scattered about the countryside and a couple of small textile factories that have relocated here over the last few years. And there's a regional hospital that's well known for its innovative health care. Some people come here from Cooper's Corner instead of going to Boston when they need surgery."

Jake waited for them at the entrance. Ethan pulled out his wallet and paid for their tickets. The only thing he needed help with was putting his change back in the proper compartments. The tens went in one section, the fives in another. She'd never seen a wallet quite like it.

Her irritation with him eased. Life couldn't be easy for him, yet he certainly made the most of it. He was upbeat, intelligent and fun. And incredibly sexy. None of which changed the fact that she was not going to become the next conquest on his undoubtably lengthy list.

Alison had never been to this particular school carnival before, but the sounds, sights and smells were all familiar.

"I hear the hawkers and smell the roasted nuts," Ethan said as they walked into the action. "And I feel the sun on the back of my neck. It's got to be a great day for a carnival."

"Yeah," Jake answered, slowing to watch someone try to toss rings around bottle tops. "They have cotton candy, too. Do you want some?"

"Not yet. What else am I missing?"

"Game booths. All kinds of ways to win stuffed animals and little trinkets. The game booths at this end all belong to the carnival," Jake said, "but the ones our school sponsors are past the carousel, near the rides for the little kids. I'm going to wait until I get down there and try to dunk Coach Reynolds.''

''Now, that I really wish I could see.''

Jake started describing everything to Ethan, and the way Ethan reacted, you'd have thought they were at Disney World instead of a school carnival.

''You ought to go up there and buy a ticket for the bumper cars,'' Jake said. ''And take Longfellow with you. Bet the ticket guy would have a cow.''

''Don't dare me,'' Ethan said. ''I've done worse.''

''Yeah? What?''

''Back in college the gang was going snowmobiling one day, and I decided to join them. I figured I could follow the sound of the person in front of me and stay on the trail.''

''What happened?''

''I ran the thing smack into a tree.''

''Did you get hurt?''

''Luckily, I didn't break anything, but I spent a night in the hospital—and gave up every spare dime I had for the next two years to pay for damages to the snowmobile.''

Jake got a big laugh from the story. ''Want to go on the Mega Drop? You don't have to see to ride that.''

''What's the Mega Drop?''

''It's a new ride. You go up really high and then it drops straight down, just like you're free-falling, but it slows down before you hit bottom.''

''No, not me. I'll leave that one for you to ride with your friends.''

''How about you, Aunt Alison?

''So I can feel like I'm falling six stories? No thanks.'' Who needed a ride? She had Ethan for that.

"So what are you going to go on? Not the carousel," Jake said. "That's so corny."

"I might take Alison on the Ferris wheel if you'll watch Longfellow for us," Ethan announced.

"Yeah, sure. I'm not supposed to meet Ben for another fifteen minutes."

"How about it, Alison? I'll keep both hands on the safety rail."

A ride to the top of the world with Ethan. At least it would feel that way to Alison. They'd be so close their bodies would touch. And when they touched, her mind and body did strange things, blurred her ability to reason, made her warm in all the wrong places.

"It's only a ride, Alison. What are you afraid of?"

"Yeah, Aunt Alison, it's only a ride, and you've ridden it with me before. You weren't scared at all."

"Okay. One ride."

"I'll get the tickets," Jake said, running to the ticket stand before she had a chance to change her mind.

Funny, your stomach wasn't supposed to do flip-flops until you actually started down from the top of the Ferris wheel. But hers was already in motion, quivering like mad and making her weak.

ETHAN SLID INTO THE SEAT beside Alison. The attendant had given no indication he realized Ethan was blind. Everyone had on sunglasses today, and Alison's hand on his arm was much less conspicuous than walking with a cane or a guide dog at his side.

His first impulse was to stretch his arm along the back of the seat, let his fingers tangle in the silky swirl of Alison's hair. But he'd promised to keep his hands on the safety bar. And he would—for a while.

The movement was stop and go as they finished filling

the swaying gondolas. As the cars climbed upward, the wind increased, tousling Alison's hair and blowing flower-scented strands into his face. It took real effort to keep his gaze focused straight ahead when he wanted to turn and look at her.

"Who was the first boy you ever rode a Ferris wheel with?" he asked as they stopped almost near the top.

"Jake."

"Your nephew?"

"That's right. When he was six. Madge had a date that night, and I drove Jake to a carnival in New Ashford much like this one. I thought he'd be scared to death. He was fearless. We rode it three times before he was ready to move to something else."

"You did date in high school, didn't you?"

"A time or two. I had a lot of friends, both sexes, but I wasn't Miss Popularity. Besides my snowman nose, I was skinny and awkward. The guys went for the pretty girls."

"Their loss."

"I'm sure they didn't think so."

"What about in college?"

"I dated some, but no one special."

"Then you've never been serious about anyone?"

"Not yet. But I will." She reached up and touched her nose, as if it were the good luck charm that was going to turn her life around and bring her true love. He caught the movement from the corner of his eye.

The wheel rotated up to the highest point. This time he did turn and face her, staring into her beautiful, expressive eyes through the amber glow of his glasses. His heart kicked up and lodged somewhere in the vicinity of his throat.

She was glowing like the North Star on a clear night.

In her mind, the nose job had set her free to be herself, yet she was still afraid to let go and give in to her emotions. His hand left the safety bar and he touched the fingers of his right hand to the bridge of her cute little nose.

She sucked in a shaky breath, trembling a little as if something intimate had passed between them.

"I'm not going to hurt you, Alison."

"Not unless I let you."

"Not even then. Why would I?"

"Because this is all a game to you. You just drop into my life and then you'll drop out. Easy come, easy go."

"Lots of things in life are temporary. An ice-cream cone. A spring breeze like the one that's sifting through your hair right now. The first time for anything—like a kiss at the top of a Ferris wheel. Being temporary doesn't make them bad." He trailed his index finger down the line of her nose, not stopping until he reached her lips.

Only he wasn't sure he believed what he was saying anymore.

She leaned in close. "Kiss me, Ethan."

"Are you sure?" He must be crazy, sitting here talking her out of the very thing he'd been hoping for all along.

"Yes. I want my first kiss on the top of a Ferris wheel. It's long past due."

He touched his lips to hers just as the wheel started to spin. And once their lips met, he dissolved in the sweet taste of her. The world passed in a blur, and he closed his eyes as the motion carried them over the top again and then down, a revolving, pulsing sensation of everything moving at once and yet time standing still.

He was totally breathless when she pushed against his chest with her hand and pulled her lips away. "We better stop now. What will Jake think if he sees us?"

''That I'm the luckiest man at the Woodstown carnival. And he'll be right.''

She cuddled against him, making a nook for herself in the cradle of his arms. Ethan had an incredible urge to give out one of those wild warrior roars.

Alison was still snuggled against him when they halted at the top for the first people to get off. He started to kiss her again, then stopped, his attention caught by a group of boys past the last food tent. Four big kids had a boy on the ground, two of them kicking him in the stomach and head while the others held him down. The kid on the ground was smaller than his attackers, about Jake's size. Ethan's muscles tightened into painful knots. But it wasn't Jake. The shirt was different.

Damn. He was blind, by order of the FBI. He wasn't supposed to be able to see anything but shadows and light. How could he scream for help for a victim so far away? But he had to do something.

A couple of men came out of the back of the tent. The boys took off running, scattering like buzzards chased from roadkill. The men were leaning over the kid on the ground now, helping him up. Ethan released the breath he hadn't realized he'd been holding.

''Is something wrong?'' Alison asked. ''Don't tell me the Ferris wheel made you sick?''

''You took my breath away and left me dizzy,'' he teased. He kissed her again. It was still magic, still sweet, but it couldn't brush away the sick feeling left by the violence he'd just witnessed. Two years of intensive training and work in the field and he still wasn't used to the hard reality of seeing what teenagers were capable of doing to each other.

He spotted Jake in the crowd gathered around the exit. Safe, standing there with Longfellow. Ethan smiled gratefully, but the relief didn't overshadow his concern. The other boy, the one on the ground who'd had the stuffing beaten out of him, was somebody's kid, too. Someone's grandson. Someone's nephew.

It was their turn to get off, and Alison took Ethan's arm as they walked down the exit ramp. It felt good to have her beside him, even if she was the one leading. A brief touch of heaven was better than no heaven at all.

"WHAT WAS THAT ALL ABOUT?" Alison asked Ethan as Jake walked off, talking a mile a minute to his friend Ben. "You sounded like Jake's father, the way you were giving orders about what he should and shouldn't do."

"Boys that age think they're immune to danger. You have to remind them every now and then that they're not."

"It's a carnival. There are crowds of people everywhere. I'm sure it's safe enough."

"I'm sure it is, too. I was just reminding them to be cautious."

But it had been more than that. Ethan had sounded genuinely worried as he'd lectured Jake. Alison could never quite figure him out. When she'd met him, she'd expected him to be a quiet, docile man. Instead he'd teased and touched and kissed her senseless. She'd expected him to go berserk sharing the house with Madge and Jake. In reality, he'd jumped right in with them like one of the family. She'd accepted the fact that he and Jake were friends. Then he'd come on like a strict uncle or a stern schoolteacher, revealing a side of him that had been hidden until now.

The only thing she was certain of was that she was falling hard for love 'em and leave 'em Ethan. She could tell herself all day long that she could resist him, but the minute she got close to him, her willpower crumbled like stale cookies. A few minutes ago on the Ferris wheel, she'd melted completely. It had taken a colossal effort to pull away, even in a public place with people staring.

He was messing up her mind and there didn't seem to be a lot she could do about it, short of ordering him out of the house. She should be walking around in the clouds today, thinking about her date with Kevin Bosco. Instead she was still trembling inside over kissing Ethan on the Ferris wheel.

"You're quiet," he said. "Are you mad at me for breaking the no-touch rule?"

"No. That was my fault as much as yours."

"Except I don't think of it as anyone's fault. I thought the timing was perfect. I suggest we find a private place and take up where we left off."

She stopped and tugged him to a stop as well. "Why is it so important that you seduce me, Ethan? Do you have some kind of quota that you have to make? Five hearts in a year? Or is it just that you consider every woman you meet a challenge?"

"So that's what this is about. You think I'm just looking for a conquest and you're handy."

"I don't know what else to think. This started from the very first night we met. You were the best man. I was the maid of honor. Wendy asked me to drive you back to Twin Oaks, so you must have thought I was being handed to you like a canapé on a silver platter."

The muscles in his arms bunched and strained against the fabric of his shirt. "You really haven't been around, have you?" His voice was low and harsh and almost drowned out by the squeal of kids on the roller coaster.

"What's that supposed to mean?"

"Let's get out of here, find somewhere quiet where we can be alone, and I'll tell you exactly what I mean."

"The only place like that is the car."

"Then lead me to it. It's time we get this misunderstanding cleared up once and for all. And time you learned how to tell when a man's so crazy about you he can't think straight, and not just attracted to your cute little turned-up nose and killer body."

Crazy about her? Ethan? Her heart raced faster than the last car on the speeding roller coaster. This she had to hear.

CHAPTER ELEVEN

ALISON LOWERED the front windows of the car and moved her seat back as far as it would go. Positioning herself against the door, she turned so that she could face Ethan but keep a reasonable amount of space between them. He still wore his glasses, and his gaze appeared to be directed over her left shoulder.

Perhaps the fact that he could never look her in the eye when they talked added to the feeling of distrust she experienced with him, the sense that he was never leveling with her. If so, she was being unfair. It must be a hundred times worse for him not to be able to look directly into someone's eyes.

He rested his left arm against the back of the seat and opened and closed his fist, as if he were ready for a fight or else trying hard to keep some inner demon in check. It struck her again how virile he looked. Lean and hard bodied, he could have just stepped from the pages of a catalog of clothes for rugged outdoorsmen. The worn jeans that fit to perfection, the rolled sleeves of his sport shirt and the scuffed loafers all added to the illusion. The crowning touch was his confident air. It was clear he knew who he was and was comfortable with that.

But she didn't know who he was, and had only just began to learn who *she* was. Her emotions seemed as new as her nose, her reactions to Ethan as unfamiliar as the trendy clothes she'd bought in New York. One minute she felt attractive and sure of herself, the next she longed to crawl back into her old clothes and identity.

The old Alison had never gotten dizzy and light-headed at a man's touch, had never lain awake at night reliving the thrill of a kiss. But then, the old Alison had never encountered someone like Ethan Granger. The man was a master at turning every meeting between them into a rendezvous, making even the most incidental touch a loaded sensual experience. No wonder she was so afraid of giving in to this need for him that never let up.

"So, Ethan, you can start talking anytime now. If I've got everything all wrong, why don't you straighten me out? If the seduction of Miss Alison Fairchild, small-town postmistress, isn't a game to you, what would you call it?"

"How the hell would I know what to call it? I came here for a wedding, remember, not to improve my love life. Cooper's Corner is hardly considered the hot spot of the world for singles action."

"No, but you sure didn't waste any time. I drive you home and you come onto me as if we're two teenagers with raging hormones. Even at the restaurant you were monopolizing my time and attention. I was there, so you did what evidently comes naturally to you—use your disability to seduce women."

"Okay, I admit it started out as something of a game. You all but asked for it."

"I beg your pardon?"

"You were flitting around the church, showing off your new nose and flirting with every man there."

She swallowed hard, knowing he was right but not realizing she'd been that obvious. "But I didn't flirt with you," she said, making the only valid point she could come up with.

"Only because you didn't want to waste your efforts on a man who couldn't admire you. You had that poor Barry guy panting after you, the same way you had Kevin Bosco doing at the wedding reception. So, if you want to talk about games, Alison, you need to examine your own motives a little closer."

"I may have been enjoying myself, but I didn't stoop to lying the way you did when you came up with that absurd story about the plane tickets. Admit it, Ethan, that was a calculated lie told for the sole purpose of getting me alone in your room."

He shrugged. "I admit I may have stretched the truth a little."

"There wasn't a thread of truth in that story."

"Seth and Wendy *were* flying out the next morning."

"And Seth had the tickets in his bag."

"Okay, I shouldn't have lied, but how was I supposed to compete with Kevin when he could whirl you around the dance floor and gaze into your eyes?"

"You compete with your magical hands and your lips, that's how, and you do a damned good job of it."

"They're all I have, Alison."

Her heart constricted and she almost reached out to him. A shadow of doubt stopped her. He was doing it again, getting to her, destroying her resistance, awakening that need inside her that drove her over the edge. She ached to crawl into his arms and drown in his kisses. But nothing he'd said had changed anything about their relationship.

"Why me, Ethan? Why did you decide to concentrate all your efforts on me? Why not Maggie Porter or one of the other women at the reception? They were all after you. Even without being able to see them, you had to know that."

"Why you? Are you trying to tell me that you don't feel the crackle in the air every time we get within ten feet of one another? That you don't grow weak when we kiss?"

Her mouth grew so dry she couldn't swallow. "But if it's just a game…"

"It might have started as a game, Alison, but it didn't stay one for long. Do you think I'd turn my life upside down over a game? I wake up in the morning thinking about you, and lie there every night in pure agony, knowing you're sleeping just down the hall and I can't crawl into bed beside you. I've taken so many cold showers over the last few days that it's a wonder I don't have frostbite."

He put his hand on her shoulder, gripping and massaging her flesh. "Do you really think these kinds of feelings happen every day, that anytime I take a woman into my arms, fireworks explode and I go out of my mind with wanting her?"

"I don't know, Ethan. I don't know what I think anymore." Only she did know what she was thinking now. She was thinking that she wanted him in the same way he wanted her. She didn't know if she would ever feel this way again, but she knew if she didn't kiss Ethan soon, her heart might leap right out of her chest.

"I'm crazy about you, Alison. I don't know any other way to say it, and apparently I don't do a very good job of showing it. If you want me to leave just—"

She put a finger to his lips. The reasons she should avoid him were probably all still there, but she couldn't keep fighting the hunger that consumed her. Couldn't keep analyzing her feelings and trying to make rational judgments about emotions that had no rational basis.

"No more talking, Ethan. Just kiss me." She moved into the circle of his arms, protecting her sore wrist. Desire

swelled inside her, took her breath away, swallowed up
her fears. She parted her lips and welcomed his tongue,
wanted to feel every beautiful sensation of taste and tex-
ture, the whole spectrum of desire. When they came up
for air, he kissed her eyelids, her nose, her chin, the curve
of her neck, stopping to nibble and suck her earlobe, ever
mindful of her arm and careful not to hurt it.

She was on fire with wanting him, but not here, not
like this. No one was around this area of the parking lot
right now, but someone could walk up at any time. "We
better stop," she said, "while we can."

Longfellow barked once from the back seat.

"See, even Longfellow thinks so."

Ethan turned toward the door. "Watch it, buddy. I'm
the one who controls the flow of doggie treats." Then he
leaned toward Alison, touched his forehead to hers and
fitted his hands beneath the swell of her breasts. "Is there
anyone around watching our show?"

"No, but people will start leaving soon. I really think
we should go back to the carnival area."

He squirmed and tugged on his jeans, drawing her attention to the obvious bulge. She blushed, thankful he
couldn't see her.

"I guess you're right," he admitted. "Jake would probably get embarrassed if we were arrested for indecent be-
havior."

She shuddered. "I'd never live it down. The Cooper's
Corner postmistress arrested for getting it on in public at
the Woodstown School Carnival. My mother could never
show her face at her bridge club again."

"Madge would get a kick out of it."

"You're right," Alison agreed. "Vindication for all the
times Mom's told her she should be more like me, settled
and boring."

"Your mom doesn't think you're boring."

"She does. Only she thinks staying home alone night after night is a virtue."

"Then she must be changing her mind. She seems awfully excited about going out to dinner tonight with her new beau."

"Let's not get into that now."

Ethan kissed the tip of Alison's nose. "It's probably your fault, you know. You and your new nose. Your magic is contagious."

"There's nothing magic about my nose."

"Couldn't prove it by me or by the action your phone's been getting. Let's see, how many requests for a date have you gotten this week?"

"You've been talking to Madge."

"*Listening* to Madge," he corrected, tangling his fingers in her hair. "So, do you want to neck again? Because if we stay here, I'm not going to be able to keep my hands off you."

"Then we better head back to the carnival. Are you hungry?"

"Famished."

She wasn't. When Ethan was around she was giddy with excitement, drunk on pure titillation, impervious to hunger. No wonder women in love always lost weight.

Love. The word stalled front and center in her mind, flashing as if it were lit in neon. She couldn't say it, couldn't even think it, not with Ethan. It reeked of permanence, when he offered none.

Still, they walked hand in hand back toward the carnival, separating them only long enough to flash their wrists to the gatekeeper and show the stamp that proved they'd already paid. Alison was still confused by her feelings for Ethan, still unsure and somewhat frightened, but she knew it was useless to fight them. She'd given it her best shot and had come up short.

The only thing left was to take advantage of her time with him, revel in the moments that stole her breath away and the passion that erupted inside her like a volcano spewing molten lava.

She'd miss him when he left, but she'd get over him. She would.

Somehow.

THE RIDE BACK to Cooper's Corner was much quieter than the one to Woodstown a few hours earlier. Alison seemed lost in her own thoughts, and that concerned Ethan. When they'd talked in the parking lot, she'd seemed to accept that what they shared was too good to toss away just because he'd be leaving soon.

But her withdrawing this way worried him. Was she reconsidering and deciding she could do without anything that wasn't permanent? Or was she thinking of her date tonight with the smooth-talking attorney from Boston?

"So how was the Mega Drop?" Alison asked Jake.

Alison and Ethan had both tried to initiate a conversation with Jake several times. He'd answered them, but he wasn't the funny, talkative kid he usually was, and Ethan couldn't help but wonder if the fight he'd witnessed had anything to do with it.

He knew from his training that news traveled fast among kids within a school. Violence, intimidation, a fight—the impact of any one of them could cover an entire campus like a gathering storm cloud.

It chafed at him that he couldn't just talk about what he'd seen and ask Jake about it, but there was no backing out of his assumed role at this point. If anything, seeing the beating made his commitment to his latest assignment even stronger. He had to become totally convincing as a blind schoolteacher. When he hit the inner city school in New Orleans, he had to observe everything yet appear to see nothing. In the meantime, he'd try to get Jake to open up about whatever it was that was bothering him.

And as eager as he was to get started on his new assignment, Ethan was not looking forward to leaving Cooper's Corner. Alison had definitely crawled under his skin, gotten to him the way no woman had in a long, long time. Maybe God just hit a man with a sensual wallop like this once or twice in his life to show him how weak he really was. Made the sparks so intense that the only thing a man could do was quiver and beg.

All Ethan knew was that he couldn't get enough of Alison, and that he was going to have a miserable night knowing she was out with Kevin Bosco. But it was her choice. See if he'd wait up for her again while she was out infatuating some jerk who had shunned her when her nose was a little large. See if he'd worry that she was kissing the guy good-night, or worse yet, enjoying it. See if he'd care.

But of course he did care. A lot.

NORA HAD WORRIED all afternoon that she was making a big mistake. She was too old to date, too set in her ways. She'd had a great marriage and that had been enough. She should never have colored her hair, either. If you dyed an old egg, it was still an old egg on the inside.

The doorbell rang. She fumbled for the key, reaching shaking fingers along the mantel, behind the crystal vase Alison had bought her for her birthday last year, and practically sending the beautiful piece of glass shattering to the floor. Key in hand, she checked her image in the mirror one last time.

She was a jittery old fool. Patting her hair into place, she took the key and opened the door. Ron stood there, a bouquet of pink roses in his hand.

"Hello, Nora." He extended the hand with the flowers. "I guess men still give flowers, don't they?"

His voice was strained. The guy was as nervous as she was. Somehow that made her feel better. "I have no idea what men do these days, Ron, but they're pretty. Pink roses were always my favorite."

"I remember."

"You remembered for all these years that I like pink roses?"

"Yeah. I swiped one for you once, out of the yard of that old woman who lived back of Tipsy's."

"Tipsy's. The campus hangout. I haven't thought of that place in years, but I do remember the rose episode. There were a whole group of us walking to Tipsy's for burgers, and you just jumped the fence and grabbed the rose. The woman came chasing after you with her broom, and you called her a witch."

"She did look like one."

They both laughed. Nora especially liked the sound of Ron's laughter. Easy and genuine. He hadn't changed all that much. "Face it, Ron, you were bad. Stealing an old woman's roses."

"Hey, you said you wanted it. Besides, she had lots more."

"You didn't steal these, did you?"

"I thought about it. I'm not sure I could take a fence that fast anymore."

"I've never seen anyone jump one so fast."

She started to the kitchen to retrieve a vase, then changed her mind. The crystal one on the mantel would be perfect for the roses. She turned to reach for it, but Ron was there first. "I'll get that for you."

He did, then followed her to the kitchen. His footsteps sounded strange to her ear. It had been a long time since she'd had a man in her home, other than the handyman the supervisor sent over for repairs. And he was so young, she wasn't sure he even counted.

"I made reservations at the Red Maple in New Ashford, but I couldn't get them until eight o'clock. I hope that's not too late for you."

"Eight will be fine." She placed the flowers on the counter while she filled the vase with water. "Would you like a glass of wine? I have a bottle of cabernet. It's not opened, though. I could get us some cheese and crackers to munch on. Wine on an empty stomach makes me giddy."

"Nothing wrong with giddy, and a glass of wine would be great. I can't handle jumping fences anymore, but I'm a real pro with a corkscrew. Just point me to it."

"Top drawer under the coffeepot. And there are some goblets in the hutch in the dining room."

A minute or so later, she heard the soft pop of the cork as it cleared the bottle, and the sputtering sound of the wine flowed into the glasses. The kitchen seemed warm and cozy. The nervousness had vanished, replaced by a sensation she didn't quite recognize. But whatever it was, she liked it.

She placed the last rose in the vase and made a few touches to give the arrangement a finished look. "What do you think?" she asked, holding the vase up for him to admire his roses and her handiwork.

"They're lovely. Let's set them in the middle of the kitchen table and have a toast."

"We could put them in the dining room and have our cheese and wine in there."

"We could, but I like it in here. Dining room tables need a crowd to feel right, but kitchen tables seem perfect for two."

She carried the roses and he carried the wine, handing her a glass once the flowers took their place of honor in the center of the small wooden table. He held up his glass for the toast. "You first."

"To old friends, pink roses and memories," she said.

"And to new beginnings," he added. "And shorter fences."

They clinked their glasses and Nora took a sip of the wine, letting its warm glow seep inside her. It was going to be a nice night.

KEVIN PULLED his red sports car to a stop in front of Alison's house. He killed the motor, leaned toward her and snaked his arm across the back of the seat. "You'll have to come to Boston soon, Alison. I'd like you to see my apartment and meet some of the attorneys I work with. Besides, there's so much more to do there—theater, night-clubs, museums, great restaurants. And on Sunday, we can have breakfast at the club and get in a set of tennis. I'll be preparing for a case next weekend, but the weekend after that would be perfect."

Alison stared at the lights from an oncoming car and wished she could muster up a little enthusiasm. Swoon-worthy Kevin Bosco was inviting her to Boston to meet his friends. He wanted to show her off. She'd paid out big bucks for cosmetic surgery and sunk a bundle into a new wardrobe for a moment like this. Now that the moment had arrived, it felt like the biggest letdown since she'd discovered that the tooth fairy was a fraud.

"What do you say, Alison? Can I put you on my calendar?"

"And have me replace the Patriot cheerleaders? I don't have an outfit quite that skimpy."

"You don't need a skimpy outfit to look great. Besides, I haven't had a cheerleader calendar in years. I have an appointment planner in a leather binder."

"Of course you do. I was only teasing." And deciding how to say she didn't want to see him again. It wasn't that Kevin had done anything wrong, it was just that he wasn't...

He wasn't Ethan. And therein lay the rub. Boston wasn't all that far away. If she and Kevin hit it off, they could have a real relationship, one with a chance to grow into something permanent.

Ethan was a moment in a lifetime. He thought temporary was great. After all, who'd want an ice-cream cone in winter or fireworks all year round. Those weren't exactly his words, but they captured his meaning, all right.

"I won't be able to make it that weekend, Kevin." She reached for the door handle.

Kevin laid a hand on her arm. "Are you in a hurry to go in?"

As a matter of fact she was. "It's been a long day."

He crawled from behind the wheel. She'd already opened her door and was standing by the time he reached her side of the car. Before she could react, he put his arms around her and pulled her close. She could feel his body against hers, smell his aftershave, sweet and just a little nauseating. She looked up, met his gaze and knew he was going to kiss her.

Her first impulse was to pull away, but she reconsidered. She should give him a chance. Maybe she'd just been in too much pain from her wrist to react the other night. Perhaps his kisses were a hundred times more thrilling than Ethan's. She closed her eyes and waited.

No magic at all.

She finished the kiss, then pushed away from him, amazed that two similar actions could affect her so differently. When Ethan kissed her, the world stood still, or else it exploded with such a burst of passion that she went totally weak. Kevin's kiss left nothing more than a taste of the herbs that had spiced his broiled fish.

"I really have to go, Kevin. But thanks. It was a…" She thought for a minute, trying to find a word that was truthful and not insulting. "It was an enlightening evening."

"I'll walk you to the door," he said, obviously upset by her lack of enthusiasm.

"No need. Why don't we just say good-night here?"

"Okay. I'll call you."

They both knew he wouldn't. She'd had her chance with Kevin Bosco, the experience she'd waited ten years for. The best thing she could say was that the food at the Purple Panda was delicious.

She hurried up the walk and opened the front door, anticipation already swelling inside her at the prospect of finding Ethan waiting up for her again. But the house was quiet and dark except for the glow of the hall night-light. She slipped out of her shoes and stepped silently across the polished floor so as not to wake anyone, hating to admit just how disappointed she was not to find Ethan stretched out on the couch.

As she headed up the stairs to her room, the only illumination came from the strips of light that peeked from around the edges of Ethan's door. She could just walk down there, knock on his door and tell him she wanted to talk. And then what?

He'd touch her and she'd become so aroused she'd melt into his arms. He'd kiss her and she'd kiss him back. The magic would explode inside them. The *temporary,* sensual, dazzlingly erotic magic that she'd never known before and might never know again.

Take it or leave it? It was her call.

She took a deep breath, touched a finger to the tip of her nose for luck and walked right past her own door. The new Alison Fairchild was going to take it.

CHAPTER TWELVE

ALISON STOPPED in front of Ethan's door, summoned up all her courage and tapped lightly.

"Come in."

Heart racing like an Olympic sprinter's, she turned the knob and stepped inside. Ethan was stretched out on the bed. Shirtless, his jeans unsnapped at the waist, his big, manly bare feet poking up. Heat suffused her, and she started to tremble so much that she had to hold on to the door for support.

"Good evening, Alison."

"How did you know it was me?"

"From the scent. Passion, isn't it?"

"You have a good memory."

"How was the evening with lover boy?"

"It was okay."

"Just okay?"

"We had dinner. The food was good, but there was no magic."

He smiled. "Did that surprise you?"

"Not really, but I gave it a shot."

"So what do we do, Alison? Keep waltzing around the issue of whether or not we make love, or admit that we have something most people only dream of finding and make the most of it?"

"What do you want to do?"

"Hold you in my arms. Make love with you. Explore

your body with my hands and my mouth and find out what gives you pleasure.''

The image that his words formed in her mind made her want him with an even greater urgency, but still she held back. ''I need to know one thing, Ethan.''

''I'll answer if I can.''

''Is there someone else? A wife? A lover?''

''There's no one else. There hasn't been in a long, long time.'' He put out his hand to her. ''I can't promise you forever, Alison, any more than you can promise that you'd want me around forever. You're just beginning to discover your new self. But I care for you, more than I ever thought possible, and I really want to hold you. That's all I know for certain.''

She took his hand. ''If that's your best offer, I'll take it.'' She stretched out beside him on the bed, her insides quivering in anticipation, her left hand trembling as she splayed it across his chest.

He rolled over and gathered her in his arms, gently this time, as if she might crumble if he held her too tightly. Only she didn't want him to treat her gently. She wanted to soar straight up to the pinnacle and even higher. If the fireworks were brief, then she wanted them to explode with such brilliance that she'd remember this moment in time for as long as she lived. ''Don't hold back, Ethan. Make love with me the way you said. Touch me all over, and let me do the same to you.''

And then he kissed her as even Ethan had never kissed her before. Incredibly sweet for a few seconds, then deep and demanding, as if he were laying claim to her soul.

Forever didn't matter any longer. Time ceased to exist. There was only here and now, and Ethan. His hand brushed the smooth fabric of her blouse, then moved lower until he slipped his fingers beneath her skirt and stroked her thighs. As the familiar heat pooled within her, Alison became impatient. She started to slip her panties off herself, but he took her hand and held it.

"Let me undress you, Alison. Slowly, inch by inch, so that I can memorize every part of you."

Reluctantly she moaned and lay back on the pillow while his fingers skimmed up her arms. He fumbled with the buttons of her blouse, loosening them and pushing the fabric back. While his tongue ran along the lacy edge of her bra, he eased the blouse down her arms and tossed it to the floor.

The bra came next. Once the clasp was loose, he slid the straps down and released her breasts. They fell against his bare chest, her nipples already pebbled and erect. His fingers caressed the rounded flesh, and his tongue laved the rosy tips, driving her crazy with desire.

Ethan raised his head and his voice was strained. "I'd like to keep going this slow, Alison, but I can't. My body won't let me."

"I feel the same," Alison said, her breath quickening, and thrusting her hands through his hair, she pulled his mouth to hers. Their kisses were urgent, frenzied. Ethan practically tore off her skirt and her panties in quick, jerky movements. His fingers explored the delicate folds of flesh hidden beneath the fiery triangle he'd revealed, and then his tongue took over. Alison had to bite back squeals of pure ecstasy as warm waves of pleasure rose to a crest within her.

She was desperate to have him inside her, and finally he pulled away. As she watched, her breath coming in jagged, painful puffs he stood by the bed and peeled the jeans from his body, stripped until he was totally naked. He was beautiful. All of him. Lean, muscular, virile. Hard in all the right places.

She touched his erection and he moaned softly. "Finally a night with no cold shower."

"Oh, Ethan. I've waited so long."

"It's only been a week."

"No. It's been all my life."

"This is it? Your first time?"

She swallowed hard and touched her lips to the smooth flesh of his abdomen. "I had chances, though not all that many. They were never right. I knew it would happen someday. I just didn't know when or with whom."

"Oh, Alison." He cupped her face in his hands and kissed her tenderly. "I'll try my best to make sure this was worth waiting for."

And then he lay down beside her, took her in his arms and fitted himself inside her. Her body rocked with an overwhelming need as Ethan touched parts of her that had never been touched before. She pushed her hips toward him in rhythm with his quick, steady thrusts. She couldn't think, couldn't savor the moment the way she wanted. All she could do was feel and react and go along for the ride of her life.

She heard Ethan gasp, and then she was overwhelmed by a rush of heat that seemed to consume her. Long minutes later, her pulse was still racing, her emotions teetering on the edge of delirium. "Oh, mi'gosh, Ethan. That was great. It was… Wow. It was just…wow."

He laughed and rolled her over on top of him. "Guess that means you liked it."

"I loved it. Can we do it again?"

He ran his fingers through her hair, brushing loose, wispy locks back from her face. He was looking right at her, and for the first time she felt as if he were meeting her gaze, that she could see her happiness reflected in his eyes.

"*You* could probably do it again. I need a few minutes to regroup." He touched a finger to the tip of her nose. "The new Alison Fairchild, femme fatale just crawling from the cocoon. I'll always be thankful that I came along at just the right time."

"But you can't see my nose, Ethan. You would never have been able to tell the new me from the old me."

"If what Madge says is true, I would have known."

"What does she say?"

"That the surgeon slipped and cut the nerve that leads to your inhibition control. That before you got your nose clipped, you were a mousy little postmistress who didn't seem to know men were a separate sex."

"I was never that bad. Close, but not quite that bad."

"Now you're wanton."

"I certainly am not."

"Ready to make love again the second you finish? I don't know what else you'd call it."

"Happy, Ethan. Really happy. I guess I should sneak back into my bedroom, though. It wouldn't do to fall asleep and have Madge or Jake find me here in the morning." She kissed him again, then started to slide from his arms.

"Not just yet," he said, easing his hand down the smooth flesh of her belly.

"I thought you couldn't do it again so quickly."

"So did I." He held her close and she felt the hardness of him pressing against her. "But there's no accounting for magic."

ETHAN STOOD IN FRONT of the bedroom window, staring up at the stars. They seemed almost close enough to reach out and touch. In the city they were never so bright, not in D.C., at least, and probably not in New Orleans. He'd never thought a lot about stars before. He was sure he would after tonight. Mostly he'd remember Alison's moans of pleasure, the softness of her flesh, the abandon with which she'd given herself to him, not once, but twice.

He'd fallen asleep after that, so totally relaxed he couldn't stay awake. But he'd woken up aroused again, and when he had, Alison was gone. It was only 4:00 a.m. now, and he was wide awake, grappling with the situation he'd gotten himself into, feeling the bitterness of guilt.

He had no choice but to lie to Alison about his blindness, yet he felt as if he'd deliberately deceived her. She was so open about everything. His whole identity was made up. Thomas had warned him it would be a mistake to travel to Cooper's Corner and take part in Seth's wedding when he'd already assumed his undercover identity. A smart man. Guess that was why he was the boss.

But Seth had been so insistent, and no one involved in the wedding party had ever met him, so how could anything possibly go wrong?

Only it had, and it was all Ethan's fault. The problem would have been avoided if he'd been honest with himself from the first, admitted that what he felt for Alison wasn't mere physical attraction. And it certainly wasn't a damn honorable attempt to give her a little harmless experience.

Truth was, he'd been hooked from the first moment he'd spotted her flitting around the church. Cute, fun, glowing with excitement. And then he'd touched her, let his fingers slide down her cheek, and had felt her tremble.

Blind. He was blind, all right. Blinded by a killer attraction that he hadn't had enough sense to run from. "You should have bitten me on the ankle, Longfellow. Every time I got close to Alison, you should have nipped me until you drew blood. It's your duty to protect me, you know. What kind of guide dog are you, anyway?''

Longfellow whimpered and put his head between his paws. Ethan leaned over and gave him a few pats. ''That's okay, boy. I probably wouldn't have listened to you, anyway. I'm a very hardheaded man. It's job training. We butt our heads against a lot of walls.''

If he had half a brain he'd leave tomorrow, before things got even more complicated between him and Alison. But if he'd had half a brain, he would never have stayed in the first place, not when he had nothing of value to offer. Even if she could forgive him for letting her think he was blind, he could never give her the permanence she wanted, not as long as he worked in covert operations for the FBI.

They'd be good for a while. No, they'd be dynamite. And then he'd have to leave, take on a new identity, disappear into a secret life that she couldn't share. It was the life he loved, the only one he knew. But Alison would get lonely, and there would be plenty of men eager to take his place. And finally one cold, lonesome night, she'd give in. And then...

No. God help him, he couldn't go through that again. And he couldn't put Alison through it either. Whatever time they had together now would have to be enough. When he left Cooper's Corner, it would be for good.

He dropped to the side of the bed. Longfellow put his head in Ethan's lap and licked his hand as if he understood what his master was going through. ''Don't let me start believing I could make it work with Alison, old buddy. Don't let my heart make a fool of me again. Alison deserves better.''

Ethan stretched out and closed his eyes, wishing sleep would come and give him a reprieve. It didn't. So he settled for the next best thing. He concentrated on how it had felt making love with Alison. But the image skipped into the future and he saw himself in an efficiency apartment in New Orleans, sleeping alone and going out of his mind missing Alison.

Longfellow had his work cut out for him.

ALISON WOKE to the trill of a bird outside her bedroom window. The moment she opened her eyes, she was fully alert, tingling with life and full of thoughts of Ethan. Memories of last night swam through her consciousness, and she felt a gentle ache between her thighs. The discomfort assured her that making love with Ethan had been the real thing and not another of the erotic dreams he'd starred in all week.

She stretched, running her feet between the crisp sheets and poking her arms from beneath the covers. The house was quiet, but sunlight streamed through her open window and painted long rectangles of light across her floor and bed. The morning was much too beautiful to waste sleeping.

If Madge and Jake weren't here, she'd dance down to Ethan's room, slip out of her nightshirt and crawl in bed with him. If Madge and Jake hadn't been there last night, she'd have stayed in Ethan's room, woken up this morning in his arms. Both thoughts were utterly delicious. She touched her hands to her stomach, remembering how Ethan's hands and mouth had explored her body.

He'd called her wanton, and she was. Even now, in the early morning quiet, she longed to make love to him again and again. She couldn't imagine ever getting enough of him.

A week ago she'd sat in this same bed, remembered the thrill of his kisses and the way he'd lured her to his room at Twin Oaks. She'd tried to convince herself she was glad he was leaving Cooper's Corner. Only she hadn't been glad. Even then she'd woken with the taste of his kiss on her lips and had ached for more.

They had been magnificent together from the very beginning. They would be until the end. *The end.* Her chest constricted and her heart seemed to turn inside out at the thought of his leaving.

She exhaled slowly, threw her legs over the side of the bed and walked to the window. It was a glorious morning, and she was not nearly finished basking in the afterglow of making love with Ethan. Besides, her dad used to say it was never over until the fat lady sang, and the only sound she heard was the song of the birds nesting in her backyard.

A raw energy coursed through her, quelled her doubts and filled her with anticipation. She couldn't go to Ethan, but she couldn't stay in bed, not with her body so alive she could barely keep from dancing. And cavorting across the creaky floor of an old house at daybreak on a Sunday morning would wake the entire household and have both Jake and Madge howling in protest.

She hit the bathroom, brushed her teeth, washed her face and changed into a pair of grass-stained sweats, not part of the new Alison's wardrobe but her favorites for working in the garden. Even sexy, provocative women had to have a few knockabout outfits. Besides, Ethan couldn't see her.

A good half hour later she'd started the coffee and was settled into the flower bed that bordered the front of the house. Her crocuses and tulips had already bloomed, but her summer perennials were just poking their neat little heads up to the sunshine. Every winter they withered away, only to revive the next spring and burst forth in an avalanche of brilliant color all over again.

Their survival against such odds seemed like an omen to Alison. Her heart lifted and her spirits soared as she dug into the damp earth and loosened the dirt around the roots of some of the plants that needed to be thinned.

Ethan admitted he was crazy about her, that what they shared was magical and unique. After last night, she knew it was so. If this was all they had, it would be a million times better than nothing. But *temporary* was only a word. Magic was forever. She just had to trust the magic.

"Hey, I thought Jake was supposed to do that for you."

Alison looked up. Madge was standing on the front steps, a mug in each hand. "It was too pretty to stay inside," Alison answered. "I'll leave the back garden for him."

"I brought you coffee."

"Thanks. I could use a cup."

"You haven't had one yet?"

"No, I just started the brewing process and came out here."

"You never do anything without your shot of caffeine. So are you working off frustration from your date with Kevin last night or celebrating a victory?"

"Neither." She stood, dusted her hands together, then headed to the hose to wash them off before she joined Madge. "I'm enjoying a spring morning."

"By weeding a garden. Yuck!"

Alison let the cold stream of water run over her hands. "I'm inside five days a week. It's nice to get a chance to work in the sunshine."

Madge held out a cup of coffee from her perch on the top step. "The flowers can wait. I want to hear all about the night with Kevin Bosco. And then I'll tell you about Mom's date.''

That piqued her interest. Alison turned off the water and wiped her hands across the front of her shirt. ''When did you talk to Mom?'' she asked, joining Madge on the steps.

''A few minutes ago.''

''She's already called this morning? What did she say?''

''She said that she and Ron Pickering had an enjoyable evening.''

''Enjoyable,'' Alison mused. ''That could mean anything from fantastic to barely passable. How did she sound?''

''In a word—luminous. I think Mr. Pickering has charmed his way right into her life.''

''Maybe *weaseled* is a better word,'' Alison grumbled.

Madge groaned. ''He's good for Mom. And you'll get a chance to see for yourself in a little while, because we're meeting her and Ron at Twin Oaks. Mom and Ron ran into Clint, his son, Keegan, and one of Keegan's friends at the ice-cream parlor, and Clint invited us all to Twin Oaks for Sunday brunch. You can take Ethan. The gossip mills will buzz tomorrow with both you and Mom out with guys. Or would you rather take Kevin Bosco? Did you and Mr. Boston Attorney do the lover's tango last night?''

''We didn't do the lover's tango, whatever that might be.''

Madge put her arm around Alison's shoulder. ''C'mon, sis. You can tell me. You did at least get kissed last night, didn't you?''

Kissed. Oh, yeah. She'd been kissed all over her body. Kissed, sucked, nibbled. And if dancing the lover's tango meant what she thought it meant, she'd danced that, too—just not with Kevin. Heat suffused her body, making her blood run hot and her cheeks turn crimson.

Madge pulled away and scrutinized her. "You did do something last night, didn't you?"

"You're being absurd."

"You can't fool me, Alison." Madge smiled broadly. "I know the signs. You made love and you liked it. I should have known it when I caught you out here singing in the garden before you had your morning coffee. And now you're as red as a boiled lobster. So when are you seeing Kevin again?"

"I'm not."

She narrowed her eyes. "Why not?"

"I did kiss Kevin. It was about as exciting as kissing a baked potato."

"That good, huh? But I don't understand why you're so—" Madge leaped up as if she'd been stung by a bumblebee. "It's Ethan. You slept with Ethan last night."

Alison stood and turned away, trying to hide her feelings and knowing the truth was probably written all over her face. "Get a life, Madge."

"I don't need one now. I'm having too much fun watching you and Mom get yours." She hugged Alison. "The new Alison Fairchild. Boy, when you come around, you do it big-time. Stealing the heart of gorgeous, hunky Ethan."

Alison gave up trying to deny it. It was no surprise that her happiness showed. She felt as if she were floating in a state of euphoria, kind of like the old musicals where people just burst into song and a whole symphony orchestra joined in.

"Don't say anything in front of Ethan, Madge. And don't talk like this in front of Mom and Jake, either."

"I wouldn't dream of it."

"Good."

Madge linked her arm with Alison's as they walked back into the house. "Finally I get to be the sane sister."

"I'm sane," Alison assured her.

"No one is sane when they're falling in love."

Alison started to correct her, to explain that she wasn't in love, but Madge was already opening the front door, and Alison could see Ethan and Longfellow making their way down the stairs. Her heart jumped at the sight. She hurried inside, eager to see him, to touch him, to tell him good-morning. And she wondered how in the world she'd ever last until night before making love with him again.

MAUREEN SAT AT ONE END of the grand old mahogany dining table, which overflowed this morning with Clint's famed walnut griddle cakes, sliced Virginia ham, fresh croissants, and a baked egg and cheese dish that was her favorite. A selection of jams, jellies, fruits and pastries was spread out on the antique buffet, along with a silver urn of coffee and a pitcher of freshly squeezed orange juice. A bouquet of flowers that she'd grown and arranged herself graced the middle of the table, and all around her were family and friends, chattering amiably and lingering over the last of the breakfast. The only one who was missing was Clint's son, Keegan. He'd stayed in town to spend the night with his friend.

It was at moments like this that Maureen marveled at how well her life in Cooper's Corner had turned out. From New York detective to lady of the manor at Twin Oaks had been like moving from one world to another.

The serenity of the rural setting had provided a balm for her troubled soul and given her time to think about and deal with issues that affected every aspect of her life.

She was a single mother whose ex-husband didn't even know he was a father. And somewhere out there was a man who was evil to the core, and who had sworn to kill her in revenge for sending his brother to prison for life.

She could never put any of that totally behind her, especially when events over the past few months had proved to her that Owen Nevil had discovered her new home. But Maureen refused to live in fear. She and her brother, Clint, had found a satisfying life here in the house their great-uncle had willed to them. They'd made wonderful friends like the Fairchilds, who were here for brunch, and most of all her precious twin daughters were surrounded by people who loved them.

"I'm all done, Mommy." Three-year-old Randi pointed to her nearly empty plate.

"I'm done, too," Robin announced. "Can I go play now?"

"As soon as you wash your hands."

They climbed down from their seats simultaneously, and Randi stopped by Ethan's chair to pet Longfellow.

"Can your dog come outside and play with us, Mr. Granger?"

"He's supposed to stay with me, but I'll bring him outside when I finish my coffee."

"Why's he have to stay with you?" Robin asked.

"Because he helps me get around, since I can't see."

"Why can't you see?" Randi asked. "Are your eyes sick?"

"In a way. But even if I can't see, I can hear and feel and taste. I'm still a lucky man."

"You can come outside and play in a minute," Randi said to Longfellow, bending low to look the dog in the eye. "You can help us see, too."

"They are so adorable," Alison said as the twins ran

out of the room holding hands. "Do you always dress them alike?"

"I try. I'm not sure they'll want to keep it up when they're older, but they don't complain now."

Ethan finished the last of his griddle cakes and wiped his hands on his napkin. "Another great meal. No wonder your rooms are all filled. It's worth the price of the lodging just to eat your breakfasts."

"Then maybe I should up the price," Clint joked.

"This was a real treat," Nora said from her seat between Ron Pickering and her grandson, Jake. "It must be like a busman's holiday for you, though. Inviting people in for brunch after feeding all your guests."

"I like cooking," Clint said, "and I've done these breakfasts so many times I could probably do them in my sleep."

"Some mornings he does," Maureen teased. She turned to Alison and Ethan. "Has anyone heard from the honeymooners?"

"Not a word," Alison said. "I suppose that means things are going well."

"No surprise there," Clint said. "The guy had stars in his eyes. It'll be months before he comes back down to earth."

"The look of love," Maureen added.

And speaking of the look of love, she thought, there was definitely something going on between Alison and Ethan. She sat back and studied them while the conversation at the table continued. There was an undeniable chemistry between the two of them, the same as she'd noticed when they'd returned from the picnic.

Since Ethan couldn't see, there were no furtive glances to give them away. But a good detective could pick up on other clues—the way they talked, the way they touched, the expression on Alison's face when she looked at him. And he was still in town after a week, a sure sign that he'd found something in Cooper's Corner that intrigued him.

Maureen liked Ethan, but something about him didn't ring true. She couldn't put her finger on it, not yet anyway, but she hoped Alison wasn't moving into a relationship with him too quickly. She'd hate to see Alison hurt, especially now, when she was blossoming into such a vivacious young woman. The nose job had done wonders for her self-confidence—had unleashed a tiger, as Maureen's partner on the force used to say.

But there were no doubts about Nora and Ron Pickering. They went together like butter and biscuits. Clint had said the same when he'd run into them at the ice-cream parlor late last night. That's why he'd invited them over for brunch. He wanted Maureen to see what a great couple they made. She was glad he had. Besides, she liked all the Fairchilds, and it was a rare treat to have them over when they had time to sit and visit.

Once everyone had eaten their fill and then some, Alison and Madge joined her in the kitchen for cleanup duties, while Clint took Ron on a tour of the house and Nora went outside to play with the girls. Ethan had asked Jake to go for a walk with him. That was the first she'd seen of Ethan's serious side, but he definitely looked concerned as he and Jake headed outside.

Randi came running into the kitchen as Maureen was putting away the jellies and jams. "What's this, Mommy?"

Maureen took the box from her. "It's candy, sweetie. Where did you get it?"

"In the rocking chair."

"Which rocking chair?"

"On the porch. Can I eat some?"

"I don't think you need sweets now. We just had breakfast."

"Why?"

"Because sweets aren't good for growing children."

Maureen pulled out the note that was tucked under the bow. "Thanks for being a great hostess," she read aloud. She turned to Alison and Madge. "How thoughtful. Did you bring this?"

"Not me," Madge said. "I'd never do that to a friend, not with bikini time just around the corner."

"I didn't bring it," Alison said, "and I'm certain Mother didn't, either."

"I had a surprise party here last night for Mrs. Stanton's sixtieth birthday. Just a few of her close friends and relatives. One of the guests must have left it. But you're right. I don't dare open it. I'd only be tempted to indulge, and I don't need any extra pounds to stuff into my bathing suit. I found this drop-dead-sexy little suit on sale at the end of the season last year. It's been a long time since I've worn anything nearly that revealing, but for some reason I couldn't resist it."

"Good for you," Madge exclaimed. "You have the body for it. Stir up these guys around Cooper's Corner a little. God knows they need it."

"And once I stir them up, what will I do with them? The girls and Twin Oaks keep me too busy to have time for a man."

"You'll change your mind if the right one comes along," Madge assured her. "Now go get the bathing suit while we finish up in the kitchen. I'd like to see it."

"And show Madge that dress you wore to Wendy's wedding," Alison added. "That was a scrumptious number."

Maureen went off to retrieve the bathing suit and the dress. Living with Clint was nice, but it was great to have females around to talk clothes for a change.

She took the box of candy with her and stashed it in the hall closet as she passed. Temptation should always be kept out of sight, at least until she decided who to give the candy to.

ETHAN AND JAKE STARTED down a path that led to the garden. Jake had been unusually quiet ever since they'd left the carnival yesterday, and Ethan was certain something was bothering him. If he could mention seeing the attack from the top of the Ferris wheel, he would have a perfect lead in. As it was, he'd have to handle the situation with kid gloves.

Longfellow trotted alongside them, a reminder to Ethan that he was to look straight ahead and sweep the area in front of him with his cane. He tried to think of a good lead-in. None came to mind, so he just plunged ahead the way he did with most things in life.

"Did something happen at the carnival yesterday?"

"What kind of something?"

"I don't know. You were unusually quiet on the way home and you seem worried today."

Jake exhaled sharply. "Why do some people have to cause so much trouble, Ethan? Just because they're bigger and tougher, they think they can do anything they want."

"I know what you mean. Some people can make it really tough on others."

"Yeah. You just wonder what they get out of it."

"Probably trying to make up for something missing in their own life, but that doesn't make it any easier to deal with them. Does this have something to do with the troublemakers you were telling me about the other night?"

"Yeah. I suppose I can tell you the truth, but you have to promise not to tell my mom or Aunt Alison."

"Why is that?"

"They'd go ape, probably yank me out of Woodstown or go up there whining to the principal and making me look like a wimpy kid. I can take care of myself. At least I hope I can."

"I'm not following you."

Jake nodded. "It started like this."

CHAPTER THIRTEEN

JAKE MEANDERED AROUND some shrubs and dropped onto an iron garden bench. Ethan had to remind himself not to cut across the grass and follow. He stayed on the path until Jake noticed and came back for him.

"There's a seat over here, but you'll have to watch your step," Jake said. "Here, take my arm and I'll guide you."

Ethan poked at the shrubs with his cane and followed Jake's lead. When he reached the bench, he ran his hand along the back and the seat as if getting his bearings before he sat down. Jake perched on the other end and leaned forward, propping his elbows on his knees and staring at the ground.

"I was in the wrong place at the wrong time." Jake muttered the words half under his breath.

"At the carnival?"

"No, at school. Actually, behind the school. The catcher and me had stayed late at practice one day a couple of weeks ago to work on my pitching. We were heading back to get our books and we walked up on this group of guys standing by the back door. Right away we could tell something was up."

"Students?"

"Yeah. Tough guys. You know, the kind that like to bully everyone they can."

"So you know them?"

"I know their names, but they aren't friends or any-

thing like that. They're seniors, so they don't have much
to do with us freshmen unless they're pushing us around.
That's what they were doing then—harassing this younger
kid.''

Ethan's muscles tightened. Next to home, schools were
the one place kids should feel safe. ''What did you do?''

''Laney—that's the catcher—me and him stopped in
our tracks when we saw them. At first they didn't see us.
They just kept threatening this kid, telling him if he didn't
pay up, they were going to beat him into a bloody pulp.
Except they didn't say it like that. They were using every
swear word they knew. The younger boy was scared. He
wasn't saying nothing.''

''What did they want him to pay for?''

''They never said, but I figure they were talking about
drugs. The school's supposed to be a drug-free zone, but
that doesn't mean anything. Everybody knows you can
buy any kind of uppers or downers you want. That's just
the way it is.''

The story sounded all too familiar, like a page from
Ethan's research files. Guys on the inside protecting their
turf. Guys on the outside trying to belong. It was push
and shove and threats and payback for real or perceived
injustices. Lots of other factors figured in, but all too often, illegal substances were involved.

''You're not messing around with any of that stuff, are
you?''

''Heck, no. The coach would kill me. Mom, too. Besides, I have better sense than that.''

''Good. But I have a feeling there's more to this story.''

''Yeah, there is. The guys saw Laney and me and they
started chasing us. We ran and hid under the bleachers in
the back by the ball field, but they found us. They roughed
us up a little, but didn't really hurt us. Said if we kept our

mouths shut we'd be fine. If we didn't, they'd beat the crap out of us."

"And this was two weeks ago?"

"Yeah. We didn't say a word to anyone, but then a few days before spring break, that same boy we saw getting harassed behind the gym was attacked while walking home from school. He ended up in the hospital with a concussion and a broken collarbone. As soon as Laney and I heard about it, we knew those guys had made good on their threats."

"Did you tell anyone that?"

"Laney didn't want to. He was more scared than ever."

"How about you?"

"I was scared, but I just kept thinking about the kid. I mean, he was in the hospital and those guys were still walking around school like big shots."

Ethan could see what was coming and it filled him with a dread so caustic it seemed to burn away the lining of his stomach. "Who did you tell, Jake?"

"The school principal."

"What did he say?"

"He beat around the bush, said that just because I saw the seniors picking on the boy behind the school didn't prove they were responsible for the attack that put him in the hospital. He knows they did it, though. He just didn't admit it. I did hear later that he suspended them for three days for roughing up Laney and me."

"So they know you're the one who told?"

"Yeah, but they're not just blaming me. They're blaming Laney, too, and he had nothing to do with this. It's all my fault."

Ethan put an arm around the boy's shoulder. "Nothing is your fault, Jake. Don't ever think that it is."

"Try telling that to Laney. They got him off by himself

and jumped him at the carnival. He didn't get hurt as bad as the other boy, but only because some men in the food tent heard him yelling and came running out. Laney didn't do anything, but he got beat up. It's not fair.''

"It's not fair, but it's not your fault." Poor kid. Not only did he have to deal with fear for himself, he felt responsible for what had happened to his friend. But Ethan knew it probably wasn't over. They'd gotten back at Laney, but they didn't sound like the kind of guys who'd just let Jake off scot-free. And Ethan was the one who'd stuck his two cents worth into the situation and kept Madge from putting Jake in the school near Cooper's Corner. Worse, he'd promised Jake he wouldn't tell his mother what they were talking about now.

"Maybe you should think about changing schools, Jake."

He shook his head. "I can take care of myself. I know karate."

Jake was fooling himself if he thought a few karate chops would stop a gang of thugs. But then, kids his age frequently thought they were invincible. "What's the name of the boy who's ended up in the hospital?"

"Billy Clayton. He's in my class, but I don't know him well."

"I think you should talk to your mother about this."

Jake clenched and unclenched his right fist. "You promised you wouldn't tell, Ethan. You can't go back on a promise."

"I wouldn't, Jake. You can trust me on that. I just think you should go to her."

"She'll yank me out of the school, especially now that we're living in Cooper's Corner. I can't let that happen, not now. I'm the *pitcher,* Ethan, the best pitcher on the team. Besides, a guy can't go through life running from trouble. Only wimps do that.''

But a guy Jake's age shouldn't have to worry about dealing with this kind of trouble on his own, either. Ethan decided he would make a few phone calls when they got back to Alison's, see what he could find out about the attack and about the school. The FBI wouldn't have any files on Woodstown, but Thomas had friends in law enforcement all over the country. He had unofficial ways to get information.

''I shouldn't have said anything,'' Jake said. ''I can handle this myself.''

''I'm glad you told me, Jake. School's my business, you know, and I've handled problems like this before.''

''Yeah. So what would you do in my shoes?''

Ethan wanted to say, ''Change schools and move to Cooper's Corner,'' but he knew that would be a lie. He'd stay and stand up for himself the way Jake was doing, but still he hated to see Jake in that position. ''Let me think about it. We'll talk again later.''

''I sure wish you could come to the game tomorrow afternoon. I'm pitching.''

''I wish I could, too, but it would be a long walk for me and Longfellow.''

''Yeah, a real long walk.'' Jake laughed, but it lacked the genuineness it would have had before the episode at the carnival.

''Guess we better get back to the group,'' Ethan said, giving Jake a manly punch on the arm. ''You ready?''

''Yeah.''

ALISON STOOD with the rest of the crowd on the walkway in front of Twin Oaks, soaking up the brilliance and warmth of the sun and watching her mother and Ron drive away. Her mother had looked happier than she had in a long, long time. It was still difficult to see her with another man, but it was nice to see her so happy, especially when Alison was brimming with joy herself.

She was absolutely enchanted by Ethan. All he had to do was walk into the room and she grew warm and tingly inside. And while part of her didn't want the day to end, another part couldn't wait until night, when she could sneak down the hall and crawl into bed beside him.

She refused to let thoughts of his leaving spoil her bliss. If they were meant to be together, it would happen. And every tiny particle of her being told her they were meant to be together—if not forever, then at least for now. She was seizing the magnificent, glorious, thrilling moment.

"It was a lovely brunch," Alison said at the first lull in the conversation. "Thanks so much for inviting us."

"Just glad you could come on such short notice," Clint said. "It was a spur of the moment idea when I ran into your mother and her new beau last night. I like that guy."

Madge put a hand to Alison's shoulder. "Everyone likes him but my little sister here."

"He's growing on me," she admitted.

"Fantastic food and even better company," Ethan said. "Thanks for including me in the invitation."

They continued to talk as they approached the car, all present and accounted for except the twins and Longfellow.

"Guess I better find my dog," Ethan said.

"Absolutely," Maureen agreed. "Robin and Randi have probably hidden him somewhere, hoping you'll forget him." She called, and a few minutes later the twins came running from the house, Longfellow at their heels, his tongue working overtime as he tried to reach a huge smear of pink frosting that covered his mouth and nose.

"Longfellow sure does like cake," Robin said. "He gobbled up all of his."

"And where did he get cake?" Maureen asked.

Randi twirled a lock of her hair and slid it between her lips, looking adorably innocent. "He barked at it and licked my hand. He was hungry."

"He barked at the cake and you gave him some?"

"It was already cut," Robin volunteered. "We didn't touch a knife."

"Never let animals go hungry," Randi said, shaking her finger the way she must have seen her mother do. "Remember?"

"I do say that," Maureen agreed. "I'm just not sure cake is the best thing for hungry animals. I'm sorry, Ethan. I guess I should have specified that they shouldn't feed him. It just never occurred to me that they would."

"I don't think one little piece of cake will hurt him. Of course, now he'll be licking the hand of every little girl he meets, hoping for a treat."

They all laughed as they piled into Alison's car, Jake, Madge and Longfellow in the back, Ethan up front beside her. She reached over and put a hand on his thigh for a brief second before sticking the key into the ignition, for absolutely no reason except that she could and she wanted to.

Truth was, she wanted to do a lot more than that. It was probably a good thing Jake and Madge were with them or she might have driven to some secluded area and seduced him on the spot. The idea cavorted through her mind and she let her imagination run wild until it shocked even her.

Ethan was right. She was wanton. Definitely wanton.

ETHAN MADE THE PHONE CALL to his supervisor from his bedroom at the Fairchild home. He was about to hang up when Thomas finally picked up. "Hello."

"It's Ethan Granger." He waited for Thomas's usual tirade about calling at home on Sunday. It didn't come.

"What's up, Ethan? Are you tired of the idyllic life in Cooper's Corner and ready to see some action?"

"I'm in no hurry."

"That worries me. Why do I smell a woman behind this?"

"You have a remarkable sense of smell." He could hear Thomas' sigh of concern over the phone and could imagine his face twisting into a scowl.

"You're in the middle of an assignment, Ethan. Well, not the middle, but your identity has already been established. It's no time for you to get serious about some female. Not that we don't all know it's going to happen sooner or later. We have a pool on you down at the office. I think I have March of next year for you to bite into the wedding cake."

"You guys are sick."

"Did you call to tell me that?"

"No. There's a little problem here."

"What kind of problem?"

"A kid named Billy Clayton was attacked by some older students on his way home from Woodstown High School. He ended up in the hospital."

"Where is Woodstown High School?"

"In Woodstown, Massachuetts. It's a small town about sixty miles from Cooper's Corner."

"The FBI has no business getting into their problems. You know that."

"I don't want you to get into it. I'd just like some information, and I figured you'd have a cop friend upstate somewhere who could dig up the facts for you."

"What do you want to know?"

"If the cops know who was responsible. If any charges have been filed. That kind of thing. I'd also be interested in knowing what the principal told the cops, assuming they've questioned him. It should all be in the police records."

"Any particular reason you're interested in this case?"

"Yeah. The nephew of the lady I'm staying with has been threatened by the punks he believes attacked the other kid."

"The nephew? It sounds as if you're getting in deep, Ethan."

Deep? Hell, he was so far over his head he needed scuba gear, but he'd handle it. "I've got everything under control."

"You better have. Things are heating up in New Orleans. When they call, I'll expect you on the job in twenty-four hours."

"Have I ever let you down?"

"No. And don't start now."

"Get back to me as quickly as you can on this? Tomorrow would be great."

"I'll see what I can do."

They said their goodbyes and Ethan broke the connection. "Come on, Longfellow," he said, "we've done all we can do up here. Let's go back and join the party."

An odor so divine he thought he was dreaming hit him the second he opened the bedroom door. He followed it to the kitchen. Alison was bent over, pulling a tray of fresh baked peanut butter cookies out of the oven. The sight was as good as the smell. She'd changed into a pair of snug-fitting jeans that curved over her tight little behind, and a light blue sweater that fell to her shapely hips. When she turned to him, it seemed that her gorgeous eyes had turned the color of the Caribbean on a bright, cloud-less day. For a second he forgot not to stare.

When he regained a fragment of good sense, he turned away and leaned against the counter. "Cute, sexy, wan-ton, and she bakes, too."

"Shh. Someone might hear you."

But she was giving him that seductive smile that made his heart start pumping like mad. She set the cookie sheet on top of a cooling rack and sashayed toward him, her hips swaying, her nipples at full attention, outlined against the fabric of her sweater. When she got close, she fit her hands around his buttocks and squeezed.

"I take it we're alone," he said, knowing full well that they were.

"For the time being. Madge and Jake went to the store to get some milk."

"Can't have peanut butter cookies without milk."

"How did you know they're peanut butter? By the smell?"

"I'm psychic."

"Then tell me what I'm thinking."

"That you're dying to kiss me and try to talk me into a quickie before Madge and Jake get back."

"Hey, you are psychic." She rose up on tiptoe and fitted her lips to his.

He wrapped his arms around her and held her close, kissing her back and thinking how right it felt to be with her in a kitchen that smelled of cookies and a home that was cozy and warm and filled with love and laughter. All the hard, ugly things he dealt with every day in his job seemed to dissolve. He was fondling her breasts and kissing his way down her neck when he heard a car door slam.

''The spoilers have returned,'' she whispered in a husky voice.

''We could lock the door.''

''Madge has a key.''

''Foiled again.''

''But not for long. Tonight it's your turn to sneak into my room.''

''Why? I thought we were great in mine.''

''I have candles and a huge tub for bubble baths.''

''And a little rubber duck to play with?''

''I'll have something for you to play with, but it won't be a duck.''

''You decadent temptress.''

''You're not complaining, are you?''

''Not on your life.''

They pulled away as Madge and Jake came banging though the back door, each carrying a paper bag of groceries.

Jake grabbed a cookie from the cooling rack. ''Boy, Aunt Alison, you make the best peanut butter cookies in the world. Can I take some to my coach tomorrow?''

''I don't see why not.''

''Cookies for the coach,'' Madge said. ''I may need to meet this guy you're so crazy about. What's he like?''

''Awesome, and he's not married, either.''

''Then I should definitely meet him.''

''Why don't all of you come to my game tomorrow? Then you could meet Coach Reynolds and see me pitch. *Pleeze* come. You want to, don't you, Ethan?''

''I'd love to come and *hear* you pitch.'' More than that, he'd like to check out the situation at Woodstown High for himself. He'd promised not to talk to Madge or Alison about the trouble, but he hadn't promised not to talk to Jake's coach.

"I'd like to get there in time for the game," Madge said, "but I can't cut class. I'm a serious student."

Alison opened the carton of milk and started pouring it into tall glasses. "I'm afraid I can't make it this time, either, Jake. I missed two days of work last week with my sprained wrist. The wrist is doing fine, but I can't take off any more time."

Ethan took the glass of milk Alison was handing him while he considered the idea spinning around in his brain. He wasn't sure he could pull it off, but it was worth a try. "Tell you what, sport. I'm not doing a thing tomorrow. I'll ask around and see if I can hire someone to drive me to Woodstown. If I can, I'll be there for the game."

Madge looked at him as if he had flipped out. Alison looked at him as if he were a knight on a white horse. Jake looked at him as if he'd risen to superhero status. Ethan just stared straight ahead. After all, he was blind.

Jake jumped from his chair, the look on his face changing abruptly. "Oh, gross! Look at Longfellow."

The dog retched as if he were choking. "What's wrong?" Ethan asked, twisting around in his chair.

Alison plopped the carton of milk down on the counter and ran to Longfellow. "Poor thing. He's throwing up. Does he do this often?"

"Never." Ethan turned. "Where is he?"

"About a foot behind your chair," Alison said. She took Ethan's hand and led him to Longfellow, then grabbed a handful of paper towels and started cleaning up the mess.

Longfellow made a low, howling noise and looked up at them as if they should know what to do.

"I think he should see a vet," Alison said.

"Where can we find one on Sunday afternoon?" Ethan asked.

"I can call Alex McAlester at home. I'm sure he'll see him or tell us what to do."

Alison didn't wait for a response from Ethan, not that he would have objected. Here he had a helpless little animal in his care and he'd let him get sick. He wanted to pace the floor while she made the call, but it was next to impossible for a blind man to pace in a crowded kitchen. He drummed his fingers on the table until she deposited the phone back in its wall cradle.

"What did he say?"

"He asked if we'd been feeding him table scraps."

"No, I never do that. I keep him on the diet the guide dog association recommended. Except for…"

"Cake."

He and Alison said it in unison. He stooped over to stroke Longfellow's neck. "You wouldn't think a bite or two of cake would make him this sick."

"If it was a bite or two. The twins are only three. There's no telling how much they gave him, but I'm sure they never meant to make him sick."

"Those little angels? I'm sure they didn't. Besides, we don't know if that's what made him throw up. We're only guessing. What do we do now?"

"Alex is meeting us at his clinic. It's only about ten minutes from here."

"I'll get Longfellow to the car," he said, bending to pick him up.

Jake flew to his side. "Hey, let me do that. You have to carry your cane."

"Yeah, right. Thanks, buddy."

Ethan grabbed his cane and followed Jake to the car. The guilt, the worry, the deception seemed to hit him all at once, like a hard blow below the belt. What in the devil was he doing in this house, in the midst of this terrific family, pretending to be something he wasn't?

He had to get out of here fast, whether New Orleans needed him or not. It probably wasn't the cake that had made Longfellow sick, after all. It was disgust with his master.

LONGFELLOW SLEPT in the back seat. Dr. McAlester had given him a shot for nausea and said it would probably relax him to the point where he slept most of the night. The cake was likely the culprit, especially since Longfellow was not used to that type of food. Ethan was just thankful it didn't appear to be anything serious, and vowed to make sure Longfellow had no more cake.

Longfellow's problems were a lot easier to solve than his own. In a couple of hours he'd be alone with Alison. They'd make love, and it would be beautiful and wonderful the way it had been last night. She thought she was making love with Ethan Granger, a blind schoolteacher. She might even be falling in love with him. Except Ethan Granger did not exist.

If she ever found out the truth, she'd hate him. Only she wouldn't find out, because he was going to walk off and leave her with nothing but a bunch of lies.

His heart seemed to sink to the bottom of his gut. He'd walk away from Alison and never see her or hold her or kiss her again. Whoever said it was better to have loved and lost than never to have loved at all was obviously in serious self-denial. Or else just plain crazy.

All he knew was that he couldn't stay here much longer. It was becoming too difficult to keep up the ruse. Too hard to lie to Alison. Too hard not to fall in love with her, if he hadn't already.

His cell phone rang. He pulled it from his pocket and took the call.

"It's time, Ethan."

CHAPTER FOURTEEN

THE LIGHT FROM a half-dozen candles cast a shimmery glow across the luxurious mounds of scented bubbles. The effect was sensual, almost surreal. Ethan had difficulty believing it was more than a vivid dream.

He stretched his long legs and pulled Alison into the cradle of his arms, fitting her back and buttocks against his body with just the slick glaze of soapy water between them. He kissed the back of her neck and buried his face in the silky softness of her hair while his hands explored her body.

Alison turned to him, playfully scooped up a handful of bubbles and blew, sending them airborne until they came to rest in the hairs of his chest. She splayed her hand across them and squashed them against him, then kissed her way up his chest.

"I wish we could stay like this forever," she whispered.

Forever. The word was sharp and jagged, a cutting reminder that his time with Alison was almost over. "Who'd get the mail out?" he teased, trying hard to keep the hoarseness from his voice.

"I wouldn't know or care. Not if all my days and nights were like this."

But they wouldn't be, not with him. There would be weeks, sometimes months at a time when he wouldn't be home at all. She'd be left all alone while he lived a life she couldn't share. No matter how wonderful it seemed now, she'd grow tired of being without him, tired of sleeping alone. Still, he ached to promise her more than the brief moments they shared now, longed to believe there was a chance for them to make it.

But aching and longing weren't enough to make a marriage work. He'd learned that the hard way. Walking away from Alison after one week was going to be the most difficult thing he'd ever done. Losing her once he'd built his world around her would be a million times worse.

"We have now, Alison," he whispered. "And after this, we'll have the memories." He kissed her, a long, slow kiss that seemed to taunt his soul the way the memories would when he left Cooper's Corner and Alison for good.

"You said that the way we feel about each other happens rarely in a lifetime. Has it ever happened for you before now?"

The question caught him unprepared. He could lie, but there were already way too many lies between them. "I was in love once," he admitted, still holding her close. "It was never like this, but it had its moments. It was a long time ago."

"And do those memories still warm you?"

"No."

"Then what makes you think our memories will be different?"

"Because all of our memories will be wonderful."

"What happened before? If you were in love, it must have been good at first."

He rested his head on the bath pillow behind him, closed his eyes and let the images from his past slip back into his mind. He and Sylvia had been good together, although their initial attraction had not been as instantly intense and consuming as what he'd felt with Alison. He had been much younger then, and believed that love could overcome any problems. How he'd ever arrived at such a conclusion, he had no idea. Certainly not from the experiences of his childhood.

"We got married," he said, being as honest as he could. "It didn't work out."

"Why not?"

He opened his eyes, wishing he could look into hers, but settled for taking her hands in his. "This has nothing to do with us, Alison. It's an ugly story, and it's not important."

"It is to me. It's not that I'm prying. I'm just trying to understand you."

"Lots of luck with that. I don't understand myself."

"Maybe you don't want to."

"Could be. I just know that if you analyze things long enough, you can come up with seemingly rational reasons for anything. But that doesn't make them true."

"Were you the one who wanted the divorce?"

"I was the one who filed. Nothing was the way I wanted it. It was just the way things turned out."

She grew quiet, and he knew he'd probably gone too far to stop here. The mood had already changed.

"What else do you want to know?" he asked.

"What made you give up on the relationship?"

"I didn't so much give up on it as I just plain failed it. I didn't keep my wife satisfied. She went looking for what she needed somewhere else. I came home unexpectedly one night and found her in *our* bed with another man."

"Oh, Ethan, how terrible. What did you do?"

"It wasn't one of my finer moments. I muttered a few choice words, none of which bear repeating, and I stormed out of the house. When I returned three days later, she'd moved out, taking all the furniture and our belongings with her. There wasn't a lot of trust left to work with at that point.''

"You must have been devastated.''

"Devastated. Humiliated. Angry. I went the whole route, but eventually I got over it.''

"What was her name?''

"Sylvia.''

"Sylvia lost a lot when she lost you.'' Alison trailed her finger down his chest. "You can't spend your life running from love because of one bad experience, not even when it was as destructive as that must have been.''

"But I have to face facts. There's more,'' he said, ready now to get everything he could out in the open. If they made love tonight, he wanted her to do it knowing there would never be anything permanent between them. "I have to be on the job in New Orleans Wednesday morning.''

She drew away from him. "When were you going to tell me?''

"Tonight. I only found out when we got home from the vet. And then you brought up the bubble bath and I didn't want to spoil it for you.''

"So you were going to make love with me to keep me happy?''

"You know I didn't mean it like that. This isn't any easier on me than it is on you.''

"It doesn't matter if it's easy or difficult. You're calling the shots. But you were honest. You promised one explosive, breathtaking moment, and you've delivered that and more.''

"So what do we do now?''

She climbed from the tub and pulled a fluffy green

towel from the rack. Her wet body shimmered and glowed in the soft light of the candles, so beautiful it hurt to look at her. She couldn't know the effect it had on him—she thought he couldn't even see her. Another of the deceptions between them, sealing the finality of their upcoming parting.

She dabbed at her face with the towel. When she lowered it, he could see the moisture in her eyes and knew she was fighting back tears. He stepped from the tub, picked her up and carried her carefully to her bed. He placed her on top of the quilt, then crawled onto the bed and stretched out beside her. Soap bubbles still clung to his damp skin, but he hardly noticed as he held her close and kissed her.

They didn't talk. They just made love. Sweetly. Completely. And he knew that if he lived to be a hundred, there would never be a moment this perfect, and yet this bittersweet, again. There would never be another Alison.

ETHAN SAT AT THE TABLE in Alison's kitchen, taking advantage of the empty house to read the morning paper. It was difficult to get into current events in light of what was going on in his own life. Alison had been quiet this morning. Pensive. She hadn't mentioned his leaving, but had changed her mind about going to Jake's game. She would take off work early and drive Ethan to Woodstown.

Woodstown. Yet another secret between them. As if on cue, his cell phone rang and the display identified the caller. "Good morning, Thomas."

"Not sure it's going to be here, but it's hopping."

"New problems?"

"Always, but no more than usual."

"Do you have news for me?"

"You have an 8:00 a.m. flight tomorrow morning.

Lynn will get back to you with the details, and she can arrange a driver from Boston to pick you up. I'd suggest you go over today and get a room near the airport.''

"Yeah. I'll be there, but later tonight. Did you find out anything about Woodstown?''

"I did. The principal gave the cops the names of four seniors who he thought might be responsible for the attack on Billy Clayton. Apparently it was the same guys who got suspended for roughing up your young buddy. Two of the guys have already had dealings with juvenile court. The cops questioned all four of them individually. Three denied everything. One squealed.''

"So where are we now?''

"Billy Clayton's parents have filed charges against all four. You probably won't have to worry about them for a while. I imagine they'll lie low until after their court date. They're not likely to risk more trouble with the law right now.''

"That's what I wanted to hear. Thanks.''

"You can't get involved in this, Ethan. It's not FBI business.''

"I'm well aware of that.''

"It's all going okay in Cooper's Corner, isn't it?''

"Define okay.''

"Not blowing your cover. Having everyone believe you're Ethan Granger, blind schoolteacher ready to return to New Orleans.''

"Then everything is going okay. The real Ethan Greenway from Tupelo, Mississippi, and a couple of dozen other spots around the country, has not surfaced. I'm not even sure he still exists.''

"You sound down.''

"I haven't learned any of the school cheers yet.''

"Don't get smart with me, Ethan. I know you too well.

You're ordinarily reeking with excitement when you're starting a new assignment."

"I'm excited about the assignment."

"But not about leaving Cooper's Corner?"

"You're right. You know me too well. Let it ride for now. I'll tell you all about it over a beer someday. Actually, over a lot of beers. You get over everything if you live long enough, right?"

"You're asking the wrong man."

"Yeah. Sorry."

He finished the conversation, then bent to give Longfellow a good ear scratching. "Glad you're feeling better this morning, buddy. No need for both of us to be scraping the bottom."

He took the stairs slowly, Longfellow at his side. The house was quiet, but not lonely. Alison filled every corner. He could smell her fragrance, hear her soft laughter, see her shining eyes and seductive smile, feel her body pressing against his.

"You let me down, Longfellow. We were supposed to have a few days of fun. You should have never let me fall in love."

ALISON'S SPIRITS had lifted considerably by the time she pulled into the parking lot of Woodstown High and found a spot near the back of the school. She'd thought a lot about Ethan's confessions last night, and the more she thought about what he'd said, the more convinced she was that it was pure fear that made him avoid any suggestion of permanence in a relationship. He'd been betrayed in the worst way. That would scar anyone.

Sylvia had been a fool, but Alison wasn't Sylvia, and given enough time, she could convince Ethan that all women were not the same. It wouldn't be easy nurturing a relationship with so many miles separating them, but it could be done. A chance was all she would ask for.

She killed the engine and turned to look at him, stirred as always by his rugged good looks and the depth of her feelings for him. "I know you're leaving tomorrow," she said.

He turned toward her. "Actually, I have to leave tonight. I have a driver picking me up at your house at nine to drive me to Boston. I have an early flight in the morning."

"I want to see you again."

He groaned. "You don't give up easily, do you?"

"I don't give up at all."

He shook his head. "I'm not the man you think I am, Alison. I wish I was, but I'm not."

"You're the only man I'm interested in. I'm not asking for any kind of commitment, Ethan. I know you're not ready for that. All I'm asking is that you don't close the door on us, that you'll give us a chance. If you care about me at all, you'll do that for me."

"You know how I feel about you."

"Then you'll come back to Cooper's Corner when the school semester is finished?"

"You may not want me then."

"I'll take my chances."

"I'm a damn poor risk."

"I don't see you that way. We're fantastic together. You can't deny that."

"I wouldn't try."

"Then don't give up on us. If you do, you might be walking away from a lifetime of love."

He stretched his hand across the back of the seat and tangled his fingers in her hair. "In that case, how can I say no?"

He leaned over and touched his lips to hers, a sweet, thorough kiss that whispered of promises and passion. The words I love you sprang from her heart as she melted into the kiss, but she swallowed them back. She didn't want to scare him off now.

Reluctantly she pulled away. "We're here with time to spare," she said, opening her door. "The game doesn't start for another half hour."

"Good. Let's go find Jake and get you a big glass of water. You'll have to be my play-by-play commentator, so I'll know when to cheer. Bet I'll be the only blind man in the stands."

"Bet you'll be the only man who just got kissed in the school parking lot."

"Shall we tell Jake that his aunt is wanton?"

"You wouldn't dare."

"You do have a lot to learn about me."

And she couldn't wait to learn it all. How could he possibly have any secrets that would destroy the love that swelled inside her right now?

IT WAS CLOSE TO GAME TIME when Alison, Ethan and Longfellow made the long walk to the wooden bleachers. The Warriors were on the field getting in some batting and fielding practice. Ethan tried to be as inconspicuous as he could when he let his gaze move to the bull pen, where Jake should be throwing warm-up pitches. He wasn't there, and Ethan didn't dare start searching for him.

"Let's go down to the dugout area and let Jake know we're here before the game starts," he said. "He's probably already looking for us."

"It looks like most of the team is there, but I don't see Jake."

Apprehension shot through Ethan the way it did when he was on a case and sensed something wasn't right. He worked at keeping calm. Guys looked different in their ball uniforms. Alison probably just hadn't spotted him yet.

They halted at the backstop fence, and Alison waved one of the Warrior players over. "I'm looking for Jake Hodge. Have you seen him?"

"No, ma'am, but he better get out here on the double. If he doesn't, Coach Reynolds is going to put in a new pitcher."

The apprehension swelled to a choking knot in Ethan's throat. "Go find the coach," Ethan said to the boy. "I want to talk to him a minute."

"Are you Jake's dad?"

"No, but I want to talk to the coach all the same. Get him *now*."

Alison stared at him as the boy ran out on the field to deliver Ethan's message to the coach. "I can't imagine why Jake's not here. He was so excited about pitching."

"He's probably on his way."

Coach Reynolds hurried over to the sidelines and introduced himself. "You must be Jake's Aunt Alison and his friend Ethan," he said, extending a hand. "Jake was excited that you were coming to the game."

"Where is Jake now?" Ethan asked.

"He hasn't shown up yet. I was hoping he was with you."

Ethan's muscles coiled like a spring in spite of Thomas's theory that the kids who'd threatened Jake wouldn't strike again. There was never any way to know what guys like that would do. "Have any of his teammates seen him?"

"Ben said they left the dressing room together, but Jake was going to stop by his hall locker and pick up his algebra book. That's the last anyone's seen of him. I just called the school and alerted the principal. He has people searching the premises for Jake.'' Concern was etched in the coach's ruddy face.

''I need to talk to Ben,'' Ethan said.

''Better than that, I'll have him take you to the principal. He's probably located Jake by now.''

The coach didn't look as if he believed that any more than Ethan did. Only one thing would keep Jake away from this game, and they both knew it.

Ethan didn't wait for Ben, Longfellow or even Alison, and he didn't bother to knock that white cane around in front of him. He took off racing toward the school. Jake was in trouble and he needed help. That was all that mattered now.

CHAPTER FIFTEEN

JAKE COULD HEAR his heart pounding, as loud as that bass drum in the school·band. He hadn't expected to be this afraid, but he was. That group of thugs were after him, and if they found him, they were going to hurt him bad.

He might even wind up in the hospital or have his pitching arm broken. He wanted to cry, but he wouldn't. He hadn't cried in two years now, not since his dog, Tumble, had died. Jake curled himself in a tight ball under the teacher's desk, the scissors he'd found in the drawer clutched in his hand like a knife.

He'd tried to lock the door, but he needed a key. He'd settled for sticking a chair under the doorknob, hoping that if they tried the door, they'd think it was locked. If they found him, he'd have to fight. The only other option was to jump from the window, but he was on the third floor and there was nothing but a concrete basketball court to break his fall. The jump would kill him for sure.

He wondered if the baseball game had started yet. Coach Reynolds would be upset with him for not showing up. Aunt Alison and Ethan would be wondering what had happened to him, too. Aunt Alison would probably be all worried, like that time he'd had the wreck with his bike and come in with blood pouring from the wound on his head. That had been bad. This could end up a whole lot worse.

He could hear voices now, right outside the door.

"It's not locked. There's a chair blocking it. The dirty little fink is in there, and he's ours." A different voice followed with a string of swear words.

The door started moving, the chair scratching across the bare wood floor. They were coming in. Jake's lungs burned and he felt as if someone had knocked the breath out of him.

He had to do something, but what? If he stayed under the desk, he'd be a sitting duck. He crawled out, took the scissors in his hand and willed his body to stop trembling. He might get killed, but he'd go down fighting.

The door flew open all the way, and three guys almost twice Jake's size rushed inside. The last one kicked the door closed as the first one hurled a chair at Jake. The fight was on, and there was no way on earth Jake was going to win.

"JAKE'S LOCKER'S ON the third floor," Ben puffed breathlessly.

Ethan didn't even slow down as he took the wide steps. The building was old and dark, and the lights had already been turned off for the day. Alison wasn't far behind. She had kept up better than he'd have expected. He hadn't had time to explain what was going on, only that Jake might be in a fight and they had to hurry. She'd have a hundred questions when this was over, but the only thing that mattered now was finding Jake.

Adrenaline coursed through Ethan, speeding both his heart rate and his legs as he passed the second-floor landing and headed up another flight of stairs. He scanned the hallway when he reached the top. Both sides were lined with doors, all closed. Jake could be behind any or none of them.

Ethan was alert for sounds, yells, the crash of furniture—anything to lead him to Jake. Then he heard a steady clunk, clunk, clunk and the rattle of something solid hitting against metal. A tall, muscular student in worn jeans and a fleece pullover slouched against one of the metal lockers that lined the wall. His gloved fist was hitting rhythmically against the side of the locker.

Ethan knew immediately that this was the lookout, on guard. His knocking was warning the attackers that someone was in the hall. These guys were not novices to violence.

"Where's Jake Hodge?" he demanded, grabbing the guy by the back of his collar.

"Hey, leggo of me, man. I don't know no Jake Hodge."

"I asked you a question." Ethan pushed the boy against the metal door. "Unless you want me to use your head as a battering ram against that locker, you better come up with an answer."

Alison and Ben had joined him now. Alison fell against the wall, her breath coming out in uneven gasps, confusion and fear clouding her usually sparkling eyes. He turned back to the guy. "Start talking while you have teeth left in your mouth."

The boy tried to jerk away from him. Ethan tightened his grip around the youth's collar until he could barely breathe. Ethan had to convince him he meant business.

A piercing yell came from down the hall. Ethan let go of the kid and took off running. He had no trouble finding the right room now. The scream had been followed by a stream of loud curses and the sound of cracking wood. He kicked the door open and assessed the situation with the trained eye of an FBI agent.

One boy was cradling a bleeding hand in his shirt. Another was holding Jake, while a third, the largest of the bunch, was getting ready to plant his fist in Jake's stomach. Jake and the other boys all saw Ethan at the same time. The boy with the bleeding hand picked up a chair and heaved it at Ethan. He ducked in time to miss being hit in the eye by one leg.

"Leave him alone," Jake shouted. "He's blind. He didn't do anything to you."

The boy who'd been about to hit Jake broke into a raucous laugh. "Blind? Won't this be fun. After we finish Jake, we'll take care of him, too." He pulled back his fist, ready to pound it into Jake.

Ethan grabbed his arm. "Why don't you just finish with me first?"

The boy swung at Ethan but missed. Ethan grabbed his arms and pinned them behind his back.

"Hey, I thought you said he was blind."

Jake stared, his eyes wide as saucers. The boy with the bleeding hand took off running just as Ben stepped inside the door. He tripped the boy and sent him sprawling at Alison's feet. The kid literally crawled past Alison and out the door.

She headed toward Jake. "Are you all right?"

"I'm fine," he declared, "but I'm sure glad to see you guys."

"Stand back, lady." The boy holding Jake in a wrestler's grip gave the order, but his voice was shaky. He knew he was no longer in control.

"Let Jake go," Ethan said calmly.

"Who says?"

"I do."

The boy shoved Jake toward Ethan and ran for the door. But Ethan was too fast for him. He kicked the door shut while still holding on to the largest of the attackers. Ben and Jake jumped the boy at once, each of them grabbing one arm and holding on for dear life. It took both of them to restrain him.

And that's the way they were when the principal and two cops showed up at the door. They had the lookout and the boy with the bleeding hand in tow, both in handcuffs.

Jake and Ben let go of the boy they were holding. Jake rushed to Ethan. "That was awesome. How did you do that when you can't even see?"

One of the cops stared at Longfellow, then back at Ethan. "Is that true? Are you really blind?"

Ethan glanced at Alison. "No, but it's a long story."

Jake looked him straight in the eye. "You're not blind?"

"Afraid not, buddy."

"I don't understand."

"I'll tell you all about it later."

"We're going to need you to answer some questions," the cop said. "Principal Gothard filled us in on a few details, but we'll still need an official statement. Are you Jake Hodge's father?"

"No, but I'm his aunt," Alison answered for him. "And I'd like to know what's going on here."

Jake explained to her as best he could, though he was talking fast. The kid really was a hero. He'd taken on the worst of the thugs and he'd done it knowing full well the risk to himself. He'd done it just because it was the right thing to do.

"Can I give my statement right now?" Jake asked, when he'd finished giving Alison the lowdown. "I've got to pitch a baseball game."

Alison put an arm around his shoulder. "You can't play today. You're hurt." She took a clean tissue from her pocket and dabbed at a bloody scratch on his chin.

"I'm not hurt that bad. I have to pitch. Tell her, Ethan. I *have* to pitch."

"I think he's earned the right," Ethan agreed.

"I think so, too," the cop said. "Go to it—that is, if it's okay with your aunt. We'll take care of the fighting four here and then come out to the ball field and take your statement."

"I guess if you want to pitch, you should pitch," Alison said.

Ben and Jake both gave a war whoop and took off running. Jake stopped at the door just long enough to flash a big grin and give Ethan a thumbs-up. "You're not blind. Awesome! We can play catch."

Alison did not look impressed.

ALISON FELT AS IF her emotions had been riddled with bullets or pricked again and again by a sharp ice pick. She would be forever grateful to Ethan for rushing to Jake's aid and saving him from a horrible beating or worse. She'd told him that inside the school. Yet when she looked at him, she felt sick at her stomach, betrayed and used by a man she'd didn't know at all. She'd fallen in love with a total stranger.

A stranger she'd taken into her home. Into her life. Into her heart. They were at the top of the bleachers now, away from the prying eyes and ears of the other fans. That was Ethan's idea. He wanted an opportunity to explain everything to her, but her heart and mind had shut down, as if protecting her from any more of his lies.

"I have good reasons for everything I've done, Alison."

"I'm sure you have."

"Then face me and look me in the eye. Give me a chance to make you understand."

The irony of his statement mixed with the pain and disillusionment that rolled and pitched inside her. Even when they'd made love, she'd never suspected that he could see her body or return her gaze. Now when she looked him in the eye, she saw a man she didn't even recognize.

"I didn't just make up an identity as part of some screwy seduction game. Like I told the cops, I'm an FBI agent involved in covert operations. When I'm on an assignment, I go undercover, assume the identity of whoever the FBI says that I am. Right now I'm Ethan Granger, blind high school history teacher."

"So you're not even Ethan Granger."

"No. My name is Ethan Greenway. It's not often we use our first name, but they made an exception this time since they were afraid Seth would give me away by calling me by the wrong name."

"What about the story of how you were betrayed by your wife? Is that part of your identity?"

"No. I wish it were, but that's all true. She couldn't take being married to an agent in covert operations. The long separations were too much for her, and the inability to be part of so much of my life was something she could never adjust to. Not many women can."

"And you automatically lumped me with those women?"

"I did at first. Look, Alison. I'm not the best at understanding women. My mother was married four times and never stayed married to any of her husbands for more than five years. She was always searching and never seemed to find what she was looking for, so we moved around a lot, never put down any roots. Even before I met Sylvia, I didn't have a lot of reasons to trust a woman's staying power."

"You should have told me all this before, Ethan. Before we made…" She hesitated, unable to say the word *love* now, when all she felt was a cold, lonely emptiness deep inside her heart.

He took her hand in his. "Please try to understand, Alison. If you don't want to have anything to do with me, I can accept that, but you have to know that I never meant to hurt you."

"All I understand is that you came to town and had your little vacation fling. The best man and the maid of honor. It was a cozy setup, and you had nothing to lose."

"I had as much to lose as anyone."

"How could you? The real you was never even on the scene. You must have had a lot of laughs. 'Let me touch your face. It's the way I see.'" She mocked his words the way he'd mocked her feelings, played her for a fool.

"I was a jerk, Alison, but I never meant it to come down to this."

"No? Exactly what was it you meant to do? Give the poor virgin a little experience? Treat me to a little sex? While away the time by becoming part of my family before you reported to New Orleans? Tell me, Ethan. Now that you've brought it up, I'd really like to know."

"I was attracted to you. You were attracted to me. I didn't see what harm it could do for us to enjoy each other's company."

"And you didn't ever feel the least bit of guilt over sleeping with me and letting me believe you were someone else entirely?"

"I felt guilty about lying to you, but I convinced myself I was doing my job."

"I fell in…love. I may as well say it. I fell in love with a blind schoolteacher. He doesn't exist." She turned away, fighting back the tears that burned her eyes. "In your mind I was always temporary, Ethan, so it didn't matter to you that I loved the temporary man. But you were much more than that to me. You were part of my life, part of my heart. Now there's nothing.''

"I have to leave tonight, Alison. I don't want us to say goodbye like this. I never meant to hurt you.''

"Then I guess that makes everything all right.'' The tears slid from her eyes and rolled down her cheeks. It hurt so damn much. "I'll meet you in the car when the game is over, Ethan. Right now, I just want to be alone.'' She stood and made her way down the bleachers and back to the car.

Tears continued to drip down her cheeks. She blew her nose on a tissue. The cute, upturned nose that she'd wanted all her life. Now it felt like a curse. The old Alison might have missed out on a lot, but she had never felt this kind of heartbreak. The old Alison had never loved and lost.

EHAN TOSSED THE LAST of his clothes into his suitcase. The driver would be here momentarily and Ethan would walk out of the Fairchild house for the last time. He hadn't expected it to end like this, with Alison hurting so badly.

She wasn't the only one who was hurting. He'd been a fool to think he was impervious to the kind of attraction that existed between them. Now all he felt was a painful emptiness so strong it seemed it might swallow him. He would miss Nora, Madge and especially Jake. But most of all he'd miss Alison. Miss her cute little walk, the way she wiggled her new nose, her enthusiasm for life. Miss the way she fitted in his arms and in his heart.

He stood at the window and watched until his ride pulled up in front of the house. He didn't want any long goodbyes. They would be too painful. Picking up his suitcase, he walked out the bedroom door and down the hall.

Alison's scent wafted from beneath her bedroom door and into the hallway, flowery and light as springtime. Passion... It fit her perfectly. He stopped, unable to help himself. He knocked once and she came to the door. Her eyes were red and swollen. God, he wanted to hold her one last time, but he knew she'd never let him.

"What is it, Ethan?"

He shuffled his feet, struggling with the words he'd never thought he'd say. "Today, on the way to the game, you asked me to give us a chance. Now I'm asking you to do the same. Don't make this goodbye. Let me come back in the summer and we'll start all over again. No games. No lies."

"I can't do that."

"Why? The only difference between the real me and the one you fell in love with is that I can see."

"No. The difference is trust. It's gone for me now, the way it was gone for you after you found Sylvia in another man's arms."

She turned and went back inside the room. He heard her sobs as he walked down the stairs and out of her life for good. He'd been a fool. Now he was alone—again.

CHAPTER SIXTEEN

MAUREEN STOPPED in front of Ed Taylor's house. She wished he could afford to fix up the place. Ed worked so hard, but the house was practically falling down around him. Maureen had grown fond of Ed since she'd come to Cooper's Corner. He was a nice, thoughtful neighbor and he raised the best free-range chickens she'd found anywhere. She was supposed to pick up two for Clint and then make a run into town to take care of a couple of errands before meeting Madge, Alison and Nora Fairchild at Tubb's Café for lunch.

Nora had called and asked her to join them. She was worried about Alison and thought maybe Maureen could help cheer her up. Maureen didn't know the whole story, but she knew that Ethan Granger had fooled them all. She'd suspected he wasn't totally on the up-and-up, a sign her detective instincts were still intact.

Maureen wasn't sure exactly what Nora wanted from her, but if it was to convince Alison that she should forgive and forget, Nora had called on the wrong person. Maureen had thought she'd known the twins' father as well as any woman could know a man, and in the end, she hadn't known him at all. Alison was lucky she'd found out about Ethan before she'd married him.

But Maureen could empathize with Alison. Nothing hurt more than discovering that the man you loved was not what he seemed. And even now, after her own bitter heartbreak, she wouldn't change the fact that she'd married Chance and given birth to their beautiful twin daughters.

She stepped onto the porch, knocked on Ed's door and waited. When he didn't answer she knocked again, louder this time. She'd told him yesterday she'd be stopping by this morning, and he'd said he'd be here. She tried the knob. It turned and the door squeaked open.

She started to call his name, then stopped. Ed was sprawled across the floor, clutching his stomach, not moving, his eyes open wide and locked in a blank stare. She rushed to him and checked his pulse. There was none, and his hands were cold and lifeless.

"Oh, God, no." Shock hit her in tumultuous waves. He couldn't be dead. It was too sudden. He was too young.

Her years of training with the NYPD kicked in and she forced her arms and legs to move as the initial shock subsided. She wasn't a forensics expert, but it was clear from his body temperature and coloring that he'd been dead for a while, probably since late last night or the wee hours of the morning.

He'd died all alone, perhaps while trying to reach his phone and call for help. She grabbed her own cell phone and called the emergency number. Ed had been fine yesterday. He'd stopped by Twin Oaks to talk to Clint, and she'd given him the box of candy someone had left her last week. The candy was on the table by his chair, open, a few pieces missing. The chocolates had been the last thing he'd enjoyed.

Tears filled her eyes and ran down her cheeks. She'd faced death lots of times as an NYPD detective, but not like this. Not when the person was a neighbor and friend, a good man who should have lived years longer.

Life was so short, so uncertain.

Maybe Nora was right, and Alison was wrong not to forgive and forget. Maybe a person should just reach out and grab all the happiness he or she could find.

Maybe Maureen had been wrong, too. Perhaps she'd been too quick to give up on her own marriage. Real love came along so seldom, and the pain of losing it lasted such a long time.

ALISON SAT AT THE TABLE in Tubb's Café, picking at her chicken salad and listening to Maureen tell how she had walked into Ed's house and found him dead. Maureen was shaken. They all were.

Ed was a nice guy and couldn't have been more than sixty years old. Her own heartbreak should pale in comparison with death, but even after two weeks, life without Ethan seemed unbearably desolate and empty.

She shouldn't have let herself fall so hard for a man who'd never claimed to be more than a temporary thrill. In spite of what he'd said, it was evident the whole relationship had been a sham, no more than a deceitful game to him.

She could understand why he'd posed as blind when they'd first met. It was his job and he was doing what was expected of him. But how could he have made love with her the way he did with those lies between them? He couldn't, unless the lovemaking had meant far less to him than it had to her. She had bared her body and soul. He hadn't even shared his true identity.

And yet she missed him so.

She tried to concentrate on the conversation going on around her. The talk moved from Ed to Madge and her classes, which were going amazingly well, before touching on Nora's relationship with Ron Pickering. Apparently Nora was much better at choosing men than Alison.

"And we owe it all to Alison," Madge said. "If she hadn't started the ball rolling, both Mother and I would probably still be muddling around in our same old lives."

"I had nothing to do with your taking classes," Alison said. "You did it all on your own."

"Not true," Madge protested. "It was your nose job that gave me courage to try something new. I'd wanted to make changes in my life before, but I was always afraid I'd fail. Then when I saw how you got your nose fixed and let your personality blossom, I decided to go for the gusto."

"The same with me," Nora added. "My life was comfortable and I would have been content to leave it that way if Alison hadn't been brave enough to have her plastic surgery and change her whole attitude and look. I would have seen Ron that one weekend, but I wouldn't have had the nerve to go out on a real date with him, or to color my hair and lose a few pounds, if I hadn't seen the new Alison emerge from her cocoon."

"Guess the new nose did work magic," Maureen said. "The Fairchild women will never be the same." She put down her fork and wiped her mouth on her napkin. "And what about you, Alison? Is the nose still magic for you?"

"I'm not sorry I had the surgery, but it certainly isn't magic."

"It was," Madge protested. "As long as Ethan was around."

"We agreed not to talk about that subject."

"I know, but you make me crazy, little sis. If a man like Ethan Granger was as nuts about me as he is about you, I'd never let him get away."

"I don't know the whole story," Maureen said, "but Madge may have a point. When you came to brunch, you were glowing with happiness. Today, you're miserable.

Maybe it wasn't the nose job that was magic at all. Maybe it was Ethan Granger who changed your life.''

"Only there is no Ethan Granger." She tried to hold back the frustration, but failed. "There's only a *seeing* FBI agent whom I don't know at all."

"I know him," Madge said. "He befriended my son and saved him from losing out on the time of his life, pitching for the Woodstown Warriors. Not only that, he risked his whole undercover identity to save Jake from being brutally attacked by a gang of thugs. He was just lucky that his supervisor let his assignment continue and didn't can him for that action."

"I liked his sense of humor," Nora said, "and the way he fit into the family. But I guess what I liked best about him was that he seemed so enthralled with Alison. A mother likes to see that in a man her daughter is interested in."

Alison shook her head, hoping the tears didn't escape to slide down her cheeks and give her away. She liked all the things Madge and her mother liked about Ethan, but that only scratched the surface of her emotions. The man she'd known as Ethan Granger had quite simply taken her breath away. She would never forget that man and would probably never feel the same way about anyone new.

But that man had been a sensitive, blind teacher who could rock her world with a touch or a kiss. "It's over," she whispered. "It was all a game to Ethan, and we both lost."

Maureen laid her hand on top of Alison's. "You don't have to lose, not if you have the courage to go after what you want. Maybe it won't work, maybe you'll find that your feelings aren't the same for the FBI agent as they were for Ethan Granger, but you'll never know if you throw your love away without giving it a chance. Love is worth fighting for. It's everything.''

A lone tear escaped and rolled down Alison's cheek. ''I don't know. I just don't know.''

Maureen squeezed Alison's hand. ''What could it hurt to give the man a chance? If you don't, if you just stand by and do nothing, you definitely lose. And you'll have the rest of your life to wonder if you made a mistake.''

ALISON SAT on the back porch swing, sipping a cup of hot tea and staring at the basketball hoop where she'd played one-on-one with Ethan just a few weeks ago—weeks that seemed like months. She'd had lots of time to think since he'd left, sleepless nights, long boring weekends.

Eventually, she knew she'd go on with her life, but she hadn't reached that point yet. The memories were too poignant, the dreams of him too vivid. It was ludicrous that one week in her life could change her so completely, but the week with Ethan had.

Not only that, but Maureen's words kept echoing in her mind. If she did nothing, she'd lose.

The doorbell rang. She ignored it. Jake and Madge were in the house. One of them would get it.

A few minutes later, Jake pushed open the back door, a wrapped package in his hands. ''Mom said this is for you.''

''What is it?''

''I don't know. It came in a brown shipping box, but the card inside said the present is for you.''

''Who sent it?''

''Guess you should open it and see.''

She detected the teasing in his voice and knew something was up. Surely this wasn't from Ethan. If it was, she didn't want to open it. It would only pull all the hurt out and lay it bare again. "You open it, Jake."

"Nah. That wouldn't be right. It's for you."

She tore the shimmering red paper from the package and lifted the lid off a small cardboard box. There was nothing between inside but a pair of men's socks and a note. Her fingers shook as she unfolded the slip of paper.

You knocked my socks off the moment I met you. They're still off and it looks as if they always will be. I want to step into the cold stream with you again, kiss you and feel the thrill of it all the way to my toes.

I love you, Alison, and all I know is that one explosive, awesome, breathtaking moment isn't enough. It never would have been. We need forever. Ethan

The socks fell from her hand. The hunger swelled inside her. She didn't know all there was to know about Ethan—maybe she never would. But she knew that life without him was a miserable existence. He'd made a mistake, but he loved her. And she loved him. All her life she'd lived in a protected, sensible world, and even a new nose hadn't fully changed that. Now it was time to take a chance on love.

She turned the note over, looking for a phone number or an address. They were both on the back.

"Who sent you a pair of men's socks?" Jake asked.

"Ethan."

"That's a weird present. But Ethan's a funny guy. I sure hope he comes back to see us, Aunt Alison."

"You know what, Jake? I think he just might."

ETHAN TRUDGED UP the stairs to his apartment, Longfellow at his side. It was only early June, but the temperature was already in the high eighties in New Orleans and the humidity was pushing a hundred percent. That kind of weather added to the problems that were brewing in the high school where he was sharing duties with a teacher who actually knew all about American history.

But he was doing what he did best, too, and he was making progress in identifying the ringleaders and finding out who was behind the threats on the lives of students and teachers. He wasn't, however, making any progress in getting over Alison Fairchild.

When he crawled into bed at night, he ached to hold her. When he woke in the morning, her image danced in his mind. Cute, bubbly, smiling at him in that way she had, making his heart skip a few beats and his breath catch. Life without her was a poor excuse for living. He'd never thought he would give up the job he loved for any woman, but he'd been wrong. He'd give it up in a minute for a lifetime with Alison.

He'd hoped his note and present might touch her heart-strings, but apparently he'd been wrong. She hadn't called and hadn't written.

Longfellow's head shot up as they reached the door, and he started barking. Ethan tensed. He wasn't expecting trouble this afternoon, but that didn't mean it wouldn't find him.

And then he caught the familiar, intoxicating scent of spring flowers. Passion. His heart raced and his hands trembled as he unlocked the door and pushed it open. The small living room was just as he'd left it. Empty. Even his nose was playing cruel tricks on him now.

Longfellow left his side and went racing to the bed-room. Ethan followed cautiously. But like the living room, the bedroom was the same lonely place it always was. "She's not here, Longfellow. Maybe the cleaning lady wears Passion."

But Longfellow was not to be swayed. He stuck his nose to the bathroom door.

"Sorry, boy. It's just the two of us. The lady doesn't want us." Still, he opened the bathroom door for Longfellow to see for himself.

The room was bathed in candlelight, and the tub was filled with mountains of glistening bubbles. Bubbles and Alison. He went weak.

"Hello, Ethan."

Her voice reached inside him, turned him inside out. Still he could barely believe she was actually here. "Hello, Alison."

"Hope you don't mind my borrowing your bathtub."

"Does this mean you've forgiven me?"

She swooped up a handful of bubbles and blew them his way. "It means I'm willing to give us a chance if you are."

"I've thought a lot about that. I'd miss being an undercover agent for the FBI, but I've had my fun. There's no reason I can't work at a desk. That way we could have a normal life."

She shook her head. "I don't want a normal life. I want you the way you are. Doing what you love."

"It would mean long periods of separation."

"I'm not Sylvia, Ethan. I'm the sensible Alison Fairchild. I can handle your being gone as long as I know you'll always come back to me. And when you come home, we'll have lots to talk about and we'll make love all night long."

He kicked off his shoes. "You are wanton."

"And in love."

"In that case, move over."

He climbed in with her, clothes and all, and took her in his arms. They laughed and kissed and touched until he was too hungry for her to wait another minute. Then he picked her up, dried her off and shed his own wet clothes before carrying her to his bed.

"I love you, Alison Fairchild."

"And I love you. So let the fireworks begin."

They did, and they lit up the bedroom all night long.

Welcome to Twin Oaks—
the new B and B in Cooper's Corner,
Massachusetts. Bed-and-breakfast
will never be the same!
COOPER'S CORNER,
a new Harlequin continuity series,
continues May 2003 with
FOR BETTER OR FOR WORSE
by Debbi Rawlins

Veterinarian Alex McAlester is the man to go
to in Cooper's Corner for sound advice and a
shoulder to lean on. But don't ask him to get
emotionally involved. Since his wife's death
eight years ago, his closest relationship has
been with his dog, Bagel—until he insists on
"helping out" Jenny Taylor…by marrying her!

Here's a preview!

CHAPTER ONE

THE STEP CREAKED, and they both looked toward the door. It must have been a floorboard, because Jenny was already standing there, her gaze trained on the hand Maureen had laid over Alex's.

Maureen quickly withdrew. "Good morning."

"Hi." Jenny's gaze went to Alex. "I didn't know you'd be here."

"Have a seat." Maureen got up. "I'll get you some coffee. The other guests have eaten, but I'll fix you some strawberries and cantaloupe, and freshly baked blueberry muffins."

"Just coffee will be fine."

"Wrong." Alex rose from the table and went over to the counter to retrieve the bowl of fruit.

"Excuse me?" Her hair was still a little disheveled, as if she'd only just awoken and ran a quick brush through it. She wore no makeup, and the freckles stood out across her nose, making her look really young.

"You have to eat, Jenny."

Her gaze skittered to Maureen, who busied herself with the coffee.

"I'm going to be leaving soon," Jenny said, her voice tight with annoyance. "I'll pick something up while I'm on the road."

"I need to talk to you," he insisted.

Her gaze flew to Maureen again.

He took Jenny by the elbow. "Let's go sit in the living room. Okay with you, Maureen?"

"Be my guest." She didn't even look up.

"Wait a minute…!" Jenny tried to put the brakes on.

"Would you rather we talk in here?" He sent a meaningful look toward Maureen.

Jenny glared at him, then led the way into the large gathering room. She didn't sit on the sofa, but stood with her arms folded. "It's not that I don't appreciate you taking me to the hospital yesterday, and waiting for me and all that, but you can't ride roughshod over me. I won't let you."

Alex wondered how much of his conversation she'd overheard. He didn't want Maureen's suspicions hanging over her head—she had enough on her plate.

"Did you know Maureen found your father?" he asked, testing the waters.

"Maureen?" Her eyes widened in genuine surprise and her gaze drifted toward the kitchen. "Oh, my God, she didn't tell me."

"It's not that important. I just wondered if you knew. She was good to him, inviting him for holiday dinners and stocking him up with food whenever he delivered his free-range chickens to her. She was actually picking up her order at Ed's place when she found him."

"I had no idea. Thank you for telling me." Jenny started to return to the kitchen.

"Wait," he said, satisfied she hadn't overheard anything upsetting. "That's not what I wanted to talk to you about."

Alarm flashed in her eyes again.

"Why don't we sit?"

She shook her head. "I'll be sitting the entire ride back to New York."

"Okay." He paused, knowing she wasn't going to make this easy. "I think I have a solution to your problem."

Interest sparked in her eyes. But then she drew back, subtly, with a wary expression. "I didn't ask for your help."

Alex had expected her to balk. Both father and daughter were as stubborn as they came. "Will you at least listen, or are you going to let pride stand in the way of your health?"

Her expression turned sheepish. "Okay. I'll listen."

Alex cleared his throat. He really wished they were sitting down. "Marry me."

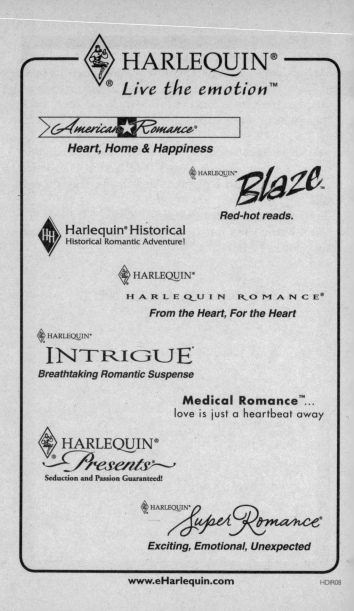

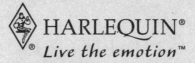

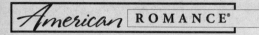
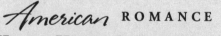
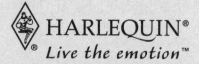

HARLEQUIN®
INTRIGUE®

BREATHTAKING ROMANTIC SUSPENSE

Shared dangers and passions lead to electrifying
romance and heart-stopping suspense!

Every month, you'll meet six new heroes
who are guaranteed to make your spine tingle
and your pulse pound. With them you'll enter
into the exciting world of Harlequin Intrigue—
where your life is on the line
and so is your heart!

THAT'S INTRIGUE—
ROMANTIC SUSPENSE
AT ITS BEST!

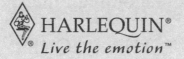

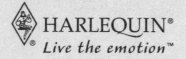